I0782207

Mark of Clover

JUDITH BARCZY "KELLY"

Countess Gyurky

XENOPHON PRESS

Introduction

Judith with Mokus, one of the last mark of clover horses.
The clover-shaped mark is visible on the tip of her nose.

Mark of Clover by Countess Judith Barczy Gyürky is a delightful collection of folklore chronicling one-thousand years of Hungarian horse history. The work is a testimony of a very special breed of horses, called by Hungarians the "marked horses" or "Mark of Clover horses" in Judith's book. Each chapter follows one of these horses beginning with ninth century foundation stock to the flight and survival of a few of her own horses to rural Virginia at the end of World War II.

As a child, Judith first heard of the Clover horses from her father, who liked to spend time around the stables on the estate of Count Kálmán Forgách. His parents spent summers there with Forgách who was a famous horse breeder; his best stallion was a Derby winner named Kettledrum. A family tragedy is related in one of the chapters.

Many years later, at the foot of the Tatra Mountains on another estate belonging to the great horseman of the time, Count Géza Andrássy, Judith enjoyed long summer vacations as a wild young tomboy. It was there that she discovered the mare, Sárga (meaning *yellow* in Hungarian) that she learned to ride on; "Uncle" Géza himself gave her the first lessons.

Count Géza Andrássy

Sárga had a sort of clover mark on her lip, so Judith and her playmates became curious. They had the good fortune that an old retired groom living there, knew the story of Sárga in detail and that of her dam, Rézust. This groom knew the history from his time working for the Counts Forgách, which were now relations of Judith on her mother's side. In the evenings, after supper, the children headed to the stable and assembled around the old groom to hear the stories of the Clover horses. Already a horse fan, Judith was captivated to such an extent that half a lifetime later she was able to recall and retell these same stories in this book.

The stories start so far back that they fall into the category of legend but each successive generation gets closer to actual facts. Bayram, whose owner, the great Miklós Zrínyi, national hero of Hungary and Croatia, is a direct ancestor of Judith. In 1566, with 2,500 men, Zrínyi held the frontier fortress of Szigetvár and blocked the advance of Sultan Suleiman the Magnificent's army of 100,000 who were headed to Vienna. Ultimately, the besieged defenders were killed, only seven managed to escape but the Ottomans lost between twenty and thirty thousand men. Most importantly, Sultan Suleiman died in his tent and Vienna was saved.

The more recent stories include violence, theft and bloodshed like the murder of the English trainer who came with Kettledrum to the stable of Rézust. Judith took care to disguise the names of people whose children were still living to protect their reputations. To entertain her younger readers, she indulged in some coloring and enhancements of the stories but all from the 19th century onwards are based on actual facts. The last three dramatic stories were from Judith own life experience.

Judith was fond of describing herself as an adventuress. Her life imparted more than she could have wished for, fleeing twice from the Communists, first escaping from jail and torture by the Commune of 1919 disguised as the singing and dancing "Miss Arizona" as part of a traveling vaudeville group.

When she entered the international show circuit, she often found her mounts couldn't match the strength of their foreign rivals. This limitation led her to breed more versatile and stronger jumpers on the estate of her first husband, Count Aladár Gyürky. She was so successful that by the end of the 1930s not only the Hungarian but also the German, Swiss and Italian cavalry schools had become her regular customers.

We might wonder what invisible force brought Judith and the Clover horses together, not once, but three times. All of these "meetings" were blind dates: the first, a compassionate purchase to save an old hack from mistreatment, another by choosing a mean beast that the cavalry failed to tame but to Judith's eye showed jumping qualities. With the third, she won the trials for the 1936 Olympic Games but at that time, only men could be nominated to compete. She was a passionate horse rider and between the two world wars became one of Hungary's top equestrians and a national champion. Nevertheless, unlike some of her colleagues, she didn't focus solely on winning tournaments but instead, saw them as just part of an interesting life in enchanting places among intelligent and amusing people.

After many productive years building up their estate with diversification into multiple product lines and modern farming methods while simultaneously developing her stud farm, she was not exempt from tragedy. She experienced the devastating loss of her daughter, and the cataclysm of World War II destroyed all she had worked for.

In 1945, she again had to flee with a selected group of sixty-four horses trecking just a few miles ahead of the Red Army.

However, success in escaping the Russian terror to the West was just the beginning of the most traumatic period of her life. The great devastation and misery after World War II fully impacted her herd. Her work horses were used by farmers but all the others were classified as "surplus horses" and couldn't get allowances for the then scarce, rationed feed. Judith had to suffer unbearable pain, first from the theft and maiming of sixteen young horses she'd carefully bred to become first rate jumpers and hunters. Despite bartering her stash of family jewels for feed, she had to almost helplessly watch the slow starvation of the horses, with some even dying. Her motto at the time was: "free us from the liberators, who liberated us from the liberators!" A few horses were stabled with the Lipizzaners of Alois Podhajsky but she never forgave him for failing to pass her letter of appeal to General George Patton proposing gainful use of the horses nor for him diverting a shipment of her hay to his horses.

Her fighting spirit attracted U.S. Army Captain Howard Kelly who became her guardian angel. It was only thanks to him that she avoided repatriation back to Communist Hungary and the possible auctioning off of her horses yet even he couldn't secure feed for them.

Her tireless efforts brought some relief by getting some horses drafted to the equestrian team of the U.S. Army in Austria led by Colonel John Meade. At great risk of confiscation, she shipped the others through the Russian controlled zone, to Vienna where they were accepted by the Austrian Jockey Club to run in steeplechases and flat races at Freudenau racetrack. Judith was amazed that her pitiful horses, with their ribs showing and many with coughs from deprivation, had such fighting spirit left that they were making out pretty well in the races. Ultimately, with no future for her and the Clover horses in post-war Austria, she chose the only apparent way out by accepting Captain Kelly's offer of a marriage of convenience to realize her dream of starting a new life in America. But one thing that she couldn't bear to miss was watching her stallion, Sobri compete in the 1948 Olympic Games in Aldershot, England. Sobri was lucky that the Russian sentries missed their shots while he was being rowed at night across the Danube as described in one of the chapters.

Her last difficult decision was to select which horses were to be sold to pay for the shipment of the thirteen who would become Judith's foundation stock at their new home in central Virginia.

Once in America, she rented farms to stable the horses, took odd jobs, sold eggs and chickens, ran a "pig factory," and authored, self-published, printed, and sold *Mark of Clover* all as fund raising efforts. She illustrated *Mark of Clover* with her own drawings and watercolors. She sent out hand-made Christmas cards of her drawings, paintings, poems, and jokes.

For several years, with her thirty-six horses, Judith ran the equitation program at Hollins College. She was very popular with the students; one of them became her top rider, another her daughter-in-law.

She was a natural leader and already in her younger days was respectfully addressed by family, friends and the young cavalry officers coming in droves to ride on her estate, as 'Judith mama,' a name equivalent to 'Aunt Judith' which was used affectionately by her new American students and mentees.

While teaching at Hollins College she finally found her dream place, Port-A-Ferry Farm, which she purchased on a Friday, sold the timber from the land on Saturday and closed on the sale of the farm on the following Monday with the proceeds of the timber sale. This farm became home and heaven for her Clover horses. They never went hungry again and revived their ancient traits of jumping and hunting at the foot of the Blue Ridge Mountains. This finally brought peace to Judith as well.

Laslo "Leslie" Sorg
Budapest 2023

Judith jumping with Sobri sidesaddle.

Csusza, a mare aged 32. This mare was an FEI jumper that was retired at age 21 and had 6 foals starting from the age of 22. At the age of 33 she broke her leg on the way back from fox hunting.

Captain Kelly and Judith Kelly out for a pleasure ride in Europe.

Horses in the barn, shortly after arrival in Virginia.

Judith (center) hunting at Farmington, 1960s.

One of Judith's Christmas illustrations that she drew and colored herself. These went out every year to friends and clients.

With Csusza "We had enough of teaching - we got back to the farm."

XMAS EXCUSES

August was the month that Judith
Went to get her insides out it· .
Was no fun but with the help
Of her friends returned to health
Now she hunts and puts on weight
She could save the Xmas cake.

September we spent all our time
Getting jumps and rig in line
Saw and hammers, spade and hatchet
Where at work and stones we scratched
Out with finger nails all bleeding
Epus was foremost leading.

October was a month of peace
Scarcely had money for lease
Only Blondie Dog was killed
By a driver not too skilled
My best colt died and our barn
Half colapsed on Dollars arm.

November Dollar broke his jaw
Reason that he did not saw
Sobri's kick that sent him flying
To hospital where he's lying
Cost us all our saved money
Now he has to eat some honey.

December Judith broke four ribs
But we hoped to kill some pigs
Have a feast and forget all
Our troubles of this fall
But the flood came and the storm
Washed away our rig and corn.

Now we are completely broke
Have to sell our winter coat
Get Bulldozer and repair
All the damage and we dare
Not spend money on nice gifts
But get all our damage fixed.

Here's the reason dearest friends
That we wash our dirty hands
Of not sending you but wishes
And it seemly Xmas Kisses
May be next year luck will leap
To our side and we can heap
Gifts on Neighbors and Old Friends
With this hope the poem ends.

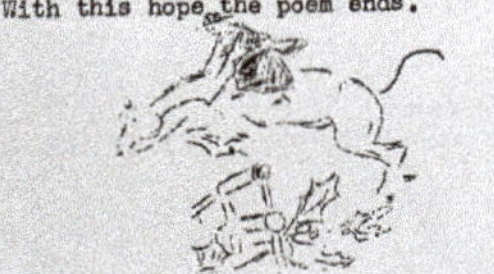

In a particularly difficult year, Judith composed and sent out this humorous newsy poem explaining away the lack of gift giving. This example reveals her incredible determination, resiliency, optimism and sense of humor.

Aunt Judith at home with the hounds.

Mark of Clover

by

JUDITH B. KELLY

XENOPHON PRESS

Franktown, Virginia
2022

Mokus I. Mark of Clover. Ernst Peterson

Contents

MARK OF CLOVER

Jegyes

IN the ninth century, before they entered middle Europe, under the leadership of Chieftain Arpad, and settled in the rich valley of the Danube that is now Hungary, the Magyars lived in an Asiatic land that suffered a great drought. The Taltos, or High-Priest, slaughtered many snow-white horses and kept the sacrificial fires burning day and night to appease the evil spirits that kept the rain away from the pastures and fields, but it was all in vain, for no rain fell upon the parched and barren lands. At last, in desperation, they sacrificed an offering to Hadur, the God of warfare and justice. After the rites were completed, the Taltos read, as he always did, the message of the god from the intestines of the slaughtered horse. The interpretation of these messages was often ambiguous, and, this time, Hadur sent them one with two decidedly different meanings. As a result the tribe of the Magyar's was split in two by an argument over what the great god, Hadur, had meant.

The young warriors were tired of the peaceful life of caring for the herds of cattle and sheep, battling only occasionally with a neighboring tribe over land rights. They were driven by their wild and adventurous nature, and they were eager to explore new lands. They interpreted the message of the God to read, "Go and conquer new lands between the two silver rivers! There you will become great and prosperous!" The older people and the aged ruler of the Magyars' said that the message was a warning to stay on their land, or disaster would destroy them. In spite of the advice of the elders, the younger people of the country decided to obey their own interpretation, and they began to prepare to move. They elected a young and wealthy chieftain named Takos, as their leader. Tokos still in his early thirties, loved nothing better than a fight, unless it was a dangerous adventure. From the time of the reading of the message, he had taken the initiative in encouraging the young Magyars to break away. He was strong and courageous, and it was quite obvious to all that he was the one to lead the band of adventurers in their search for the land between the two silver rivers.

The next few days were full of confusion and excitement as preparations were made for the departure of the explorers. They hitched their oxen to the primitive wagons that were to carry provisions, equipment, the younger children, and the older women, for a few of the old warriors had decided to go also. The men loaded the wagons, while the women prepared the clothes and food they were to take with them. The people who remained behind did not object to the departure of half the population of the country, for then there would be enough to keep them and their stock alive through the year until the rains came again. Perhaps Hadur had deliberately sent them the double message to save them from starvation and death. But the separation brought sorrow to many, for there were mothers whose husbands stayed, and whose children left; and there were girls who were parted from the young men they loved, perhaps forever.

The unhappiest of all was Ilka, the fair-haired 14 year-old daughter of the high-priest, Bera. She was the only child of the Taltos by a Germanic woman, Terlinda, whom he had captured in a raid on a Teutonic tribe. Ilka was engaged to marry Almos, the son of Tokos, but Bera had taken advantage of an argument with Tokos over the prophecy of Hadur to break the engagement, when he found that the Chieftain and his son had decided to leave for the land between the two silver rivers. Ilka was the image of her mother, who had died when her daughter was five, and Bera could not bring himself to part with the only thing that was left to him of the woman he had loved. In spite of this love that the elderly priest had born his wife, Terlinda had never relented in her hatred on the man who had destroyed her people and forced her to live as his wife, in his barbaric nation. Ilka sensed that the Taltos made the life of her adored mother miserable, and she had instinctively disliked her father all her life, though he indulged her in every whim. After each raid on neighboring tribes or on the convoys that traveled through Magyar lands, Bera always chose the things that his daughter would want as his share of the loot. He gave her richly embroidered materials, spices, perfumes, delicately carved pieces made of ivory and jade, tropical birds with brightly colored plumages, slim Oriental horses, and the beautifully wrought golden jewelry that he knew she loved. Ilka was envied by all the girls of the tribe for her many beautiful possessions, but still Bera was not able to buy the love of his daughter. If the old priest had spent more time with his only child instead of scheming continually how to increase his wealth and importance he might have succeeded in winning her affection, but as it was, the extravagant gifts were not sufficient for an unhappy and lonely little girl.

Ilka's memories of her mother were very vague. She remembered a gentle, golden-haired person who sang her to sleep with German lullabies, and, because gold was so closely associated with the only warmth and love she had known, she loved golden things. Her dresses and her saddles and bridles were trimmed with gold. Her thin, childish arms were weighted with heavy gold bracelets, and the horses she rode were always golden in color. She had everything she wanted except the two things she wanted most. Ever since the death of Terlinda, Ilka had given her love to her childhood companion, Almos, who was three years older than she. She had grown up believing that they would marry, for the two fathers had agreed upon this when their children were infants, but now Bera had deliberately fought with Tokos and the pact was broken. The girl knew that when Almos left, it was probable that she would never see him again, for no one knew how far it was to the land

between the two silver rivers. The second thing that Ilka wanted was a golden filly from Tokos' famous breed of horses.

The Magyar's were a horse-loving nation, and each family sought to surpass the other in breeding a superior line of animals. The competition was strong, but for some years Tokos had been the undisputed owner of the best breed. These horses were fast, cunning, and brave. In endurance and speed tests against the other Magyar animals they always won. Tokos was taking all of his horses with him, for none was ever sold or given away. A few mares were carefully bred each year, and, if the colts were not perfect or did not live up to the standard set by Tokos, they were destroyed. Many of these horses bore a strange sign upon the tips of their muzzles, a mark in the shape of a four leaf clover. It was rumored among the Magyars that it was the mark of the Gods, and, as long as the Gods favored the clan of Tokos, no one could hope to breed a better horse.

Ilka had seen the golden filly she wanted so much two years before on the day it was born. She and Almos had ridden out to make sure the mares that were in foal were all right when they saw a horse grazing alone in a distant part of the pasture. They had galloped over to see what was wrong and found the mare proudly licking her new-born foal dry. The little filly was a true golden chestnut, and on her nose she bore the slate-blue mark of the clover. The girl had immediately fallen in love with the filly and she had longed to ask Almos to give it to her, but she knew that the horses never left the family.

Almos was a wise young man, for his years, and he had immediately seen the longing in the girl's eyes. "I'll tell you what I'll do", he had said, "this foal is by my stallion, Kurd, so she is part mine, and, on the day of our marriage, I will give it to you as a wedding present. She'll be ready to break then, and you can train her. Would you like that?" Ilka had never been so happy as she was that day, and now her father had ruined everything. He had taken both Almos and the golden filly from her, and he thought he could make her forget them by giving her trinkets.

A slow anger began to rise in Ilka. She was not quick-tempered like the Magyars, ready to kill one moment and laughing the next. She had her mother's cold, unforgiving temper and determination.

"I am not an animal to be sold or kept at will," she thought, but she said nothing. The time would come when she could take her life in her own hands. Until then she would wait.

The High-Priest, Bera, could read the future, and he knew the wisdom of the past, but he could never understand his daughter.

Though Ilka was still a child, she knew what she wanted. She did not know what she would do, but she did know she would marry Almos somehow. The night before the departure of the adventurers, Ilka and Almos met secretly in the far pasture where they had found the golden filly.

"I will disguise myself and go with you," the girl said, "my father won't find out until it is too late."

Almos smiled and took her hand. "You are too young, little Ilka, and you know that your father would come for you within a few hours after we leave. You must stay here and wait for me. I promise I will return, within a year if possible, and get you. But even if it is longer than a year, you must not worry, for I will come back. Now, stay here a few minutes. I have a surprise for you."

Almos mounted Kurd and rode off in the darkness. A short time later he returned, leading a small horse next to his brown stallion.

Ilka felt her heart leap up. "It's the golden filly," she cried.

Almos put the lead rope in the girls hand. "This is my parting gift," he said, "and the token that I will come back for you. I have smeared brown dye on her nose so that the mark of the clover won't show. My father won't miss her in the excitement of the journey, but the Taltos would take her from you if he found out I had given you one of our horses after our engagement was broken. Keep her hidden in a far pasture, and make sure the dye does not rub off... that will be a double precaution. The Taltos has so many horses, I don't think he will notice one more, but be careful! Now then, what are you going to call her?"

Ilka thought for a moment, "I will call her Jegyes," she said finally, "the name means both 'marked' and 'betrothed', and it is my token that I will wait for you to come back to me!"

The next day Tokos and his followers left to find their new country.

Almos leaned down from his horse as he passed Ilka and whispered," Wait for me, my Ilka take care of yourself and Jegyes."

Then the long line of Magyars started off. Now and again a young warrior would gallop out of the formation and race back to the mother or the girl he left behind to show off the speed of his horse and to reassure them that all would go well. Then he would gallop back, pulling his horse to a rearing halt, and once more take his place in the swiftly moving lines.

When Bera, the Taltos, saw the tall figure of Almos, mounted on his seal brown stallion, gallop away from Ilka, he walked over to the girl's side and put his hand on her shoulder.

"It is well that he goes, girl," he said gruffly. "You will soon forget the young fool. Like his father, he is a fighter with wandering blood in his veins, as wild and dangerous as those vicious horses that his family breeds. I have thanked the gods that my argument with Tokos broke the bond forever, that tied you to his son and their wild clan. It is a good thing for the rest of the Magyar people that they are leaving!"

Ilka felt an uncontrollable hatred for her father welling up in her as she listened to his words, but she held her peace. She turned and silently walked away from him.

The old priest shrugged his shoulders and let her go. "The child is always sullen when she is crossed, but she will get over it," he thought. "Perhaps a dress made from the yellow material I got from the Byzantine caravan last week would help."

The weeks and months that followed passed slowly for Ilka. She spent her time carefully and gently breaking her golden mare. Jegyes was intelligent and eager to please, so the task was a joy rather than a duty for both of them. Ilka worried that her father might question her about the mare, but he never seemed to notice what his daughter was doing. During this time men and women, who were too sick and weak to travel, or who had been wounded in battle, left the Magyar explorers and returned home. They brought back news of the venture, stories of frequent fights with fair-haired giants, who rode great warhorses twice the size of the Magyar animals. These ivory-skinned people with golden hair fought in a slow, steady manner entirely foreign to the fast strike-and-retreat method of the Magyars, and because of this clumsy style of battle, the giants were most often defeated. The people listened, incredulous and awed, to the tales of the returned warriors, and went home to pray to the gods for the protection of the members of their family who had gone on the journey. Ilka always questioned the returned travelers about Almos. They told her he was well, a brave warrior, but they brought no messages from him.

A year after the departure of the Magyars a small band of warriors returned slowly and painfully home. There were about thirty of them who were too badly wounded to continue with the others, so they had been sent back. They had traveled the great distance in carts and on horseback, stopping frequently to rest with friendly tribes along the way. The news of their return spread, and the people gathered to hear what had happened. A young warrior told them of a great battle with the blonde giants in which many of their kin had been killed and wounded.

"But most wonderful of all," he said, "was the single combat to which Almos, the son of Tokos, challenged Berenguk, the greatest warrior of the fair giants. We gathered on one side of the meadow, and Berenguk's troops stood on the other. Several old warriors, chosen from both sides, placed themselves between the two armies on the edges of the field, completing the square in which the battle was to take place. It was their duty to see that the combat was fairly fought."

As the wounded man began his story, Ilka pushed through the crowd until she stood by him.

"Yes, yes, but what happened to Almos," she cried.

"Hush, child, let him tell his tale," an old woman beside her whispered. The girl subsided and waited impatiently for the soldier to continue.

"At the signal Almos and Berenguk charged, and, as they met, the terrible impact of the giant's black charger nearly knocked Almos' small stallion off his feet. You all know the horse; Kurd was his name. He was one of the best of Tokos' excellent breed. No blow was struck in the first charge, but, on the second, Almos knew what to expect, and, as they met, he swerved quickly away so that the blow from Berenguk's heavy axe merely sliced the air. As Kurd side-stepped the giant's clumsy charger, Almos wounded his enemy in his unprotected side. Berenguk staggered in his saddle, but he was not nearly finished yet. On the third charge they used swords, and Berenguk headed straight for Kurd trying to upset him. It was a breach of the rules, but it was too late to stop them.

"Almos moved aside as fast as he could, but the giant's heavy sword whizzed through the air, cutting the tip of Kurd's ears, but missing the crouched figure of Almos completely. Both fighters were enraged and all rules were forgotten. They turned and rushed toward each other again. This time Kurd, maddened by the pain of his wound, and half

blind with the blood that poured down over his eyes, refused to obey the sharp curb. He reached out an grabbed Berenguk's unprotected leg in his teeth. The pain caused the giant to miss his blow again, and then Kurd gave a vicious jerk that unseated the big warrior and sent him crashing to the ground. The old warriors could no longer keep order. The fair giants were furious over the insult to their best warrior, and they broke ranks to avenge him. The battle that followed was bloody and costly to both sides, but the slow-moving giants were no match for our swift horses and accurate arrows. Almos and Berenguk continued to fight, and Berenguk was killed. When the giants found themselves with no leader, they surrendered. The officers came to Tokos with the tokens of peace; a handful of sod, a grain, and a gourd of water, signifying that their land was ours."

The people began to murmur among themselves. The Magyars had won the battle, surely it was a sign that they would succeed in finding the land between the two silver rivers. Then the soldier began to speak again.

"But there was no rejoicing after the battle, for our brave warrior, Almos, could not be found."

Ilka started, and she could not supress an exclamation of horror.

"With Tokos leading us we searched every inch of the battlefield, but Almos was not there. We found Kurd lying dead on the ground. He was pierced by many swords, and all around him lay dead horses and their riders who bore the mark of Kurd's teeth and of Almos' sword. They fought well before they were overcome. In the confusion of the battle, a large number of the blonde giants must have sought to avenge the death of Berenguk upon Almos and Kurd. We could not find the boy's body, so it is possible that he is a prisoner and not dead. When we left Tokos, he had not yet had any news of his son from the enemy. Now, my friends, I must return to the home of my father and rest. Tomorrow, if you come to me, I will give you what news I can of your kin."

The people moved away saddened by the news of the capture and probable death of young Almos. Ilka stood still while the others left until she was alone. Then she turned and walked toward the pasture where Jegyes was kept.

"I know he is not dead," she thought, "but if he cannot come to me, then I will go to him. It's a good thing I still have my hunting clothes on, and my bow and arrows are still attached to my saddle, so I don't have to return home and run the risk of meeting my father. I will follow the trail of Tokos until I find him. . . he can tell me where the blonde giants dwell, and there I will find Almos."

The girl went quickly to the huge smoke house and took as much of the hard smoked meat as she could carry in the leather bags on her saddle down from the hooks. Then she went to the supply tent and filled the pouch at her waist with flint arrow-heads. She took sheep and wolf skins from the drying shed for her bedding on the journey, and, when all was ready, she went down to the pasture where the three-year old Jegyes was grazing. Ilka caught the golden filly and led her back to the corral to saddle her. She remembered what Almos had told her about the little horse.

"If you are ever in danger," he had said, "trust Jegyes. She can outrun the wind, and if necessary she will defend you against any man or beast that attacks you. . . trust her, Ilka, and take care of yourself until I come for you."

But Almos could not come to her now, so she would go to him.

JEGYES

Ilka saddled the mare carefully, putting the wolf and sheep skins under the light saddle made of raw hide and wood. Then she tied the leather bags, full of supplies, to it, and led Jegyes down to the creek. She took out her hunting knife and stared at her reflection in the river. She did not look like the other Hungarian girls. She did not have the dark hair and eyes, small stature, and round face of the others. Her face was oval, framed with long golden curls. Her skin was very fair and slightly freckled, as if it were spangled with gold. Her eyes were a blue-green, and she was tall and slim, more like a young boy than a girl.

"It's a good thing I look like my mother," she thought, "otherwise I could never disguise myself as a boy."

She looked around to make sure no one was near her, then took the hunting knife, and began to cut off the thick golden curls that hung down to her waist. When she had finished, she smiled at her strange reflection in the water and shook her head, feeling the unaccustomed lightness of it. She sliced off her plain tunic, so that it looked like the hunting outfit of a young boy, and then she mounted Jegyes. She whistled softly, and two great, white Komondors, who had been dozing near the corral, ran to her side. The dogs Beles and Bundas, were her own special pets, and she knew that they would guard her from any danger on the long journey. The Komondors flanked the golden filly like two pages, as the little group moved away through the back pastures. Ilka, the daughter of Bera the Taltos was going to Almos, whom Tokos and his entire army had not been able to find.

Almos felt a terrible pain hammering inside his skull. The feeling of nausea that convulsed his aching body was unbearable, and his mind refused to function clearly. He was still on the border line of consciousness when he heard a rough voice bellow in the language he had learned when he was small from Terlinda, Ilka's mother.

"This cur ought to be drawn and quartered, not taken as a gift to Carloman the Great!"

"You hold your peace, Vizir," a gentler voice retorted. "I can hold no grudge against a mere boy who slew that brute, Berenguk. I say it's a good riddance. The man was a trouble-maker. Besides, Carloman has been trying to get an important hostage from this nomad tribe that has been overrunning our outposts. This boy is obviously important if they sent him out to fight Berenguk, and Carloman hopes to keep the nomads in check by holding him as hostage. I doubt that he'll live though, from the looks of him. . . too bad they had to nearly kill him in order to capture him."

The voices went on and on, but Almos understood very little of what they said. It had been many years since he had heard Terlinda speak the language, and for some reason he could not concentrate.

"I feel like a trapped animal while it waits for the people to decide whether they will eat him or not," he thought. "If only I could keep my mind on what they're saying. . . if I could remember. . . understand. . . what they're. . . " The room got darker and darker, and the boy lost consciousness.

When Almos came again to consciousness someone was pouring down his throat something hot and burning. He choked and tried to brush the cup away, but rough hands pushed him back against the pillow.

"Drink it, you fool, if you want to live."

Almos only partly understood the words, but the commanding tone was unmistakable. He gulped the hot liquid down, and then the darkness closed in again. Later he was vaguely conscious of a steady rocking motion, and the sound of water slapping against the boat. Somewhere, far away, someone was singing a slow, gentle melody.

He heard the song again, closer and clearer, and this time a woman was singing. He opened his eyes and saw grey stone walls, and a barred window above him. He turned his head painfully and saw a woman sitting beside his bed. She was a strange creature, dressed in a long dress of black and white. Her lovely face was framed in white linen so that her hair was completely covered. Her eyes, as they met his, shone with a strange and beautiful light, and then she smiled.

He tried to raise himself "Where am I?" Almos voice sounded strange and hoarse to himself.

The woman got up and gently pushed him back down on the couch. "It's all right, my son. You must lie still. You are too weak to get up for a while yet."

The strange woman obviously did not understand his question. She spoke in the Germanic tongue that he had learned long ago from Terlinda, when she had taught Ilka. He dimly remembered the other voices speaking this language.

"I must be a prisoner in their country," he thought. He searched for words, stuttering, and tried to sit up again.

"Lie still and rest." The woman spoke again, but her gesture conveyed more than her words. The lessons with Terlinda were too far back in his childhood to recall very much. The woman took a container from the table by his bed and gave him a drink of cool milk. The wonderful freshness of the liquid and the quiet touch of the woman's hands, as she pushed the damp hair back from his forehead, gave Almos a feeling of calmness and happiness. For some reason he knew he could trust her, and he willingly dozed off again.

Almos slowly regained his strength in the barred room, which he was not allowed to leave. Still, except for the bars, there was very little to remind him that he was in a prison. The room contained a comfortable bed and several chairs. There were books written in the strange ornate hand of the German monks, which he could not read, but the woman, whose name, he found, was Sister Magdelen, read them while he was resting. There was a strange picture on the wall of a man hung from a cross. Sister Magdelen had tried to explain it, but he could not understand the story of her God who died, she said, for her and even himself. It was ridiculous. If he had never even heard of this God, how could he die for him, Almos. On another wall there was a carved image of the God, and the same sign hung on a chain around Sister Magdelen's neck, and from the end of a rope of beads that she moved for hours on end through her gentle white fingers, mumbling words that she called a prayer. It all made no sense to the young pagan. He much preferred the picture of a mother and child to the unpleasant one of the man on the cross. Sister Magdelen said it was the same God when he was a baby. There was something very peculiar about her God, for everyone knew that gods are immortal and not born in the manner of ordinary men, and the man on the cross certainly led a very common life, not even like a king.

"He was probably a wizard, or magician of some sort, to perform the miracles Sister Magdelen says he did," Almos thought, and since he could not understand this strange religion, he ignored it.

The persistent attempts of his peaceful nurse and warden to make him join her in her prayers only made him impatient and antagonistic. "I will wait," she thought, "until he is stronger."

Sister Magdelen was with Almos almost constantly. Two silent men took care of his bodily needs, but as soon as he was washed and given clean bedding, she returned to sit and talk to him. The German words slowly came back to him, and with constant use of the language, he became more and more fluent. The sister told him he had been wounded and taken prisoner many months before. He had been transported here to Bavaria, heavily bandaged and unconscious most of the time, and put in her care. At first they had thought he would die, for he was in a coma so long, but since he was young and strong, he had responded, and now he was practically well.

"You are the guest of Carloman the Great," she finished, "he is keeping you here as a hostage to prevent your nation from moving any farther west into our territory."

Almos sat up quickly. "Then my father knows that I am alive?", he asked. "Oh yes," answered the nun, "I hear he has settled far to the east of here under the orders of Carloman, to save your life. . . but I really don't know much about it. I hear only rumors. You must ask Carloman about these things. You will see him soon."

Almos sat silently, thinking of Tokos and his followers, stopped in the middle of their search for the land between two silver rivers because of him. "I wish I had died," he muttered to himself.

Sister Magdelen looked at him with horror. "No, my son, don't ever say such a thing. The good Lord has given you life. You should be grateful."

Almos smiled. "Perhaps you are right. . . I should be grateful, but to you and not your strange god. There is a chance that I can persuade Carloman the Great to let my father continue his search, if they do not attack the tribes in his kingdom, but merely pass peacefully through. Since I am the hostage, I know my father would do it. What do you think, Sister?"

The nun shook her head slowly. The boy was a pagan, but he had a way that was hard to resist. "I don't know, Almos. Carloman is stubborn, and his ideas are not easily changed, but we shall see."

The days passed, and Almos began to walk again with the aid of Sister Magdelen. When he was strong enough to move about by himself, he left the grey stone room for short walks. The nun led him down the steps of the castle to a sunny terrace surrounded by a low stone wall. From there Almos could see the great castle he was living in and the town of Lerchfeld that stretched out all around it. The great walls with their many turrets, the lovely moat below, the sleepy little town, seemed unreal to the boy, like part of a dream he had been living in since the day of his capture. The deep, mellow tone of bells floated up to the bastion where he stood, and he turned to the sister.

"What is that? Why are they ringing now? Is something wrong?"

The nun smiled. "It is Sunday, and they call our people to the church to worship God." She pointed to a tall building that towered above the others in the town, and, on the top of it's spire, Almos again saw the sign of the cross.

The afternoon shadows lengthened and blended with the oncoming darkness, as Ilka cantered Jegyes over the vast plains with the two Komondors at her side. As the night slowly enveloped them, the girl rode on guided by the stars. She was riding westward, following the Byzantine trade routes. She knew that friendly nomad tribes would be camped all along the road, and, if she got lost, she could ask them which way the Magyars had gone. They would have stopped to rest along the way with these tribes to trade horses and cattle for supplies. "There is a tribe near here," she thought, "I can stop there for the night." As she came closer to the camp of the nomads, she saw signal fires burning. They were used to transmit messages from tribe to tribe, telling of marriages, deaths, or to give the alarm of approaching danger. Almos had taught Ilka to read the fire signals when she was very small, and she pulled Jegyes to a halt to see what news was being sent over the plains. As she watched, she knew she would not be able to stop with this tribe or any other along the way. The message read: "Look for girl on golden mare with two white dogs. Hold them where they are found." The fire signal was stopped with the sign of the Magyar nation, and then the fires were dimmed, then brightened again, repeating the message.

"So my father has found out that we have left already," she said to her companions. "From now on I must be more cunning and cautious than the fox. All the tribes will be looking for me in hope of a big reward, but if a dumb animal can out-wit the hunter, then surely I can too. I will have to find Tokos by myself, for, with the description of the trails, that the ones who returned gave, I know I can reach him."

The girl rode along a little stream that ran through the grassy plains into a grove of trees. "I can stop here for the night," she thought. "There is grass for Jegyes and water for us all."

She halted the mare, dismounted, and began to prepare for the night.

Ilka turned Jegyes loose to graze and built a small fire. Then she sat down to rest, leaning against Beles' broad back. She looked up at the sky, thinking of Almos, and saw a flock of startled doves rise out of the trees above her, then circle in a graceful spiral overhead. The girl quickly picked up her bow and arrows lying at her side.

"The fall is nearing, and they will be migrating soon. I'd better eat fresh meat while I can, and I can make my offering to Hadur, the protector of travelers, with one of these birds."

She took careful aim at a light-colored bird that could be easily seen in the darkness. The dove fell to the ground instantly. Ilka shot a few more arrows into the middle of the flock, and several more dropped to the earth, One arrow ran through two birds, an omen of good luck for hunters. The girl gathered up the doves and placed them near the fire. She added scented herbs to the blazing juniper and prepared her offering to Hadur.

Ilka crouched down in front of the fire and opened the pale grey dove, brought down with her first arrow. She chanted in a low, lovely voice calling upon Hadur for help, asking him to ride with her through her long journey. She picked out the intestines of the dove and threw them upon the ground so that they formed grotesque patterns by the fire-light. She smiled as she read the message of the God in the twisted design. Hadur would stand by her and bring her good fortune. The girl picked up the intestines and the bird and placed them on the sacrificial fire.

"Oh, Hadur," she said, "take my offering and bring me a sign tonight that Almos is alive!" The smoke curled around the bird for a moment and then rose in a billowing column to the sky. "Thank you, Great Hadur, for your kind acceptance of my sacrifice."

The girl bowed down before the fire, then rose to prepare the remaining birds for herself and the dogs.

Ilka felt completely happy as she opened the birds to dress them for cooking. She was thoroughly enjoying her outdoor life. The wild, nomadic blood in her veins made her feel exhilarated rather than tired after the long ride. She tossed the doves' intestines to Beles and Bundas, and the two dogs fought playfully over the treat. Ilka laughed merrily. She had the blessing of Hadur upon her venture, and after a year of anxiety and waiting, this positive action toward finding Almos seemed to destroy all her unhappiness. She began to sing to herself as she stuffed the doves with aromatic herbs, then dug out slabs of red·clay from the banks of the creek. She rolled each bird, feathers and all, in a ball of clay, and placed them on the fire, covering them with hot embers.

"Come on Beles and you, Bundas, we all need a bath." Ilka caught Jegyes and led her to the creek. "I'm glad to see your back is not sore, my golden horse, but you are very dusty."

The girl took off her clothes and walked into the cold water, leading the reluctant Jegyes behind her. The girl washed herself and then splashed the indignant mare, who snorted and reared in helpless rage. She was tethered to a heavy log in the stream and could not get away. When Ilka considered Jegyes and herself sufficiently clean, she went to untie the horse, but the mare was still angry over the outrageous treatment she had received. She snapped at the girl, and, when her teeth missed, she wheeled around and kicked.

Ilka jumped back laughing. "Stop, you devil, I know I was silly, but I feel so happy. . . come on, let me dry you off.

She led the mare out of the water, quickly dried herself with a sheepskin, and dressed. Then she took the sheepskin and rubbed the mare until Jegyes' coat was shining.

"You are lucky that your coats are too long for a night bath," she said to the dogs, who had watched the whole procedure with anxious eyes, afraid that they might be ordered into the creek. "But tomorrow morning you will have to wash before we leave and then dry in the sun. Now, let's go eat."

The girl ran back to the fire followed by the two Komondors, who barked joy fully, forgetting their usual dignity in their delight over the escape from a hated bath. Their deep voices echoed through the woods in accompaniment to Ilka's laughter over the antics of her pets. Jegyes watched them irritably, her sensitive ears laid back in protest over the noise, then she turned back to the more profitable business of cropping the tender grass.

Ilka knelt down by the fire and fished the hard-baked clay balls out of the fire with a stick. She hit them with her small axe, called a fokos, and the clay fell away. The feathers stuck in the shells, leaving the delicious golden-brown birds ready to be eaten. The hungry girl and her two dogs devoured their meal in a remarkably short time. Then they sat contentedly around the warm fire. Jegyes came out of the shadows and thrust a friendly muzzle into her mistress' neck, nickering softly to show her that they were friends again.

Ilka smiled. "I couldn't find any better companions than you three." And though they couldn't understand her words, the animals pressed closer to the young girl, as if to reassure her with their love.

After a while Ilka got up and prepared her bedding. She spread the wolf and sheep skins down by the fire and slipped between them. As she lay down the two dogs came and stretched out beside her. All was quiet, except for the occasional crash of a burnt log, as it fell apart in the fire, and the rhythmic crunch of Jegyes' jaws, as she grazed near her mistress. Finally the mare bent her legs and, with a groan, lay down on the soft grass. Somewhere a lonely night-bird called, and receiving no answer, called again. Ilka slept and heard none of the peaceful night sounds. She dreamed she saw Almos standing, pale and alone, in a huge stone room, a room that looked strangely like the ones in the castles her mother used to describe to her. The dream faded, and the girl sank into the restful, dreamless sleep of youth. Perhaps Hadur had given her the sign she had asked for.

The months passed as Ilka traveled westward, always following the trade routes. The leaves turned yellow and vermilion, then brown, as they fell to the ground. The winds blew colder, rattling and whistling through the bare limbs of the trees. Ilka watched the skies as she rode, wrapped warmly in a rough cape that she had fashioned from one of her sheepskins. When the sky grew grey and the months of snow were near, she turned toward the mountains to find shelter for the winter. After a week of searching she came upon an empty cave that was big enough to house the four of them. She spent her time collecting wood for the winter and storing it in the cave. She shot several deer and smoked the meat so that it would not spoil in the long months ahead. She gathered the tall grass from the slopes of the mountains, and, when it had dried, she stacked it in the cave for Jegyes. By the time the heavy snows fell, the four travelers were warm and dry in the cave, well supplied for the winter.

Ilka would have liked to travel on in spite of the snow, but she knew that it would be too deep for Jegyes and the dogs to wade through. Food would be hard to find, particularly for the mare, and so the girl stayed where she was, waiting for the spring. The snows were late in melting that year, and, in March, when they should have been moving on, a deep, white blanket still covered the earth, its hard crust sparkling in the sunshine. Ilka's supplies were low, and she was forced to go out for more wood and meat. She bridled and saddled Jegyes, who took this as a personal insult to her freedom after her long winter rest. The mare bucked playfully when the girl mounted and dumped her laughing mistress in the snow. The two Komondors joined in the play, barking and running in circles around Ilka and Jegyes. Their white, fleecy fur made them look like a pair of big snowballs, rolling and bouncing down the slope of the mountain. Ilka mounted again and sent the little mare galloping down the slope. The snow broke and rose in a silver cloud under Jegyes' hoofs, covering Beles and Bundas, who ran at her heels, with a sparkling powder.

Ilka had trouble finding meat for herself and the dogs. Jegyes could paw through the snow for grass, but the others had to have food. She finally found, and shot, two rabbits and a few birds, but they would not last very long.

"We will have to hunt again tomorrow," she said to the dogs. It's getting late, so we'd better go back to the cave before dark." She turned Jegyes back toward the shelter. "If I find some fallen limbs along the way, I can put them in the leather bags since we didn't find enough meat to fill them."

The mare was plodding on quietly through the snow when Bundas gave a low warning growl, followed by Beles' furious bark. Jegyes ears pricked forward, and she stopped, nostrils wide, sniffing, all her muscles tense. Her ears began to move back and forth, and she snorted with fear. Ilka alone did not know what the danger was; she had to depend on her eyes. She dug her heels into Jegyes side, and the mare reluctantly went forward into the thicket. Bundas and Beles streaked ahead, growling viciously, and disappeared out of sight. Then Ilka heard the sounds of a fight. She could distinguish the deep growls of the dogs, and something else was almost shrieking in a high, continuous whine.

On the other side of the thicket the girl found the two Komondors trying to pin down a small buff-colored animal that snarled and screamed at them, slashing through their thick coats with its wicked talons. It was a young lynx, not yet half grown. Ilka inserted an arrow in her bow and waited for a chance to shoot without hurting the dogs. Their coats were already flecked with red, and she was afraid they might be blinded or crippled by the lynx's sharp claws. Finally the dogs backed off for a moment, and Ilka's arrow whizzed through the air. In her excitement her aim was poor, and the arrow merely went through his right front paw, pinning him to a heavy pine log lying in the snow. The animal screamed at her in rage and pain, but it was helpless to defend himself. Suddenly, Jegyes leaped to one side so violently that Ilka was thrown to the ground. A yellow mass jumped from the tree above her and landed in the spot where the girl and horse had been only a second before. Beles and Bundas stopped worrying the lynx that was pinned to the tree, and turned on this new adversary. It was a full-grown lynx twice the size of the other. The full grown mother lynx had come to the defense of her son. Ilka scrambled toward her bow and arrows, that lay scattered in the snow a few feet away from her, but before either the dogs or Ilka could collect themselves for the attack, Jegyes tore past them toward the crouched animal. The lynx jumped, but the mare met it in mid-air with her sharp hoofs. The little golden horse was transformed into a slashing, four-legged fury. Her flying hoofs and strong teeth were everywhere as she destroyed the hated enemy.

By the time Ilka had recovered her bow and arrows the mother lynx lay dead on the ground, mashed to a bloody, unrecognizable mass. Jegyes stood trembling over the remains, while Beles and Bundas growled and worried the bits of torn fur and limbs, making sure it was dead. In the excitement of the fight with the larger animal, they had forgotten the young lynx who snarled at Ilka as she approached him, glaring at her with frightened eyes. The girl lowered her bow as she looked at the trapped animal, his torn body trembling with rage and fear. He knew he was facing death and yet the helpless animal met it defiantly without cowering. Ilka felt a great pity for the lynx, the same feeling that always came to her when she watched helpless prisoners being dragged in triumph through the streets. She heard the Komondors growling behind her as they came back to finish the fight.

"Back, Bundas! get away Beles! Leave him alone!" she commanded.

The bewildered dogs withdrew a few paces and lay down to watch their mistress. Jegyes' rage was exhausted, and she was gulping mouthfuls of snow to quench her thirst, a few yards away.

Ilka threw her heavy fur cape over the lynx and secured her trapping net over the struggling bundle. Then she took her hunting knife and cut the arrow off, leaving its head imbedded in the log. With a quick, firm jerk, she freed the paw from the painful shaft. She dragged the struggling, growling bundle of misery to Jegyes side, but the mare would have nothing to do with fiendish animals that day. She swerved away, snorting with fear every time Ilka tried to lift the lynx up on her back. Finally the girl gave up and pulled her captive over the snow behind her, as she rode an unhappy Jegyes back to the cave. Beles and Bundas watched the bundle, growling their disapproval of the procedure, but they obeyed Ilka's command, and left the animal alone.

When they reached the cave the lynx was half dead from his wounds and suffocation. The bundle barely moved, as Ilka dragged it into the shelter. While her curious pets watched from outside, the girl went to work at her prisoner. She had seen her father's skilled herdsmen treat animals that resisted any efforts to help them, so the girl knew what to do. She secured the lynx with ropes, then deftly tied his mouth shut and wrapped his feet in leather hides so he could not claw her. The animal was tied to the thick, gnarled roots of an overhead tree, that had grown through a crevice in the rock down into the cave. When she was sure that her new pet could not escape, the girl went to care for the wounds on her dogs and mare. She spread a soothing balsam salve on Jegyes' cuts and scratches, then turned the mare loose to hunt for grass in the snow. The thick coats of Beles and Bundas had protected them from any serious wounds, but she searched through their fur anyway, putting the salve on the small cuts she found to prevent an infection. She took two of the three rabbits she had killed that day and gave each of the hungry dogs one. When the dogs had eaten they stretched their sore bodies out by the fire, and slept, waking now and again to make sure the strange animal had not moved from his place in the back of the cave.

Ilka sat down by the fire to skin the third rabbit for her own meal. As she worked, she talked continuously to the lynx in low, crooning tones. At first the animal answered her with snarls of rage, but after a while his amber eyes contracted and the anger left them. His body relaxed, and he lay down on the ground, his eyes blinking sleepily in the unaccustomed warmth of the cave. The girl put her meat in the fire to roast and went to sit beside the lynx. His body stiffened as she began to stroke him, but after a while he got used to it and relaxed like a huge kitten. Ilka took the birds she had shot and then cautiously untied his mouth. The animal raised his head, watching her warily, as she impaled one of the birds on a stick, held it out to him. The lynx moved his head away, and then his hunger got the best of him. He eagerly devoured all the birds she offered him.

Ilka smiled. "I really will have to hunt tomorrow if you're going to eat like that, little beast. We don't have any meat left. Now then, I will have to give you a name." The girl thought a minute. "I will call you Vitez. You be quiet while I eat my dinner, and I will come back and talk to you later." The animal watched her walk away without fear. "I have made some progress already," Ilka thought. "Maybe I really can tame him."

The girl worked for weeks making the young lynx happy and confident in his new surroundings. The snow melted slowly, and the first spring flowers, snowdrops and golden stars, began to bloom in the green patches of grass that appeared between the drifts that kept their stubborn hold on the earth. The hunting became better as the animals came out of hibernation, and Ilka had no trouble feeding herself and her pets. At last the day came when the girl made her sacrificial offerings to the Gods, thanking them for their protection during the long winter, and then broke camp.

This time, as she rode westward on Jegyes, with Beles and Bundas at her side, she had a third follower. It was Vitez, who trotted a little behind the group in the independent manner of the canine family, his tasseled ears held high. He had recovered completely from his wounds and had grown incredibly since the day he was captured. He was a sleek, golden animal, weighing about sixty pounds, and, though Ilka had set him free to roam, after he had got gentle enough to be trusted, he refused to leave her. The dogs and Jegyes never

overcame their natural fear and distrust of the wild animal, but they tolerated him because Ilka had ordered them to leave him alone. After a while they became accustomed to his presence, and, in the way of animals, forgot that the lynx had not always been with them. Vitez left the Komondors alone because he knew the big dogs could hold their own in any fight, and he completely ignored Jegyes.

The weather had turned warm by the time Ilka reached the tribes she knew had probably traded with Tokos and his Magyar band. She knew her father's message, to hold her where she was found, had not reached this far, and she was safe in stopping with them.

Her journey was made easy from then on. The tribes along the way welcomed the lovely girl and her strange companions, and gave her an escort from one tribe to the other. All of them had traded with Tokos and his followers, and remembered the handsome leader pleasantly, for he had always been generous and fair in his business with them. They told Ilka the locations of the unfriendly German tribes, and escorts were provided to protect her from them. Each tribe gave the girl gifts of precious salves to make her skin fairer, perfumes, combs for her hair that had grown long again in the winter, for there was no need to disguise herself now that she was beyond the reach of her father. They offered her clothes, but she refused them. Her old hunting outfit was more suitable for traveling than the lively, fragile dresses they would have given her. One chieftain gave her a gold-studded, green leather collar for Vitez, for these superstitious people believed that the wild animal who walked so quietly at his mistress' side was a sign that she was favored by the Gods, and therefore one to be treated as such. They felt that if they protected her and gave her gifts, the gods would smile upon them also.

As Ilka traveled closer to the Magyars her thoughts were once more centered on Almos. The long winter months of rest were behind her, and the task of finding the boy she loved occupied her mind and crowded all else from it. The summer months were nearing as the girl rode up to the main encampment of the Hungarians. Messengers, from the tribe who escorted her, had been sent ahead to inform Tokos of her arrival, and he stood on the outskirts of the town to greet her. Ilka was shocked by the change in Almos' father as she rode near him. He had grown worn and old, his once handsome face was sallow and lined.

"He has suffered a great deal since he left to find the land between two silver rivers," she thought.

The girl greeted her elder with the proper respect and ceremony. Her words were formal, but her smile was warm and friendly, leaving the ceremonial salutes as a mere outer shell. Tokos returned her greeting, but there was no friendliness in his tone. His eyes were hard and his face, grim, as he took Ilka's hands and helped her dismount. They walked together, silently, toward the town, and Ilka saw to her surprise that there were wooden buildings and solid corrals. There was even a stone temple set on top of the tallest of the three mountains that were reflected in the broad, shining river that flowed through the middle of the village.

"Why, this is a permanent settlement," the girl thought, "and yet this couldn't be the promised land between the two silver rivers. I wonder what has happened, but Uncle Tokos is acting so strangely that I dare not ask him." They walked on in silence, but finally Ilka could stand it no longer. "Do you have any news of Almos, Uncle Tokos," she burst out.

The chieftain stopped and turned to her. "I have news, Ilka," he said gravely, "but I don't think it will make you very happy. I am sorry to find that you have left your father's house. It was a willful and foolish thing to do. You might have been killed or captured, causing no end of trouble to your father and the whole Magyar nation. . . but now that you are here, you have put me in a very difficult position. If I keep you here, violating agreement with Bera, the Taltos, by which your engagement with Almos was broken, it will cause a bad feeling between your father and myself. If he becomes angry, war may follow between the two halves of the Magyar nation, and brother will kill brother; son will kill father. I cannot help you, and I cannot turn you out. You were born under a bad star, Ilka. The price is too great to keep you here. Eventually your father will send a searching party and, if they find you, war will certainly be the result. I must send you back under escort as soon as you have rested for a few weeks. I only hope that Bera understands that I had nothing to do with this."

Tears of indignation and anger sprang to Ilka's eyes. "I did not come to stay with you, Uncle Tokos," she cried, "and I certainly did not expect such a cold reception after my long journey. I only came to find if you had any news of Almos, and then I was going on to find him. I know the blonde giants have him prisoner in one of their towns, and I will search through every one until I do find him. . . even if it takes my whole lifetime! How can you wish bad luck upon me by saying I was born under a bad star. Why, I am even riding one of your horses marked with the clover, and she has brought me luck on my trip. . . she saved my life when a lynx attacked me!"

Tokos looked at the mare's nose in surprise. "It is one of my horses, the only survivor of the breed," he muttered half to himself. Then he turned back to the girl. "Where did you get her," he shouted at her roughly, "my horses never left the family!"

Ilka started in alarm at his harsh tone. "Almos gave her to me the night before he left. I'll give her back, Uncle Tokos, only, please don't be so cross!"

The girl was tired by her long journey and upset over Tokos' cold reception. All the adult poise left her, and she was a child again, weeping with exhaustion and misery over the unexpected harshness from the man who had been so kind to her in happier times. She buried her face in Jegyes' shiny neck and sobbed.

The stern mask of Tokos' face softened, and he put his arm around her shoulders. "Don't cry, Ilka, my child, I'm sorry. . . I was just upset. I didn't mean to shout at you. Your unexpected appearance was a shock to me, and you have brought the last one of my horses, when I thought that they had all been destroyed. It is almost too much for me."

The girl turned to him with horror in her eyes. "Destroyed, Uncle Tokos.

What do you mean?"

The chieftain face was drawn with sorrow, as the terrible memories crowded back into his mind. He took Ilka's hand in his own. "Come, child, we will go into Etel together, and I will tell you what has happened on the way." The two turned and walked toward the town.

"Not many weeks after the battle with the 'blonde giants,' as you call them," Tokos began, "Carloman the Great, ruler of Bavaria sent word that he held Almos alive, as hostage. His messengers told us that we were to settle here, and cease attacking his tribes, or Almos would be put to death. Since Almos' stallion, Kurd, caused the death of Berenguk, one of 'Carloman's best warriors, he ordered the death of all that breed of horses as punishment to us. He would permit none of our fighting horses to survive, and he sent a regiment of soldiers to carry out his terrible orders. Keled. . . you remember him. . . my best herdsman, hid two of the mares, who were in foal. The soldiers of Carloman found them in the woods, and, since the mares carried the mark of the clover, they knew immediately what Keled was trying to do. They destroyed the two mares, then tortured, and finally killed, Keled, his wife, and his son." Tokos' voice grew harsh with hatred. "All the while they were doing their evil work, a man in a black sack stood with them. He carried a stick of wood in the shape of the cross and spoke continually of a God whose commandment was to love all men. He spoke of love while they tortured Keled and his family. He told us it was for our own good that all my carefully bred horses were killed, and he said our gods were evil and cruel pagan myths. When they went away not one of my horses was alive, and we are forced to live here, churning the earth like worms, because of Almos. I should go on for the good of my people, who are slaves to Carloman, but I cannot cause the death of my only son."

Ilka and Tokos reached the river where a large raft was moored. The girl was silent after the chieftain finished his story. She could find no words to express her sorrow, for she knew how Tokos adored his son, and the shock of the double loss of Almos and his beloved horses must have taken all the joy and meaning out of his life.

Tokos gestured toward the raft. "Our quarters are on the other side of the river. There the women will meet you and see to your needs. You will find many old friends, and they can give you all the details that I did not have time for but before we cross, smear mud on your mare's nose so the clover sign is covered. Carloman has a troop here to make sure we carry out his orders, and if they see a horse with the mark of clover they will kill it immediately. The mare is yours, Ilka, if Almos gave her to you, and I will not take her from you. We must rebuild the clover family together, for one day Carloman will forget, and we can bring them out in the open again. I cannot tell you what happiness it has brought me to find one of them still alive. It is a sign that the Gods will look on us with favor once more."

Ilka smiled. "Of course, Uncle Tokos. Jegyes will give you back your horses, and I know the gods will protect her foals, for they have watched over her through all the long days of my journey."

Ilka reached down and scooped up a handful of mud from the shore and covered Jegyes' nose, so that the blue mark could not be seen. She ordered the dogs onto the raft and then tried to lead the mare on. Jegyes snorted with fear. She did not mind swimming a river, but she had never been on top of one before. Finally under Ilka's coaching she stepped hesitantly onto the strange craft. Vitez stood back, snarling his disapproval, but, when he saw his mistress was leaving him, he crouched down and sprang, landing in the middle of the raft. Jegyes, nervous over her precarious balance, reared and jumped at the offending Vitez. The heavy raft rocked dangerously, and the water splashed over the sides making the footing slippery. Jegyes teeth closed on the lynx's short tail, and the snarling animal wheeled in pain, slashing the mare's nose with his sharp claws. The two animals slid against the guard rail, and it broke under the impact, so that they fell into the river. They came up coughing and choking, their fight forgotten as they battled a new adversary, the cold water. The men who were handling the raft began to laugh, and Ilka and Tokos joined them, as the angry animals turned to swim after them, sputtering and spitting out the water they had swallowed. When they reached the opposite shore, Ilka was in a much happier state of mind as a result of her pets' amusing accident.

Vitez climbed up the bank and immediately turned to lick his wounded tail, snarling all the while in rage. Jegyes' nose was badly torn with long deep slashes.

Ilka turned to Tokos. "Look," she said softly, so no one would overhear, "Vitez has taken care of the clover sign for us. Jegyes nose is so cut up that the mark will never show again."

Tokos nodded. "It is a good thing. Your lynx is surely a gift of the Gods, and they have solved our problem for us. Now, go along with the women. I know you are tired, and we will wait until you are rested to decide what to do next."

Ilka went willingly to meet her old friends, who were waiting impatiently for their chieftain to dismiss the girl.

"I will rest, but I know what I'm going to do!", Ilka thought, as she walked toward them.

The women surrounded her eagerly with affectionate greetings and many questions about their relatives in their old home. Ilka laughed as they all chatted at once, each trying to gain her attention.

"Wait a minute and let me catch my breath," she said, "after I've had a nice hot bath and some food, I will exchange my news of your families for any you have of Almos."

The women readily agreed and escorted her to the big tent set aside for the women's games and work. They poured hot water, from the kettle that was kept on the fire, into a big wooden trough, then brought clean clothes and food for their visitor. While she bathed and ate, Ilka told each of them in turn what she knew of their families. When she had finished, she turned to a girl, only a little older than she, who had been one of her playmates when they were children.

"Now, Emese, tell me the news you have of Almos, and don't leave out anything, no matter how bad it is. I want to know if he is wounded or sick, or. . . or anything."

The little dark-haired girl whom Ilka addressed looked at her old friend sadly. "You have come a long way, Ilka, to hear my bad news. He is not sick, and he has completely recovered from his wounds. What I have to tell you is much worse than that! Emese hesitated, and Ilka frowned impatiently.

"Well, what is it? Go on and tell me!"

Tears sprang to the girls eyes as she went on. "My poor Ilka, your long journey was for nothing. Almos is a traitor to his country. We have heard th. . . "

Ilka sprang to her feet. "That's impossible! I don't believe it!" she burst out. "We have proof," Emese continued, and the other women murmured their assent. "The soldiers who are sent by Carloman the Great have told us. They say that Almos has renounced our Gods and accepted a strange new religion called Christianity. He hunts and feasts with the German noblemen, while we are forced to rot here because of him. They tell us he is engaged to marry the niece of Carloman, the ruler of Bavaria, and they say that he loves this girl. He has forgotten you, Ilka he has forgotten all of us. I'm sorry I had to tell you this, but it is true. Carloman's soldiers have seen him. Even now there is bad feeling among the Magyars against Tokos, because he keeps us here to save the life of a traitor, even if the traitor is his son. Soon they will overrule his wishes and go on in search of the land between the two silver rivers. It is not right to go against the commands of the Gods for any one man. Many have died on the way. What is one more?" Emese stopped, the tears running down her face.

An older woman rose and walked to Ilka's side. "The only thing for you to do, my child, is to return to your father's house, and forget Almos. Tokos will give you a full escort, and this would please Bera, the Taltos. It will prevent a possible war between the two halves of the Magyar nation. You are young, child, there will be another brave, young warrior for you."

Ilka only half listened to the old woman. She looked at the others seated around her for a moment, then she stood up.

"There will be no war, and I am not going home. I will continue to ride westwards until I find Almos. I know you meant well, but all that you have told me is not true! I promise you that!"

Almos rose to his feet, as a tall, richly dressed man entered his room.

"I am glad to see that you have recovered, my son," he said, "I hope that you have been cared for to your satisfaction, and that you have been happy here as my guest."

Almos was immediately aware that his visitor was Carloman the Great. The boy returned the King's greeting with formal courtesy.

"Thank you, your Majesty," he said, "Everyone, especially Sister Magdelen, has been very kind to me. I have had everything I could want, but if you will pardon my question, I would like to know when I will be released to return to my people. I have had no way of communicating with them, and I want them to know I am alive and well."

The King lifted his hand and smiled. "Don't worry," he said, "they know that you are with me, but I think it is only fair to tell you that I intend to keep you here as a hostage, so that your nation will remain peaceful. You killed my cousin and my best warrior, Berenguk, but I have taken no revenge on you. You are free to go anywhere in the town that you wish, if you give me your word that you will not leave without my consent. You will be considered a member of my court, and you are invited to take part in all its activities. If you wish to communicate with your father, you must do so only through me. We will try this arrangement for a year, and then it is possible that you will be allowed to return to your people. . . if you want to go, and I hope that you will want to stay with us. Will you give me your promise to live by my terms?"

Almos thought for a moment. He was at the King's mercy anyway, and it would be better to stay in his good graces by accepting his proposal to live in his golden cage, than to make things unpleasant for himself by false heroics. He turned to the King, who was waiting patiently.

"I will do as you say, Sir, and I give you my word not to leave the town without your permission." Carloman smiled. "I knew you would be sensible about this, Almos, and I know you will find our way of life very pleasant. You will be given clothes, servants, horses. . . whatever you need. Since you are the son of a chieftain, whom I hope to have as an ally one day, you will be treated as such." The King bade him fare well and left the room.

Almos was amazed at this unexpected treatment, and an uneasy feeling, that Carloman was not acting purely out of kindness, kept him awake most of the night.

The next day Carloman fulfilled his promise. Almos was moved to a spacious apartment in the castle and given horses and servants that were suited for no one with a rank less than prince. Later in the day the King's personal tailor came to measure him for new clothes. In the excitement of this new adventure, Almos almost forgot Ilka. He hunted with the members of the court, who accepted him immediately. He learned the strange dances and games, and he joined in all the many activities. But as he be came more accustomed to his surroundings, his thoughts often wandered back to the girl. He remembered bitterly his promise to return for her within a year, for it had been almost two since that time.

"I hope the news has been carried back to her of my capture," he thought, "then she will understand. May the Gods protect her until I return, for someday I shall!"

Sister Magdelen's visits had almost completely stopped, and Almos saw her seldom. She returned to make sure her patient was not having any trouble with his old wounds. She had grown genuinely fond of the boy during his long illness, and she still hoped to convert him to Christianity. She spent her infrequent visits with him telling of the wonders of her religion. Almos listened patiently, but he still could not understand why she was not content to let him worship as he pleased.

"But I do not ask you to accept my Gods," he told her one day, and she had sighed impatiently and left the discussion of religion for another day.

The King had asked, which meant he had ordered, that Almos attend the Christian services every Sunday, and the boy obediently joined in the rites which held no meaning for him. He still believed in his pagan gods, and it was to Hadμr that he made his devotion, when the people around him knelt to pray to the man on the cross.

"I'm sure you will understand," Almos said to Him one day in church, not wishing to offend the god of his hosts, "but I am from another land, and our Gods are not the same."

In the games and tournaments Almos soon became an acknowledged leader. The heavy horses and weapons were hard to adjust to, and the dignified dances were a great test of his skill, but he succeeded in mastering both. One night at the King's table he was introduced to a tall, fair-haired girl called Juliana. She was Carloman's niece, and one of his particular favorites. Her pale hair was very different from Ilka's golden curls, but her face was strangely familiar to Almos. After he had talked with her a while, the boy realized that the princess bore a striking resemblance to Terlinda, Ilka's mother.

Juliana and Almos soon became good friends, and they attended the hunts, dances, and dinners together. Sister Magdelen would meet them in the royal gardens, and the three would walk and gossip together, telling the sister all the court news. Almos told them about Ilka and his promise to return for her. In return Juliana told him that she loved a knight called Hulderich, who was Sister Magdelen's brother. Hulderich was in disfavor with Carloman at the time, but she hoped that the situation would soon be explained so they could be married. The friendship of the two young people deepened when they found they shared a common trouble.

"Why is your Hulderich in disfavor?" asked Almos, but before the Princess could reply, a messenger came to them with a summons from the King. Carloman desired a special audience with them, and the two hurried to obey.

Carloman welcomed them pleasantly in his private chambers and bade them sit down.

"I have decided," he said, "that it would be a good thing for you two to marry and thereby unite my country with the Magyar nation. You, Almos, must renounce your pagan gods and become a Christian. I have watched you during these last few months, and I know that you have been happy here."

Juliana and Almos sat in stunned silence for a moment. Finally the girl recovered from the shock and protested. "Your Majesty, I. . . I love the knight, Hulderich. I cannot marry another, even though Almos and I are friends."

Almos nodded in agreement. "I am to marry to another in my own country, and I have promised her to return. Besides, I do not want to become a Christian, and this was not part of the promise I made the day your Majesty came into my room. I do not mean to be disrespectful. No one could have been more generous than "

"Enough," the King shouted furiously. "You are both ungrateful and willful young fools. I will give you a few days to decide, and if you don't think better of my proposal by then, I shall be forced to take unpleasant measures. As for you, you young heathen, I will have Sister Magdelen instruct you in the Christian faith, and if she does not succeed in converting you, then I will see to it that she is never made an abbess. She won't get her convent, and I'll make her a lay sister for the rest of her life. You are dismissed!"

Almos and Juliana hurried down to the gardens to inform Sister Magdelen of Carloman's sudden decision. When they had finished, the nun shook her head slowly.

"I might make a Christian of you, Almos, for I know that someday you will feel the hand of our Lord and become one of us. . . but this would not solve your problems. Carloman would still force you to marry Juliana."

Almos sat down beside the nun. "I would almost become a Christian to save you from the King's wrath, Sister Magdelen, because you have been such a good friend to me, but, you are right, it would not help us very much. There must be a solution. Juliana, what has Hulderich done to displease Carloman? Perhaps we could help get him back in the King's favor, and then he would let you marry him."

The Princess, who was always calm and poised, surprised her companion by bursting into tears. "I don't know," she whispered, "I don't know where he is, or what he has done. It's all so confusing, and no one will tell me anything."

The girl buried her face in her hands, unable to go on. Sister Magdelen explained what had happened to Almos.

"Hulderich was Carloman's best knight and warrior. He was even better than Berenguk, whom he always defeated in the tournaments. He won the hand of Juliana from Berenguk in a tournament several years ago, and the King at that time gave his blessing to the proposed marriage. They would have been married last year if Carloman had not had two great problems to settle. One was the pacification of nomad tribes, the worst of which were the Magyars, who raided the peaceful inhabitants of his kingdom on their swift, small horses and caused a great unrest among them. Carloman sent Berenguk to settle those troubles, but there was a much more serious difficulty. Basil I, ruler of the powerful Byzantine empire, was threatening war, so he sent Hulderich, disguised as a wandering minstrel, on a secret mission to Constantinople. Hulderich took with him documents and a valuable relique, with which to pacify Basil in the name of Christianity. Hulderich was chosen for his honesty and intelligence as well as for his skill in battle. This treaty between Bavaria and the Byzantine empire meant a great deal to Carloman. He told only three people about the mission beside of Hulderich; Juliana, myself, and Berenguk. He told Juliana and me to explain the postponement of their marriage, and he told Berenguk, who was to give Hulderich any military aid he might need, after the trouble with the Magyars was settled. For some time Hulderich sent messages back, telling of his progress toward Constantinople, then the messages ceased, before he reached Basil. Juliana thought at first he had stopped communicating with her for reasons of security, but then the King sent for her. He asked how long it had been since she had heard from Hulderich, and, when she told him, he became enraged. He had not had any word from his envoy either, and he thought that the knight had betrayed him. It has been nearly a year since Hulderich left, and we have had no word from him in many months. The situation between Carloman and Basil is much worse now. Basil accuses our King of having tricked him with the promise of the gift of the valuable relique and the documents, which they were to sign so, as to ensure peace."

Juliana had recovered her composure while the nun was talking, and she began to add to the story. "Berenguk returned to the capital just before you slew him in battle, Almos.

He went to the King and told him that Hulderich was guilty of treason. He brought a letter in Hulderich's writing that condemned him."

Almos looked at the girl in surprise. "Why is it that no one doubted him. Didn't the King send anyone to check on his report?"

"Oh no, Berenguk was not too smart, but he was known as an honest and courageous knight," Juliana answered. "I know that Hulderich could never be a traitor, but I thought that Berenguk had been misinformed. It is possible that Hulderich is held prisoner by enemies of Carloman, or he may have been. . . killed. There are those who wish a war between Carloman and Basil for political reasons, and if they had somehow found out about the secret mission, they would have done everything they could to stop Hulderich."

Almos frowned and turned away from the girl who sat beside him. If they thought so highly of Berenguk, he wondered if they would believe his story. "Juliana," he said at last, "from what I know of Berenguk, he was neither honest nor courageous. When we met in single combat, he fought unfairly and broke all the rules."

The boy then gave the two women a detailed account of the battle. "It is quite possible that he lied to Carloman to further his own cause, and perhaps he had something to do with the disappearance of Hulderich," Almos said when he had told his story.

Juliana clasped her hands together, and looked happily at the boy, "oh Almos, if only what you say is true; if we can find Hulderich and get proof that Berenguk was lying, then perhaps the King will let me marry my knight. But where could he be? . . . how can we find him?"

Almos shook his head sadly. "Dear Juliana, he may be dead, or sick, or in prison somewhere. I don't know what we can do, and I have given my word not to leave the town without the King's permission. If only Ilka were here, she could make an offering to Hadur and read his message that would give us a clue as to Hulderich's whereabouts. She learned that skill from her father, Bera, the high-priest of the Magyar. . . but I am a soldier and the son of a soldier. I know nothing about interpreting the word of the Gods."

Sister Magdelen started, for it was the first time the boy had ever called on his pagan gods in her presence. She started to reprimand him and then stopped. Almos was so sincere in his concern over Hulderich, that she could not bring herself to scold him.

The three decided to go to the King with their case, for it was possible that he would investigate their accusations against Berenguk just to clear Hulderich's name. Carloman was stubborn in his opinions, but he was a just man, and Sister Magdelen was sure he would want to free his favorite knight from the charge of treason. They hoped that he would permit Almos to take a small troop of soldiers out to search for Hulderich among the tribes, who lived on the route to Constantinople. Sister Magdelen told Carloman their story, who considered the matter fairly, as they had known he would. Finally he decided to consult his advisors in the matter.

The lords, who were familiar with the Hulderic treason case, gathered around the King's council table. Juliana and Sister Magdelen spoke so ardently and with such sincerity in defense of the knight, that the lords had to admit to the possibility that it was Berenguk, not Hulderich, who was the traitor. They agreed to send Almos and a band of warriors out to investigate, and Almos gave them his word that he would return. In less than a week the boy left Lerchfeld with his soldiers in search of the lost Hulderich. Just before he rounded a bend that took him out of sight of the town, he turned to look back and saw white dots, the kerchiefs of Sister Magdelen and Princess Juliana, who stood high on the walls of the castle, waving good luck and good-bye to him.

Ilka was on her way again. She had finally persuaded Tokos to let her continue her quest for Almos. She had refused his offer of an escort, saying it would only hinder her, while her four pets were more than enough protection. She had been shocked to find that Tokos also suspected his son of being a traitor.

"You are wrong, Uncle Tokos," she had said, "and I will prove it to you!"

The bewildered and unhappy chieftain had unwillingly consented to let her go on alone, hoping in his heart that her trust in Almos was not mistaken. Ilka rode toward Lerchfeld, stopping along the way with friendly tribes, but as she went farther west, the towns and villages became more frequent and more unfriendly. These were the Christian settlements under the rule of Carloman, and they looked upon the girl, who traveled alone with the huge dogs and a lynx, with suspicion and fear. As Ilka rode through a town, the people set their dogs on her, but the cowardly mongrels were no match for Beles, Bundas, and Vitez. In a short time the whole pack ran, howling with fright and pain, from the three furies, who would have torn them to pieces had they stayed much longer. The townspeople watched in amazement, then turned and ran into their homes, locking the doors behind them.

"It is surely a witch," they said to one another, "we must pray to the Lord to protect us against her evil enchantments !"

Ilka was surprised and hurt that she should be treated in such a way. "Perhaps they are afraid of wild animals. . . or they may think I have come to rob them," Ilka said to herself, and after that she avoided all settlements.

She rode through the woods, and along old trails so that she would not meet any of the unfriendly Christian people. She stayed off the well-traveled trade routes, but she always rode toward the west, parallel to them.

Late one evening Ilka was about to stop and make camp, when Beles growled warningly. The girl had strayed off her route and was not quite sure of her location, so she was deeper in the woods than she had meant to be. Bundas and Vitez stiffened suddenly as they caught the scent of danger also. Only Jegyes remained undisturbed, and Ilka knew then that the danger was of meeting humans and not animals. The girl pulled her mare to a halt and listened. She heard the snapping of brush breaking under foot and then harsh guttural voices speaking in the Germanic tongue she had learned from her mother. The voices cursed angrily, then there was the sound of blows, and Ilka heard the awful animal-like groans of someone in terrible pain.

"Be quiet. . . down!", she whispered to the snarling animals, then she dismounted and took her bow and quiver of arrows from her saddle.

She placed an arrow in the bow and then sneaked through an opening in the bushes. The girl could barely suppress an exclamation of anger and horror at the scene before her. A man was bound to a tree, and another man, dressed in a long black robe, rained blow after blow on his emaciated body with a wooden object. Near them a woman calmly lifted a cauldron from the iron peg on which it hung, then she turned and flung the boiling liquid on the bound man's legs.

The man screamed, and then muttered, "Yes, yes, I will tell. . . only let me alone."

JEGYES

The woman put her hands on her hips and sneered. "So you'll finally tell, will you. Well, you'd better not change your mind, or I'll cut you up alive."

"Where is the gem? Where are the documents? Hurry up!" The woman's companion shouted at the tied man.

"I told you I don't know. . . I don't have them. Why don't you. . .

His torturer slapped him across the face, cutting off his words. The bound man slumped against his bonds, unconscious. Ilka was enraged, and she started to interfere when another man came out of the small hut that stood in the clearing.

"What?. . . Is he unconscious again, Dinka," he said to the woman. "Well, I'll wake him up in a hurry!"

He grabbed a red-hot iron out of the fire and walked toward his victim. As he neared the bound man, Ilka's arrow pierced his chest. He made a half-turn, then fell to the ground, his hands grabbing futilely at the shaft. The second arrow went through the shoulder of the woman, but the black robed man side-stepped the third arrow and grabbed the hot iron to use as a weapon against the unexpected attackers. The dogs and Vitez came eagerly at Ilka's call and leaped into the clearing. Vitez crouched and jumped on the man as he struck at Ilka with the hot iron. The lynx's claws tore the huge brute's face, but the man grabbed the lynx around the neck and began to strangle him. Bundas leaped for the man's throat, and forced him to let go of Vitez to defend himself against his new adversary. The dog's weight bore the man to the ground, and Ilka quickly put an arrow through his heart. The woman, in her helpless rage, drew a long bladed knife that hung at her waist and jumped at the bound man. Beles, at Ilka's signal, attacked the woman and grabbed the hand that held the knife in his sharp teeth.

Ilka was about to shoot her, when another man in a soldier's uniform came out of the woods and quickly took in the scene, then he raised his bow to shoot the girl. His hastily shot arrow missed its mark but grazed Jegyes who stood behind her. The startled mare jumped forward and knocked against the woman, who was trying to free herself from Beles. When Jegyes hit her, she cried out in fear, jerked her arm free from the dog's teeth, and stabbed at the horse. Jegyes screamed, more from rage than pain, and struck the woman down with her sharp hoofs. Beles knew better than to interfere with the angry mare, and he jumped back to let Jegyes finish the job. In a short time the woman's screams stopped; she was mashed by the mare's wicked hoofs beyond all recognition. The soldier turned and tried to escape by running back into the woods, for he realized he was hopelessly outmatched by the girl and her demons. Ilka raised her bow and shot him as he ran, and he fell to the ground dead.

A strange silence followed the confused noise of the battle. Ilka felt weak and dizzy. She sat down for a moment, facing the tree where the man was tied, while the dogs and Vitez moved around the dead bodies making sure that they would cause no more trouble.

"I must get up and help him," the girl thought, but she did not have the strength to get to her feet. "I am coming to help you, only I must rest a minute," she said, in halting German.

The man did not answer, and he did not even seem to hear her words. He kept on moaning, rocking from side to side in pain. Finally Ilka got to her feet, and went to untie the man. His bearded face showed no reaction, though he looked straight at her. Ilka took her hunting knife and cut the heavy ropes that bound him to the tree. The man staggered against her, too weak to support himself, and his hands came up feeling her face and hair.

"Who. . . who are you? Where are the others?", he stammered. Then Ilka knew the reason for his strange behavior. He was blind.

"I am Ilka, the daughter of Bera, the Taltos, of the Magyar nation," she answered. "Don't be afraid. I'm going to help you. . . just lean on me, and I will take you into the hut."

As they walked slowly toward the small building, Ilka remembered that there might be more of the torturers away somewhere. "How many people kept you prisoner here," she asked.

"There were four", he said, "Three men and a woman, if such inhuman monsters can be called such. You must leave me here and escape before they come back, for they will kill you if they find you."

The girl turned to him in surprise. He must have been unconscious during the whole fight.

"You don't have to worry about them anymore," she said, "they are all dead now."

The man started and nearly fell. "Dead!. . . but who killed them?" "I did", said Ilka in her sweet voice.

The man stopped. "But that's impossible! You're nothing but a child. You couldn't possibly have slain those hired killers. . . why they were the most feared and hated ruffians in the country. You must have had help. . . didn't you? Where are they? What do they want from me?" Ilka gently urged the wounded man toward the hut, but he refused to move.

"Yes, I had help. . . from Beles, Bundas, Vitez, and Jegyes. If it hadn't been for them, I would never have rescued you. They are my. . . "

The man's fingers dug into her arm, and the girl gave an exclamation of pain. "What is it?" she said.

The man seemed to shrink from her, with an expression of terror on his face. "What do they want, I say? Why do they make you talk to me. Tell them I don't have the documents. I'll kill you, girl, if they come near me!" The man's hands moved up around her throat.

"Don't be afraid," Ilka said quickly. "Jegyes is my horse. Come here, Jegyes," she called. "Put your hand on her. Here Beles and Bundas. They are my dogs. This is Vitez. Be careful when you touch him. He is a lynx that followed me from my old country."

The man quickly made the sign of the cross with his trembling hand. "Oh God," he said, "then you are a witch."

Ilka was shocked to hear the ugly word that the Christian villagers had hurled at her when she had ridden through their towns.

"I am not a witch," she cried. "I am the daughter of the high-priest of the Magyars, and I am engaged to marry Almos, the son of Tokos, who is the leader of my people who search for the land between the two silver rivers. Almos slew Berenguk, a German knight, in battle. Almos was taken prisoner, and now he is held by Carloman the Great as a hostage. They say he is a traitor, and that he will marry the niece of Carloman, but I do not believe it. I was on my way to find him at Lerchfield, when I found you."

The girl stumbled over the foreign words in her haste to explain her situation. She was hurt and angry that the man should accuse her falsely, after she had risked her life to save him.

The man stood silently for a moment after she had finished. "I believe you, Ilka," he said at last. "This is the work of God. He has sent you to deliver me from those fiends. So Berenguk is dead. I didn't know. Let us pray, and thank God for His help."

Ilka looked startled. "Oh, no," she said, "it wasn't your God that sent me. The wicked people in the towns along the way drove me into the woods... anyway I prefer the company of wild animals to the Christians. I know how to manage the animals."

A smile broke over the tortured features of the man, and Ilka realized for the first time that he was very young, not much older than Almos.

"It was God, little Princess, whether you know it or not. He always tries the ones he loves the most, and he has burdened us both. We must thank him now for our deliverance."

The man sank to his knees, dragging her down with his weight. He began to pray to his god, asking for forgiveness and a piece of bread or something. It made no sense to Ilka.

"I wonder why he called me a princess," she thought, "my mother told me that it: was my western title, but no one else knew of it. It's very strange!"

She helped the man to his feet and led him into the little hut. "Lie down and rest," she said, and I will go get some water to wash your wounds. I have some herbs and salves in the bags on my saddle. They will lessen the pain and prevent infection."

The man nodded and smiled, but, almost before Ilka was out the door, he fell asleep from exhaustion, in spite of the pain from his injuries.

Almos rode swiftly toward the Magyar settlement. He knew that it was there, and in the nearby towns, that Berenguk had been last, before his death. The boy hoped that he might have made some reference to the missing Hulderich, if he had anything to do with the knight's mysterious disappearance. It was possible that Carloman's soldiers who were stationed at Etel might have known something about it through their former leader. Almos and his soldiers changed horses several times, as the heavy animals tired easily under the swift pace. The huge, ornate saddles were put on the fresh horses, and the tired animals were led on by grooms, who followed more slowly behind the band.

When, at last, they reached the Magyar settlement, Almos was shocked and hurt at the cold reception that awaited him. They looked at his foreign clothes, his well groomed short hair. They listened to the German expressions that he used in his conversation, and the Magyars decided he was not one of them any more. Even Tokos was unfriendly to his son, and even more so when he saw Almos' Bavarian escort, whom he had to feed and entertain.

"I am sorry to see you, my son, under these circumstances," he said. "I did not think that I would ever live to see the time when you would be a traitor to your country."

Almos looked at his father in silence for a moment. "I don't know how you could think such a thing of me... I never was and never will be a traitor, but I don't have time to explain my reasons for undertaking a mission for Carloman now," his voice matched the cold tones of his father. "But if you will call a meeting of your council, including Carloman's soldiers, I will tell you why he has sent me."

Tokos agreed, and, a few hours later, the men whom Almos wished to see were gathered in the wooden council building. The boy explained his suspicion that Berenguk had turned traitor before his death, using the knight, Hulderich, as a scape goat. He gave them a description of Hulderich, telling them that he traveled in the guise of a minstrel.

The Magyars readily agreed to help Almos search the country for the missing man, for it meant an escape from inactive life in the settlement, that had been forced upon them since the capture of Almos. They undertook the task with enthusiasm, and soon they were galloping over the plains questioning everyone they could find, asking if a minstrel had passed that way alone, or in the company of Berenguk, who was well known among the tribes around Etel. The people remembered the rough, hard-drinking leader of Carloman's soldiers, but none had seen a minstrel answering to Hulderich's description.

A few days after the searching parties had been organized and the surrounding country divided into definite areas for each to investigate, Almos at last found time to talk to his father alone. Tokos told his son of the unrest among the Magyars because of their forced inertia, and of the oppression from Carloman's guards, who were intolerant of their religion and way of life.

"They scorn us because we are not Christians, and they make us suffer because of the death of Berenguk, whom they consider a 'righteous, Christian knight'. They destroyed all my clover horses, because Carloman considered them symbols of the war like life we had lead. I thought they. . . "

Almos jumped to his feet. "Oh, no! How could they do such a thing! But I have good news for you, father, one of your horses still lives. I gave a golden filly to Ilka before I left. When we marry, I will bring Ilka here, and we can raise a new breed from her mare. I didn't tell you, for I knew that you would never let one of our horses leave the family. It is the work of the Gods that one of them has been saved!"

Tokos looked sadly at his son. "The work of the Christian gods that you have adopted, no doubt. . . and how can you marry Ilka when it is said that you will wed the niece of Carloman the Great? I have known for sometime that one of our mare's was alive. Ilka brought her here, when she came in search of you. I told her it was useless to go to you, but she. . . "

"Why didn't you tell me Ilka was here? Where is she?. . . let me see her!" Almos interrupted his father joyfully.

He was so excited he didn't bother to refute Tokos' accusation that he had become a Christian and was engaged to Juliana. Then he noticed a strange look on the Chieftain's face, and the older man did not answer his son's eager questions.

"Why, what's the matter, father?", the boy said, "Where is Ilka?".

Tokos shook his head slowly. "Against my wishes, she is on her way to Bavaria, to find you at the court of Carloman. She was the only one who had faith in you, and she would not believe you had turned against us until you told it yourself. I tried to stop her, to send her back to Bera, the Taltos, but she would not hear of it. I finally had to let her go."

Almos turned to his father in anger, his face tortured by fear for the girl he loved.

"How could you believe all that old women's gossip about me? I would never turn against my country and its people! Why did you let her go? She will meet terrible dangers. . . she may even be dead by now. Who did you send to guard her?"

Tokos sat stunned. The boy was obviously telling the truth. Ilka had been right after all.

"She refused an escort," he said, "she told me they would only be in her way. She took the ones who had protected her all the way from her father's house to Etel; the mare, Jegyes, her two dogs, Beles and Bundas, and a lynx that she caught and tamed along the way, called Vitez."

Almos' face turned white with horror. "Oh no! She will be caught and burned as a witch by those strange Christians, and you let her go. If she dies it will be your fault, father, remember that!"

The boy turned and stalked out of the tent, leaving Tokos with unspoken words of sorrow and contrition on his lips.

A week after the first searching parties had gone out, a tired rider galloped back into Etel with news of Hulderich. He told Almos that some members of a Germanic tribe that lived far off the traveled routes had seen a minstrel answering to Hulderich's description many months before. He was traveling with Berenguk, and they had thought that he had hired the minstrel to sing to him during his frequent feasts.

"Only one person saw the minstrel after that", the rider continued, "the wife of a wealthy trader was out hunting one day, escorted by a few slaves. She was traveling on a little used trail deep in the woods, and she said she was astonished to meet Berenguk, his minstrel, and three other men. She told me Berenguk greeted her cordially and said he was hunting too. She thought nothing more about the incident until I questioned her. Then she remembered that the minstrel had said nothing, though he had looked at her rather strangely."

This was the news Almos had been hoping for, and he questioned the rider eagerly. "Did she say in which direction they were riding. . . Was the minstrel bound?"

The man nodded. "They were riding toward the west, but she didn't think the minstrel was tied. The other men did have their swords drawn, but she thought that was because they were hunting."

"I see," said Almos," You have done a good job. Get some rest, and then tell the others what you have found. I want the people in that area and farther westward questioned. There's no point in looking anywhere else."

This was proof enough for Almos that Berenguk had imprisoned or killed Hulderich in order to get the fabulous relique, which Carloman had told him was a beautiful gem of unusual splendor, and the secret documents. It was possible that Berenguk had been paid by the enemies of the Bavarian king to destroy the papers and, therefore hasten war between Basil and Carloman. The thing to do now was to send the Magyars into the hills to hunt for Hulderich, but first he had to obtain permission from the king to allow them to go that far into the German hills and forests, which bordered on the boundary of Bavaria itself.

Almos dispatched messengers back to Carloman immediately, requesting permission to send the Magyars into Bavarian territory and more soldiers to protect them from the unfriendly people in the border towns. The request soon reached the King, and he called his advisors together. Most of them feared that the Magyars would take this opportunity to raid the peaceful inhabitants of the outlying villages.

"If they are attacked and find that you authorized the release of this wild tribe from their settlement, they will surely revolt against you. That will start all the tribes under your rule outside the actual borders of the country revolting," one old and trusted lord cautioned his King, "and you have more than enough trouble to handle with Basil threatening us. I don't think it would be a wise move."

Another lord spoke up. "You forget, your Majesty, that this Almos is one of them. He may be deceiving you for his own profit. We have only his word that he will return, and I doubt that a pagan's word means very much. He probably holds a grudge against Berenguk and wishes to ruin the name of our dead knight for personal reasons. How do we know we can trust the information he says he has found. He never knew Hulderich. . . why would he want to clear his name?"

The lords spoke in turn against sending aid to Almos, and Carloman listened silently to each one. Then he called upon Sister Magdelen and Juliana.

"I know we can trust Almos, your Majesty," Juliana said, "he is my friend, and he is doing this for me, for he knows I love Hulderich. He has never broken his word in the past, when he could have easily escaped from Lerchfeld. Give him permission to use his Magyars. The soldiers you send to aid them can guard them too."

Sister Magdelen turned to the King when Juliana had finished. "I know this boy well. . . I nursed him through his sickness, and I know he can be trusted. Besides this is your Majesty's only chance to recover the priceless gem and the documents Hulderich took with him."

The nun's wise argument was the deciding factor for Carloman. The recovery of the famous relique and the papers was the only way he had to prove to Basil that he was not trying to deceive him. If Carloman could send them to the angry emperor, it would once again bring about friendly relations between the two great powers. Then too, the King wanted to prove to his people that his judgment had been good in trusting Hulderich with such an important mission.

"I have decided to take the risk and give Almos permission and help to find Hulderich, if the knight still lives. I like the young pagan, and, if he proves trustworthy, he will be an invaluable assistance to us in pacifying his wild tribe." Carloman spoke with assurance, but that night he lay awake wondering if he had done the right thing.

In the cool darkness of the little hut Ilka sat beside her feverish patient and fed him broth, made from a freshly killed deer. The man was lying on a clean bed of pine needles that the girl had gathered. She had washed him and spread her soothing balsam salves on his torn body. His legs, that had been badly burned by the boiling water, were covered with sweet suet from the deer. Ilka kept the room as pleasant as possible for her patient. She put fresh flowers in an old helmet that must have belonged to one of the torturers, and she burned incense herbs all through the day and night to destroy the odor that sick people always brought into a room.

A week had passed since she had rescued the blind man, and Ilka was kept busy caring for him and Jegyes, who had been wounded in the shoulder by the knife of the evil woman, called Dinka. The dogs and the lynx had fortunately escaped injury. The mare recovered quickly, though her shoulder was still sore, and it was the strange man who worried Ilka the most. He had been unconscious most of the time. When he became conscious for a few minutes, he mumbled incoherently and didn't seem to know where he was. But he was too weak to offer any resistance to his young nurse, so she had no trouble with him. Ilka had to use all her skill to keep him alive, for the terrible fever nearly destroyed him. Finally, on the seventh morning after the fight, he came to as she was trying to feed him the hot broth. He put his hand out and felt her face, then he smiled.

"Good morning, little Princess," he said.

Ilka was overjoyed to find that he was going to recover and that he remembered her. She fed him the broth, and, while he ate, she explained how she had come there. She told him about her home, her long journey, her quest for Almos and about the great battle in which he slew the German leader, Berenguk, something which the man called a miracle. She told him about his terrible illness during the past week, and, when she had finished, she asked him about himself and how he happened into the hands of his vicious captors.

"Why, I don't even know your name," she said.

The man sat up and leaned against the pile of sheepskins Ilka had given him as a pillow.

"My story is a terrible one, little Princess. My name is Hulderich, and I was on a secret mission to Basil I, the ruler of the Byzantine empire, for the same Carloman who holds your Almos as a hostage. It is a strange thing how our lives are intertwined, for the Berenguk, whom Almos slew, was the one who held me prisoner. When I started for the east, I was to meet Berenguk in a town not far from here, and he was to give me any protection I might need. Luckily I hid the papers and the priceless relique I carried with me. I did not want to carry them with me for fear I might encounter thieves. I went with Berenguk and he began to behave very strangely. I should have suspected him then, but I was too preoccupied with my mission. He asked me to write a note for him that would complete the negotiations he had made with some Asiatic traders to buy their horses. Berenguk's writing was very poor, in fact he could scarcely write his name, so I readily agreed to do it for him. I became suspicious when he dictated an enormous price in gold and properties, far too high for any number of horses, but it was too late. I questioned him about the matter, and he became angry. He snatched the letter from me and left, but a little later he returned and apologized. His page brought us two glasses of wine to seal the friendship, and we drank. I was a fool to do it, for the wine was drugged, and I fell unconscious."

Hulderich stopped for a minute, his face sad as he remembered his misplaced trust in his fellow knight. Ilka got up and brought him a cup of cold spring water.

"Don't tire yourself," she said, "but please go on and tell me the rest, if you feel like it." Hulderich nodded and thanked her for the water, then he continued his story.

"When I woke up, Berenguk and his hirelings lifted me up on a horse and tied me to the saddle, cleverly concealing the bonds under the long cloak I wore, as part of my disguise as a wandering minstrel. They threatened to kill me if I spoke to anyone. Berenguk and the other man brought me to this place. We stopped in several villages along the way, and I was forced to act as their minstrel, but I had no chance to escape. Once we met a woman out hunting, and I tried to move so she would see I was bound, but she never sent help, so I suppose she didn't notice that anything was wrong. When we got here, the woman, Dinka, was waiting for us. One of the men was a Bavarian soldier; the others were hired thieves and murderers. They kept me chained in the cave in back of this hut. . . you must have seen it. It's in the side of the hill just beyond the trees. There were skeletons of many long dead people there, who must have been the previous victims of those evil fiends. The white bones were often broken in several places, a mute witness to the horrible torture and kill so many people.

How long have you been here?", Ilk asked.

Hulderich thought for a moment. "I don't know, Ilka, it has been many months, but I lost track of time long ago. Sometimes they would leave me in there for days at a time, giving me just enough food to keep me alive, then they would bring me out and torture me. There was one man who masqueraded as a Christian priest, and he was the cruelest of all. I think he was insane, for he actually enjoyed torturing me. I know he would have been disappointed had I broken down and given them the information they wanted, for it would have spoiled his pleasure. Berenguk did not stay here, but he came back every week to find out if I had told them the hiding place of the papers and relique yet. He always warned them not to kill me or beat me into idiocy, otherwise the treasure would be lost for good. Then one night the 'priest' left to find Berenguk, who had missed his regular visits for several weeks. When he returned he must have brought the news of Berenguk's death, although they did not tell me that. From then on the torture was much worse."

"They tore the nails off my hands, and they beat me nearly to the point of insanity. They left me tied out in the cold winter winds until a film formed over my eyes. From then on I lived in total darkness, not knowing what they would do to me next. When my nails grew back they ripped the off again. My life was an eternity of physical and mental horror. For a while I pretended I had lost my mind, and they were so afraid I would die or lose my memory, before they could find out the hiding place, that they left me alone for a few weeks. They even took the chains off, but one day the man who was guarding me, kicked me in the stomach, in his anger that his fiendish activities had been stopped. I doubled up on the floor of the cave, and, when he bent over me, I pretended to be unconscious. He knelt down in fear that he might have killed me, and I grabbed him. I don't know where I got the strength, but I threw him down on his stomach, put my knees on his back, and pulled his head up with a twist so that his back was broken."

"I got out of the cave somehow and groped my way into the woods. I was completely at a loss as to which way to turn. I kept bumping into trees and once I fell into a creek. I kept going until my strength gave out, but I soon found I had been traveling in a circle. They came and took me back the short distance to this clearing, and from then on I was chained day and night in that filthy cave. They tortured me horribly from then on, and I was on the verge of actual insanity when the good Lord sent you to deliver me from those fiends."

Ilka listened with pity and horror to the terrible things Hulderich had suffered. She wondered at his courage and his faith through all those awful days that his God would one day deliver him from his constant agony. He prayed constantly to that God and his Mother, thanking them for saving him before he had broken under the torture and given his secret away.

"I can't see how any papers and one jewel can be so important," she had told him.

"If I can get back to Carloman in time, so that he can send these things on to Basil, then I may have saved my country by my silence." he answered. "We could not survive a war against any one so powerful as Basil. That is why I must thank God for His help and ask Him to grant me the strength to return to Carloman in time. You must help me pray, little Princess."

He had taught her the prayers, and she recited them with him because it made him happy. Ilka was a good nurse, and she knew she would have to keep her patient contented if she wanted him to get well in a hurry. She watched him carefully, anxious for the day when he would be able to travel again, for she was impatient to be on her way again to find Almos.

Almos received the permission of Carloman to use his Magyars to search for Hulderich a few weeks after his request had been sent. He welcomed the extra troops and immediately started to cover the territory around the spot where the knight had last been seen, but the wandering minstrel had disappeared. No traces could be found of him. To add to this disappointment, Almos was frantic with worry over Ilka. The soldiers who had traveled over the route she must have taken had found no sign of her, so he hoped that she had already reached Lerchfeld where Juliana and Sister Magdelen would make her welcome and take care of her.

"If she has not reached the court, then she must be in trouble somewhere", he thought. "It's almost impossible for her to make the trip alone, guarded only by her animals. The dangers she encountered with wild animals and nomadic tribes will be nothing compared to that of these Christians, who kill people with the words of love and brotherhood on their lips. They are caught between their old Gods and their new one, and they don't know what they are doing."

Almos had sent a message to Carloman that the girl was on her way to his court, and asked him to send out an escort to protect her. The boy did not know that the King had immediately sent out a troop to find her, but they had been unsuccessful. Some people near the Bavarian border admitted that they had seen her, but, seeing the brilliant uniforms of the King's men, had not told them that they had driven her away with insults and stones, so the disappearance of the girl was unexplained. When she had access to the well-traveled trade routes that went from Constantinople to Lerchfeld, no one thought that she would go by way of the dangerous forests and mountains, that, for the most part, had no trails at all. When the soldiers reported their failure to find the girl, Carloman sighed and let the matter go.

"I would gladly welcome the girl in my court, but I cannot afford to send out anymore of my men to search for her. My forces are depleted now, since I sent a regiment to aid Almos," the King told Juliana. "She will have to find us by herself, if she is still alive."

As Hulderich grew stronger Ilka led him out of the hut and made him sit up in the sun, so that the 'chest-curse' would not attack him. She washed and combed his hair, and found that it was blond, nearly the color of her own.

"He must have been a handsome man," she thought, "It is a great pity that he has suffered so much, for it has taken his youth from him. He will never recover it."

One day, as she led the Knight out of the hut, the sunshine struck his face, and he turned his head away. Ilka looked at him in astonishment.

"Why did you turn your head, Hulderich?", she asked, and an impossible hope ran through her mind.

"The light bothered me. . . the light!" The man's voice trembled as he spoke. "Ilka, a miracle must be happening. I can see shades of light and dark. It's impossible, but I can. We must pray to Mary that she will cure my blindness." Hulderich sank to his knees and began to pray.

Ilka stood by him and began to think about what she could do to help Hulderich regain his sight. She had been accustomed to ask for the help of Gods. But then she also was aware of the old saying "Help yourself, so God will help you." She went to her saddle bag and took out a wonderfully clear mirror, made of metal, and another instrument with a tiny hole bored through the middle of it. She had been trained by her father to treat the eyes of animals, that often became infected when bits of foreign matter got lodged in them.

"Sit down facing the sun," she instructed the knight. "I am going to check your eyes with these instruments my father taught me to use."

Hulderich did as he was asked, and Ilka, using her tools, focused the sunlight on his eye. The sharp shafts of light centered on the pupil, and Ilka saw that under a grey film that covered the pupil and iris, the eye was intact.

"If I had a sharp knife with a tiny blade, I know I could perform the operation my father did so often on both people and animals," she told Hulderich, "but I do not have any tools delicate enough to do it here." As soon as you are strong enough we will go on to the court of your king, and there I will find the proper instruments. You will be able to see again after I operate."

Hulderich smiled. "I know you can do it, little Princess, after the miracle you performed in rescuing me, but how will we get there. I am too weak to walk, and I cannot take Jegyes from you. Perhaps you had better go on alone, and send some of Carloman's soldiers back for me."

Ilka shook her head decidedly. "No, we will go together when you are strong enough, otherwise there will be no one to take care of you. . . and I don't want to travel through the towns of your Christian friends alone. They think I'm a witch, and they might not let me pass through in safety."

Hulderich nodded sadly. "You are right, Ilka, we must go together but we shall go to my uncle's castle first. It is closer, and you can find the tools to cure my blindness there. I want to go to Juliana as a man and not as a useless cripple. She would marry me out of pity, and I could not bear that."

Ilka turned on him, her eyes gleaming with anger. "You call yourself a cripple? Why, you are worth one hundred of the frightened sheep who call themselves men in your country! I will not listen to you talk that way. Your Juliana should be glad that you are coming back to her at all!"

Hulderich laughed, forgetting his own self-pity in his amusement over the girls quick temper. She would not soon forget the treatment she had received at the hands of his countrymen.

Two weeks later they started on their trip to Huldenburg, Hulderich's ancestral home, where his uncle, Guldebrand, lived. Before they left, the knight made Ilka memorize the location of the place where the documents and the relique were hidden, so that, if something happened to one of them, the other could take the information on their way to Huldenburg. They were able to get a horse for Hulderich in return for bracelets from a Turkish caravan on its way to Constantinople. As they rode on through the Bavarian villages, the girl leading the blind man's horse, followed by the two huge, white dogs and the grey lynx, the people stared at them in horror and made the sign of the cross, as they ran to bolt their doors against the strange caravan. Hulderich said nothing, for he had decided not to tell anyone who he was. He was afraid that the story of his mission had been spread through the country, and he did not want to run the risk of being captured again. They planned to send a messenger to the King when they reached Huldenburg, but until then they had to go on slowly, avoiding as many towns as possible.

Several weeks later they reached Huldenburg, and Ilka stared in amazement at the strange buildings that surrounded a huge castle with great stone turrets and a wide moat that encircled it. She had been told of places like this by her mother, but she had never seen them before. The knight gave her directions, as she led his horse through the narrow streets toward the great fortress, where Hulderich's uncle lived. They passed by a church and a curious crowd gathered to watch them go by. They stared at Ilka and her followers, then backed away in fear to give her room.

"She is a witch," whispered an old woman and made the sign of the cross. "Yes," said another, "Look, she has devils clothed in sheepskin that guard her", and he pointed at the growling dogs.

"The lynx is her familiar, someone she has put a spell on," said one of the men. "We must drive them from the town before they work some awful enchantment on us."

Someone threw a stone and struck Hulderich on the head, then another grazed Jegyes. Ilka had trouble keeping her angry animals from attacking the crowd.

"We are almost there, Hulderich," the girl whispered, "hang on to your saddle. We will have to ride faster to get away from your Christian friends." Ilka put Jegyes into a gallop, dispersing the crowd, and the other horse obediently followed.

When they reached the drawbridge, a guard came out to meet them. "What do you want?", he shouted, "Go on away from here."

Hulderich took a ring from his finger and gave it to the guard. "Before you drive us away, take this to your lord, Guldebrand. He will have your head if you turn me away."

The man, recognizing the tone of authority in the blind man's voice, turned and went back over the drawbridge. The crowd gathered a safe distance behind the 'witch' and her companions to see what would happen. A short time later a fanfare was heard from within the castle, and then Guldebrand himself and his wife, Goldekind, started over across the moat, followed by the worried castle guards. Ilka quickly dismounted and helped Hulderich from his horse. He stood mopping the blood from the wound, caused by the stone, off his face, then he heard the footsteps as they echoed on the wooden drawbridge.

"Is that you, uncle," he cried happily.

Guldebrand stopped and stared at the strange figure before him. "It really is you, my boy. I thought you were dead, and some villain was playing a trick on me by sending your ring. What has happened to you?" But before Hulderich could answer his uncle embraced him joyfully the tears running down his face. "Speak to your aunt, Hulderich, she has done nothing but worry and pray for you since your disappearance." The knight dropped to his knees and groped for his aunt's hand, then he found it and kissed it.   ·

"Oh, Lord, he is blind. What have they done to you," Guldebrand mumbled half to himself.

Goldekind raised her nephew to his feet and started to kiss his cheek, then she drew back in horror. "Holy Virgin, protect us. You are blind!" Her eyes found Ilka and the girl's animals that stood at her side. "Who are they? Where did they come from? Did they do this to you?"

Hulderich smiled, "Not so many questions at once, good Aunt. The girl is my friend, she saved me from my torturers, and nursed me back to health. Don't be afraid."

"No, Hulderich, I'm not. It's just that the girl has such an odd gilden beauty, and that horse . . . I have never seen one like it before. . . that wild lynx and the two growling sheep. . . I don't understand. Have you made a pact with the devil? These creatures who protected you, you say, are not of this world."

Hulderich's voice rose in shocked anger, "Aunt Goldekind, how can you say such things. You sound like those ignorant, superstitious village folk."

Keep your peace, woman," Guldebrand said," anyone who helped my nephew is welcome in my house, be it the devil himself." He went to Ilka and kissed her. "Don't let this upset you, child. My wife is so glad to see our nephew return, that her emotion got the best of her. You are more than welcome here, and I am grateful to you for what you have done. Now, come along, you must be tired." Ilka felt the tears come to her eyes as she heard the kind lord's words, but she fought them back and smiled at him. Then the little group walked together into the castle.

The crowd stood silent and watched them disappear, then they hurried home to tell their neighbors what they had seen.

"Guldebrand greeted the witch with a kiss and bade her welcome," the baker's wife told her husband that night. "He ignored his good wife's warning that the girl was sent by the devil. She is the devil's bride, that's what she is. She'll bring a curse down on us, her and those three infernal monsters. She's put a spell on the knight, Hulderich, and she blinded him so he couldn't see her perform her hellish rites. You can tell by looking at her, she's evil. Somebody better do something soon, or we'll all be in the hands of the devil."

And all over the village of Huldenburg that night the story of the witch was told and enlarged upon, until the villagers had worked themselves into a frenzy of superstitious fear.

Ilka was miserable as she sat in the huge dark chamber that had been assigned to her. Her pets were separated from her for the first time since she had left her home, almost two years before. She could hear the unhappy howls of Beles and Bund as they tried to escape from the kennel, which Guldebrand had built for his hunting hounds. Vitez was snarling and clawing the wooden door of the stall, in which he was enclosed, and Jegyes, who had never been in a stable in her life, was kicking against the sides of her stall. Her manger was full of oats and clover hay, but she would not eat. The animals could not understand the separation from their mistress, and they were afraid something was wrong. The unhappiness of her pets made Ilka all the more miserable, and she longed to escape from the stuffy castle to be with them.

Someone knocked on the heavy oak door. "Come in," Ilka said sullenly.

Two maids came into the room and told the girl that they had been sent to take care of her. They brought armsful of lovely embroidered and bejeweled dresses for her use.

"The mistress says that you are to wear one of these at dinner tonight," one of the maids told her.

Ilka nodded, "I would like to have a bath first," she said, remembering with longing the huge copper tubs filled with hot water, that the servants scented with sweet perfumes from Byzantium, when she had to come in dirty and tired from a hunt back home. The maids stared at her and blushed.

"But, mistress," the youngest maid said, "Christian people do not have such immoral habits. Some are said to bathe all at once just before they marry, but never before."

Ilka was too tired to argue, and she dressed with distaste, feeling the dirt from her long trip on her body even if her hands and face were clean, washed in the cold water that stood in a small vessel on a table beside the bed. When she was dressed, the maids braided her hair with ropes of pearls. Ilka felt encumbered by the long robes and tight bodice of her costume, after the loose, comfortable hunting outfit she had worn for so long. It was tattered and ragged from many washings, but it had served its purpose well.

"I must look ridiculous," she thought, and turned to look at herself in the dim metal mirror that hung on the wall. The strange reflection stared back at her, and the girl was surprised to find that it was beautiful.

JEGYES

The ceremonies at dinner were very different from the ones Ilka was used to. Even Hulderich looked like another man, when his servant led him in. His beard had been shaved off and his hair was evenly cut. He was dressed in gold-embroidered clothes that were completely strange to the girl, and his crippled hands were encased in velvet gloves.

"Where is my wild dove," he asked as he entered the room.

Ilka ran to his side, stumbling over her long skirts. "Here I am, but I had no idea you were so handsome, Hulderich. No wonder your Juliana loves you."

Hulderich laughed and took the girl's hand. "Lead me to the table, little Princess. I am sure you have already scandalized our young Bavarian ladies, for it is usually the gentlemen who pay compliments, while the girls sit and blush in silence."

Hulderich was right, for the ladies of the court sat at their places and stared in amazement at the peculiar behavior of their lord's guest.

Ilka laughed and paid no attention. "But that's ridiculous. The women do not act like silly sheep in my country. But, Hulderich I must spend the night with my pets. The dogs and Vitez are howling and snarling, and Jegyes is about to break down her stall. I cannot bear to have them unhappy."

The knight shook his head. "You must get used to our western ways, Ilka," he said, "you cannot always remain a little savage."

"And why not?", the girl replied indignantly.

"Hush, child, and take your place at the table." Lady Goldekind interrupted. "We will talk about those things tomorrow. You must not forget that you are a princess, even if you are a pagan now. You will sit with my ladies-in-waiting."

Ilka silently took her seat and held back the angry retort she wanted to make. "I must not forget that I am her guest, and she is Hulderich's aunt," she thought, "but she is a foolish old woman anyway."

As she sat down Ilka heard one of the girls commenting on her immodest behavior to her neighbor. She turned to make an angry reply, but she was disarmed by the docile, rather stupid look in the girl's innocent, blue eyes.

"Why, the girl couldn't even begin to understand my kind of people. She looks as if she had never seen or known anything ugly in her whole life," Ilka thought, "If I said anything mean to her, she would probably cry, or do something equally stupid."

So Ilka remained silent, and concentrated on the dinner. She made several mistakes throughout the meal, because she did not understand the Bavarian ways. She did not wait for the grace to be said, and found the others staring at her in amazement, when she began eating immediately. She joined in the men's conversation about hunting, farming, and politics, for she was accustomed to the ways of Magyar women who held equal rights with the men in her country, but she could tell by the looks of her hostess and the girls around her that it was not considered proper in Bavaria. The men, however, were amazed at her knowledge and enjoyed thoroughly the novelty of a woman, who could speak intelligently on such matters.

When the meal was over, Lady Goldekind gave a signal, and the ladies rose and moved to another room. Ilka would have stayed where she was to talk to the men, but her hostess gently insisted that she go also. For the rest of the evening they chatted about little things, like the progress on a new piece of embroidery, that were of no interest to Ilka. When the other women rose to say good night to Lady Goldekind, after what seemed an interminable time, she curtsied in a clumsy imitation of the others, then hurried to the door to comfort her unhappy pets. As she started out of the castle the guard stopped her.

"The damsels are not allowed out of the castle after dark, M'lady," he said politely. Ilka opened her mouth to protest, but she realized it would do her no good, so she returned to her room. She hated the loss of her freedom and felt suffocated by the warm, stuffy chamber, the windows of which were closed to keep out the evils of the night air. Ilka tried to open them, but they had been closed for so long, that she could not move them.

"It's just like living in a prison," she thought, and she fell asleep with the howls of Beles and Bundas in her ears. For the first time in her life her sleep was restless with uneasy dreams.

Ilka bore her captivity as cheerfully as she could, but she could not get used to the restrictions that were forced upon her. She was not allowed out in the town for fear the people would burn her as a witch. Then too, Huldenburg had been attacked by a plague shortly after her arrival, so no one was allowed out for fear of contamination. A week passed, and the day came for her operation on Hulderich's eyes. Ilka was relieved to have something to occupy her mind and release her from her increasing impatience to be on her way to Almos. She felt confident of her ability to perform the operation successfully, and she sent Guldebrand to ask the castle physician to lend one of his sharp knives. She had brought the opium herbs, to brew an anesthetic, with her. Then her troubles really began.

Guldebrand came back followed by an obviously enraged man, who was protesting angrily as he walked.

"I am the physician here. How can you endanger the life of your nephew by letting this pagan girl operate on him? She may kill him. . . you can't trust her, I tell you !"

Guldebrand shook his head. "No, no, I will not stop her! I have made up my mind! Ilka, this bellowing old fool is my physician, Maguerus. He. . . "

"Where is the patient?", Maguerus interrupted, "I wish to examine his eyes. If Lord Guldebrand insists on going through with this madness, I shall supervise the operation. I don't trust you, girl, so don't try any of your trickery!"

Ilka stared at the enraged man in terror. She had heard of the cures Maguerus used, and she knew he was nothing but a licensed murderer. His methods were cruel, dangerous, and absolutely worthless. She knew she had to get rid of him, but she didn't know how. Maguerus pushed past her into Hulderich's room, and bent over the blind man.

"The eyeballs are obscured from within by the devil that fills your nephew's head," he told Guldebrand. "The only thing to do is to pour hot lead on the eyes. The devil will flee then, even though he will remain blind. . . but he will see light and happiness in the next world. If the eyes are left, shielding the devil, the knight will die in agony' and burn forever in hell," the physician finished his diagnosis in triumphant tones.

"Get out of here you butcher, you murderer, before I tear your eyes out. Don't you dare touch Hulderich! He is mine to treat. . . I saved his life!" Ilka screamed at the man, her eyes burning with anger.

Maguerus backed away from her. "Witch. . . the girl's a witch," he shouted, "she's possessed, I see the devil in her eye!"

"You won't see anything if you don't get out of here", Ilka said, and she grabbed a heavy battle axe from the wall. She started toward Maguerus, swinging the axe above her head. This was too much for the physician, and he fled in panic.

Ilka turned back to her patient, her face still set in anger. Hulderich burst out laughing.

"You're wonderful, little Princess, I wouldn't have missed that for all the gold in Carloman's treasury! It's about time someone put that blundering idiot, who calls himself a doctor, in his place. I never could understand why you let him stay here, Uncle."

"Never mind that," said Guldebrand, "But you must be careful, Ilka. You have made a dangerous enemy. You are lucky that the priest, Valentine, is on your side, but Maguerus is a powerful man. These ignorant townspeople will believe anything he tells them. From now on watch what you are doing."

Ilka felt elated over her success in scaring the evil doctor out of the room, and she did not feel a bit worried over anything that stupid man could do to her. "I will, I will," she agreed, "Now let's get started on the operation. Are you ready, Hulderich ?"

"I am ready anytime you are, little Princess," he answered.

"Good, said Ilka, now that I have Maguerus' knife I can cut the film from Hulderich's eyes that he can see again. He sees shadows, and the film over the eyeball is loose, so I don't believe the eye has been hurt at all. We've had the same thing happen to our horses when they were out in bad weather for too long. It won't be painful either, because I can brew a tea from my opium herbs that will put you to sleep."

The girl spoke with such assurance that any doubt in the minds of Guldebrand and Hulderich were replaced by complete confidence in her skill. Ilka made the tea and gave it to Hulderich, then sat down beside his bed to wait until he had fallen asleep.

The door to the room opened suddenly and Lady Goldekind stalked in.

"I thought I'd find you here, Ilka," she stormed, "I have never seen such unmaidenly behavior! Don't you know young women never go into the men's quarters. Now, come along with me. . . I will find more suitable things to occupy your time." She looked past the girl at her nephew lying on the bed. "And what is Hulderich doing asleep with you in here?"

Ilka was stung by the woman's scolding and at a complete loss for words.

She turned to Guldebrand in a silent plea for help.

"Go back to your quarters, woman, and leave us in peace. Your sharp tongue and prying eyes will get you in trouble one of these days. Ilka is here with my permission. Now go on. I will tell you what we are doing later."

Lady Goldekind turned and started out of the room. "All right," she muttered as she went, "but you'd better be careful I knew there was something strange about that girl the first day I saw her." The good woman's voice faded, still protesting irritably, as she moved down the hall.

"All right, Ilka, you can go ahead now, and I will see to it personally that you are not disturbed again" the lord said kindly.

"Oh no," the girl answered, "we must wait another hour, until midnight. According to my father, that is the time most favorable to the Gods for the performance of operations and my father is Bera, the high-priest of the Magyars. He knows about such things."

Guldebrand smiled. "You may wait as long as you wish. This is your undertaking, and I won't interfere in anything you want to do." He walked to a chair by the door and sat down there to make sure no one else would enter the room.

Ilka began her low incantations to Hadur, preparing for the operation all the while. She laid out bandages, and washed her hands in the sacrificial wine, asking Hadur to guide them and keep them steady. By the time the castle bell struck twelve she was ready. She dipped the knife in the wine that her God might grant sharpness and trueness to its blade. Ilka's hand was firm and sure as she bent over Hulderich's eyes. It took her only a second to lift the film and cut it away with the thin, delicate blade.

Guldebrand came to her side, trembling with fear, and looked into the clear blue eyes of his nephew, as Ilka held them open for him to see.

"May God eternally bless you, my child," he said, "I can never repay you for giving Hulderich back his sight. Ever since his parents were killed by a band of nomad robbers, when he was still a baby, I have loved him as a son, for I never had one of my own. My wife is barren, and Hulderich has been my greatest joy. If his life had been ruined by his blindness, it would have destroyed mine also. I and everything I own is yours to command."

Ilka turned away, embarrassed by Guldebrand's extravagant gratitude, and busied herself by tying bandages over her patients eyes to protect them from dirt and dust.

"It was really very simple, M'lord. Anyone of our herders could have easily performed the same operation. All I ask of you is to be allowed to go to Lerchfeld and to my Almos as soon as possible."

"If it were possible, Ilka, I would send you tomorrow," the old man said sadly, "but you must be patient a while longer. I didn't want to tell you, but a horrible pestilence besieges my town. It struck shortly after you came here. With that and the bad feeling my foolish people have against you, I would fear for your life, if I let you go now. The people are wild with fear of the plague, and I can no longer control them. I understand your impatience to be on your way, but I cannot let you from under my protection until it is safe. . . you understand?"

"Yes, I understand," the girl said, "I am sorry to burden you with more troubles. We will say no more about it. Now let's sit down and wait for Hulderich to wake up."

"My girl," Guldebrand said, "I will call the servants to clean up this room, and we will have a glass of wine while we wait."

He went to the door and gave his orders to the young page, who waited outside. A few minutes later two men-servants returned with the wine, and silently began to clear the room of the sacrificial wine, the instruments, and incense bowls that Ilka had used. They shuddered visibly when they saw the tiny spots of blood on Hulderich's pillow, and their hands trembled as they picked up the vessels containing the incense. They crossed themselves furtively as they left the room, and hurried to tell the other servants what they had seen.

"They were celebrating the black mass," said one. "She has bewitched our master, and put a devil in his body."

"I pray God will protect us from the evil of her vile instruments. . . we had to touch them," said the other, and crossed himself piously. "They have surely made a pact with the devil this night. She has traded Satan the lives of our neighbors for her lovers eyesight. . . that's what she did! She's the one who brought the plague on us!"

The other servants shivered in exquisite horror, and whispered among themselves that this was certainly true.

"Bunch of meddling old fools, that's what you are," said the kitchen master in his gruff way, "haven't got anything better to do than spread evil gossip. Nonsense. . . just a child. Nonsense, I say!" And he got up and stalked out of the kitchen.

"The old idiot hasn't got sense enough to see danger when it slaps him in the face," his wife said angrily, "Pay him no attention. I say something has to be done, or we'll all burn in hell."

When Hulderich woke up, he immediately put his hands to his eyes and felt the bandages there. He started to pull them away, but Ilka ran to his side and stopped him.

"No!" she exclaimed, "the room is too bright. Wait until I have blown out the candles, then I will take them off for you. We must be very careful."

The girl extinguished all but two of the tapers, so the room was in semi-darkness, then she moved to Hulderich's bed. She began to chant an incantation to Hadur in her sweet, low voice, calling on him to continue her success and give Hulderich his sight again. She reached down and gently untied the pads from the knight's eyes. In the dim light of the darkened room Hulderich saw the blurred outline of a figure, then slowly his eyes cleared and focused on the lovely face of Ilka, as she bent over him.

"I can see. . . I can see! Oh God, I can see again!" He could only repeat the words over and over, and then a choking sound came from his throat.

Guldebrand coughed, and Hulderich turned his eyes, now bright with tears, toward his uncle. "Well, what did you expect?" the old man said gruffly, "Can your eyes stand the strain of my ugly face after your physician's much prettier one?"

Hulderich looked at his uncle's ruddy, beaming face, and laughed exuberantly. "Well, Uncle," he said, "I can say this much at least. Your face is no uglier than the last time I saw it!"

In one day the news of Hulderich's recovery had spread through the town by way of the castle servants. The terrible message went from house to house. The pestilence that had come upon them so suddenly was the price the devil extracted from the witch in return for her lover's eyesight. Maguerus, the physician had been thrown out of the castle by Guldebrand, and his fanatic hatred for Ilka drove him to seek revenge upon her by the only means open to him. He further incited the people against her by spreading wild stories about the evil enchantments she had cast on the inhabitants of the castle. He told them that he had seen her talking to the devil himself, who rose from a pot of burning incense. He concocted fantastic and evil rituals, which, he swore, she performed nightly.

The people were crazed by the pestilence that each day destroyed so many of them, and Maguerus lies raised them to such a furor that they stormed the castle, demanding that Guldebrand hand over the witch to them to be burned. This was just what the wicked physician had hoped they would do, but the castle was too well fortified for them to get in. In their insane anger, they stoned and badly wounded the priest, Valentine, who tried to talk to them sensibly, telling them that the murder of an innocent girl would not rid them of the plague. No one realized that it was Maguerus who had done the most damage in spreading the horrible disease. He went into the homes of the sick in order to drive the devils from their bodies, and then he visited the houses of the well to exorcise any demons that might be lingering about their thresholds, waiting their chance to get in. He carried the plague with him everywhere he went, literally killing the people with his cures.

In a few days Hulderich's eyes were strong enough to stand sunlight, and he prepared to travel to Lerchfeld. Before he left he made Ilka promise him she would wait until Carloman sent a troop of soldiers to protect her from the people of Huldenburg, when she would leave the castle.

"It is possible that you could disguise yourself and slip out with me tonight, but you could never disguise your golden mare, or the dogs and Vitez. . . you can't leave them here, because you are the only one who can get near enough to feed and water them. And even if you could leave them, the risk is too great. Promise me that you will stay here and not try anything foolish!"

"I promise," said Ilka, "but, please hurry, Hulderich! I have waited so long. If I wait much longer, I will be an old woman, and then I know Almos will not marry me."

Hulderich laughed. "I wouldn't worry about that, little Princess, you are much too pretty for any man in his right mind to ever give up. If it weren't for Juliana, I would certainly try to take you away from him. But I will hurry, and you will be with your Almos in no time at all."

Late that night a dark hooded figure clothed in the dress of a monk, trotted over the castle drawbridge on a mule. He turned off on a road that ran along the out skirts of the town and disappeared into the darkness. It was Hulderich on his way to Carloman. The knight traveled in disguise, for he was afraid that the townspeople would hold him as hostage in return for Ilka, if they found out who he was. He expected to reach Lerchfeld within a week, and he was gloriously happy at the thought of seeing Juliana again. He remembered the ballad they used to sing together, and the melody rose spontaneously to his lips, while the "clip clop" of the mules' hoofs along the hard road beat time.

While Hulderich was on his way to Carloman, Almos sat in his tent not far from Huldenburg, moodily stroking the ear of his greyhound, as he thought unhappily of his failure to find Juliana's knight. A servant came into the tent with a vessel of wine, and asked if he would like to hear the new minstrel who had just ridden into the camp.

"Yes, yes anything," Almos said, "send him in."

The servant bowed and left the tent. A few minutes later a brightly costumed little man came into the tent.

"What would you like to hear, M'lord," he asked, "I have romances and tragic tales. I can sing of great heroes and of lovely maidens. I can tell you any tale worth the telling."

Almos was tired of the endless, detailed descriptions of battles, of the deeds of men long dead, and of the rescue's of fair maidens from fearful monsters.

"I want none of that," he said irritably. "Sing me the stories of things that have happened recently. Surely you know of something strange and interesting, some thing I haven't heard before."

The minstrel smiled delightedly. "I do, M'Lord, and gladly I will tell you the news of the country to the tune of my lute."

He began to sing of amusing incidents, improvising the song as he went and making Almos laugh with his wild tales. He sang for several hours, and then he began a story that immediately caught Almos' attention. This was the song he sang:

"Of Huldenburg I sing my song,
For sad is the suffering and sorrow there.
A wicked witch has spun her spell,
And fled far some for sanctuary,
And true is the tale that they told of their troubles.
There die many of deadly disease,
For the killing curse will last as long
As the evil enchantress flees from the fire.
She is found in a fortress, chilled by her charms,
Thus fagots cannot find a flame.
She feeds her fiend-horse and sheepskin demons
On the souls serene of simple girls
And still hot hearts of handsome lads.
She pestilence passed among these people
By demand of the Devil, who takes the dead
As his fair forfeit for certain sight,
Lost by her lover and got again,
Through terrible trickery and spurious spell,
A curse that was cast by sordid sorcery.
Her darkness has dimmed all light in the land,
For the life she leads is monstrous and mean.
Clouds of incense cover her castle,
As heavy as the hex that hangs o er the fair-folk.
But weird is the witch, for her looks are lovely,
Not white-haired and withered as witches should be.
She is gay and golden, though her gain is ill-gotten,
And her voice is soft and soothing to hear.
But all is a guise to cover her gruesomeness,
For, at midnight, comes she a crone again.
But the people have hope that God will guide
This bad-born enchantress to the burning fagots.
The flames of the fire will send her to Satan,
And save them from sorrow and dire destruction.
Her right wrist will bent be and broken badly,
That her spell may be spent and fail her forever.
The witch will wither with such white sheep
As follow her fondly to do her deeds.
The wilderness cat, that catches and claws
And devours children, will die with the rest.
Oh sad is their sorrow and lonely their life,
Whose families were fed. . . "

"That's enough!" Almos jumped to his feet and stood trembling.

The minstrel looked at him in surprise. "But I have not finished, M'Lord, there's only a little more."

"No, I don't want to hear it," Almos said sharply, "You can go now."

He gave the singer some golden trinkets for his trouble, and the bewildered man left the tent, wondering what he had done. Almos stood in the middle of the tent, his heart pounding in his throat.

"That 'witch' is Ilka, I know it," he thought. "I don't know who the blind 'lover' is, but the 'sheep' are Beles and Bundas. . . the 'cat' is that animal she tamed, and, of course, the horse is Jegyes. I've got to go to her before those insane people get their hands on her, if they haven't already. Huldenburg is only a day's ride from here. . . I've got to go at once." He walked out of the tent and shouted for his page. "Ho, Alrun, wake up! Saddle my stallion and find a horse for yourself and we'll take two extra horses in case the others get tired. We're going to Huldenburg."

The sleepy little page uncurled himself from his place beside the entrance to the tent and hurried off to do Almos' bidding. He was used to strange orders from his master, ever since the search for Hulderich had started. In less than an hour Almos was on his way, followed by Alrun, who led the two reserve horses. They galloped steadily through the darkness along the wide road to Huldenburg.

They reached the town, early the next morning. They rode past the deserted market place. There were no carts with jangling bells bringing fresh vegetables to market, and the few haggard people who stood in the street just stared at them dully as they went by. They passed a funeral procession, and Almos counted eleven coffins. The mourners looked with hatred at the richly clad nobleman on his sleek charger, and moved unwillingly out of the way to let them pass, muttering angry curses under their breath. Almos rode past the church into the town square and saw with horror the scaffold that stood there, with the wood piled around it ready for burning. He shivered with horror at the sight and quickly moved away from it. He rode up to the castle gates, and a guard shouted down from the top of the wall to ask him who he was.

"I am Almos of the Magyar people. I come under the authority of Carloman the Great. Let down the drawbridge!"

"You'll have to wait a moment, M'lord," the guard said, and he disappeared from the wall, to announce that a visitor of nobility had arrived and to get permission to open the gates to him.

While Almos waited, he noticed that there were signs of unusual vigilance about the castle. There were twice as many guards as were ordinarily used in time of peace, and it was not the custom to keep the drawbridge raised either.

"Ilka must be here," he thought, "And if the minstrel's wild tale had any truth in it, they are doing this to protect her. . . or else they're keeping her prisoner here until they decide to burn her. I will really have to rely on Carloman's name to save her then. I wonder what sort of a man this Guldebrand is. If he has any sense at all he couldn't believe such impossible lies, but these Christians are strange, even the best of them."

Finally after a long delay the heavy drawbridge was lowered, and, as Almos crossed over it, a rather short stout man, whom he realized must be Guldebrand, came to meet him. As soon as the young Magyar and his page were over the bridge, it was raised again.

Almos quickly dismounted and handed his horse to a waiting groom, then he went to meet Guldebrand.

"I am Almos," he said, "I have come from. . ."

"I know, I know, we have been waiting for you," Guldebrand interrupted jovially, "I thought if you didn't get here soon, your Ilka would have a fit. We've had a hard time keeping her here. . . wonderful girl. . . but where is Hulderich, and Carloman's soldiers. Has anything happened?"

Almos stared in astonishment at the elderly man. "You've been waiting for me? But how did you know who I was? And as for Hulderich, I've been hunting for him for months. How would I know where he is. I don't understand."

The smile faded from Guldebrand's face. "But Hulderich went to Lerchfeld to bring you back with troops to protect Ilka from my insane townspeople."

"I came from Buda. . . I haven't been in Lerchfeld for several months," Almos said, still puzzled, "I have been looking for Hulderich under orders from Carloman, but now I see the knight has found himself without my help. I heard about Ilka from a traveling minstrel. Until then I didn't know where she was."

"Oh, then that explains everything. Ilka found Hulderich for you, young man, and he has gone on to find you at Lerchfeld. He should be back any day now, but I must not keep you standing here. I know you are anxious to see Ilka. Come into the castle, and welcome. I will explain everything to you later. That is my wife who is coming toward us. She will see to your comfort, and the servants will take care of your page."

Almos was still bewildered, but he was very much relieved to find Guldebrand on Ilka's side.

From her room in the castle, Ilka heard the commotion in the courtyard. She ran to her window and saw a tall, strangely familiar figure talking to Guldebrand. Then she recognized him. "It's Almos," she screamed joyously, and she ran out of the room, her golden hair flying about her shoulders. She lost one slipper as she leaped down the steps two at a time. As she reached the door, a guard stepped out to prevent her from "rushing out half clad", as he later reported the event to his friends. Ilka stuck out her foot and tripped him, so that the poor man fell sprawling on the stone floor. She ran out into the courtyard, past the astonished soldiers and pushing everyone out of her way, she went straight into the arms of Almos. From the shelter of his shoulder, she turned her radiantly happy face to her host and hostess. They met her gaze with shocked disapproval.

"For heaven's sake, Ilka," said Lady Goldekind angrily, "can't you ever behave like a lady. What do you mean by running out here and throwing yourself on Almos' neck.. . . and in a house robe too, with your hair down and barefoot. We know you're glad to see him, but couldn't you at least wait until you were dressed properly."

Ilka turned scarlet with embarrassment, and turned to Almos beseechingly. "I am so very happy to see you, my darling," he whispered, "but we have to keep on the good side of these people. Go on back to your room. I'll talk to you later."

Almos' words were like a slap in the face to the girl. She turned in silent anger and went back into the castle and up the stairs, picking up her lost slipper as she went. The guard, who was still brushing the dirt off his clothes, watched her go by, but when he saw the tears streaming down her face, he checked the angry words that he had prepared for the girl, who had tripped him.

Late that afternoon Lady Goldekind summoned Ilka to her room. When the girl arrived, she told her that Almos and Guldebrand had explained to each other their strangely entangled stories. She told Ilka that her marriage to Almos would have to wait until Carloman gave his permission, for the king wished the young man to marry Juliana.

"But now that Hulderich is assuredly back in favor, I'm sure that every thing will be straightened out without any difficulty. It's just a matter of time. You must try to understand, Ilka, and check your wild nature," the good woman finished.

Ilka listened silently, sitting very straight in her chair, her hands folded meekly in her lap, but she was still angry.

Lady Goldekind spoke again in gentler tones. "I understand your feelings, child, and you can see Almos anytime you wish. . .under the proper circumstances. In a day or two Hulderich will be back, and he will bring good news I know. Carloman is a kind and just man. He would never deliberately ruin the lives of four people with unhappy marriages. When he finds out how much you have done for Hulderich, he will certainly be grateful enough to permit you to marry Almos."

By the time Ilka was dismissed from Lady Goldekind's chamber, she was white with anger.

"Why should I be dependent on the grace of some foreign king," she thought, as she went to her room to dress for dinner. "They say that his line of nobility is not even as old as mine. I am the daughter of the Taltos, and who are these people to dictate my life to me. I would leave this accursed castle this minute if the drawbridge weren't up. I think I will sneak out the back way to see Jegyes and the others anyway. I will wait until everyone is busy with the games and dancing after dinner, then no one will try to stop me."

In the evening Ilka was a lovely sight, as she descended the stairs that led into the main dining hall. A great feast was spread out before in honor of Almos' arrival. Stuffed fowl and wild game covered the huge table, surrounded by steaming pies and pastries. The wine bearers brought in vessels of sweet, white Moselle and heavy red wine, and poured it in the crystal goblets. The minstrels were singing merrily to the tune of their lutes, and their melodies echoed to the high stone ceilings filling every corner of the room with music. The ladies of the castle came down the stairs with Ilka last. Her proud walk, her easy carriage, and her shining, dark gold hair set her apart from the others. She had a natural royalty that the others had not been able to get in the castle school rooms.

Almos stared in amazement at the great beauty of his wild little Ilka. The love that shone in his eyes, as he bent on one knee in formal greeting, only made Ilka angrier than ever.

"He is a slave to that awful king, waiting like a coward for Carloman to say that he may or may not be in love with me," she thought, "I will teach him! I don't want the love of a slave!"

But as the evening passed Ilka forgot her rage, as she danced with Almos. He had grown taller and handsomer in the three years since she had seen him, but his deep voice brought back to her the happy times they had ridden together over the plains.

"Almos," she whispered as they danced, "Come out on the wall by the west tower after everyone has gone to bed, and we will be able to talk alone. I know I can sneak out and meet you."

Almos hesitated a moment, and then he spoke in a low, level voice. "No, dearest, that would be foolish, and you know it. If we were caught, it would only anger Guldebrand and his good wife. We will wait until Carloman sends us permission to marry. There will be plenty of time then, our whole lifetime. Be patient, my love."

"Your love? I'm not your love, you coward!" Ilka answered him in a fierce whisper, and stalked away from him in anger.

She curtsied to Lady Goldekind, and asked to be excused from the party because she had a headache. The woman consented and watched her charge walk gracefully up the stairs.

There's something strange going on," she thought, "she never had a headache before Almos came."

As soon as she reached the upper gallery, Ilka changed her direction and went over to the east end of the castle, down the steps to the stable. Jegyes poked her head over the stall door and whinnied happily, as the girl approached. She stroked the mare's nose unhappily, while Beles and Bundas howled for their share of the attention.

"At least my pets don't wait for the king's permission to love me."

The combination of rage and excitement over seeing Almos again broke through her self control. She sat down beside Vitez' cage and wept bitterly. Suddenly the lynx snarled, and Ilka looked up to see a dark figure standing in the shadows of the stable. The girl quickly brushed her tears away and stood up.

"Who is it? Who's there?" she called out.

"It's only me, Princess. It's only Rony." The woman came up to the girl, and Ilka saw with relief that it was the kitchen master's pretty young wife. Lately the serving maid had gone out of her way to be kind to Ilka. She had told her the news of the plague-ridden town and brought her special tidbits for the animals. The girl couldn't understand this, for most of the superstitious servants avoided her, but she was grateful for the attention. Rony had offered to take her out of the castle at night, by way of a secret passage, to see the beauty of the countryside and hunt in the moon light. Ilka had refused, but she was grateful to the maid for understanding her desire for freedom.

"I see you are unhappy, Princess," Rony said, "Won't you change your mind and go out hunting for a few hours? You have been closed in for so long; it will make you feel better!" Ilka started to refuse, but then she heard the music and sounds of laughter that floated out from the hall.

"I'll go! Wait for me while I put on my hunting clothes. I'll meet you here in a few minutes." When they met again, Rony had a dark scarf in her hand.

"I hope you won't mind if I blindfold you," she said, "but I want to keep the passage a secret.

Ilka wanted to object, but the maid had been so kind to her, that she didn't want to hurt her feelings. They went down by the castle dungeons, and there Rony put the blindfold on the girl. Then the maid led her down many winding stairs, where the air was cold and musty. Ilka heard the sound of water in the distance, soon the air began to smell clean again. The girl wished she had brought Beles and Bundas with her, but she knew the danger of the dogs being seen and thus giving her away was too great. Suddenly she heard the terrifying sound of a door opening and footsteps echoing along the corridor, but before she could scream, a heavy sack was thrown over her head, stifling her cries. She struggled desperately, but then someone struck her over the head, and darkness enveloped her.

Carloman's castle was ablaze with light, and the music rang through the streets of the town. Everyone was rejoicing, for their best knight, the favorite at all the tournaments was back, and his name was cleared of all the traitorous deeds attributed to him. Juliana was more beautiful than ever in her happiness over the return of Hulderich, as she danced with him that night. At dinner the knight had told the assembled company about his miraculous escape from Berenguk's hired killers. He told them of the brave young Magyar girl who had accomplished the impossible by killing his four torturers with only the help of her horse, two dogs, and a tame lynx. He spoke of her strange ways and her great courage. He told the amazed noblemen how she had wondrously saved his eyesight, and of the grave danger that threatened her life from the plague-stricken, witch-hungry people of Huldenburg.

By the time Hulderich finished his story, Carloman felt a great admiration for the little pagan princess.

"I will bring her here to safety at once," he said, "and she can marry her Almos. She well deserves any reward I can offer her. I will teach her our western ways, and I will appoint her and Almos rulers of the Magyar nation. They will keep the peace between our two countries by love instead of force."

The King felt very pleased with himself over finding such a happy solution to his problems, and he felt even more benevolent when Hulderich told him that the important documents and relique were safely hidden. They were later recovered and sent to Basil, who readily agreed to peace. Carloman suggested a quick marriage to between the knight and Juliana, then a royal excursion to Huldenburg to visit Guldebrand and his wife, and to get Ilka.

"We will have to send a message to Almos at Etel to meet us there," Carloman said, not knowing that the young man had already reached Huldenburg.

The marriage of Juliana and Hulderich was celebrated two days later, with feasting and dancing all through the night. Sister Magdelen and the nuns of the convent worked feverishly to finish Juliana's wedding gown. The good sister directed the whole wedding so beautifully, that Carloman made her abbess of a new convent near Huldenburg as her reward. The king knew she would be delighted to return to her childhood home, so he had purposely given her that particular convent. Since she could not take part in the celebrations after the wedding, Sister Magdelen decided to go on ahead to Huldenburg, to investigate her new convent. She had to admit to her self that the sin of curiosity was urging her to go, for she was anxious to see the lovely pagan, who had such courage and such an unusual knowledge of medicine. And, since she was very fond of Almos, she wanted to see the girl that he was to marry.

The nun left at dawn on the day after the religious rites that united her brother and Juliana. Two lay sisters accompanied her, mounted on black mules, that walked on either side of Sister Magedelen's small white one. A guard of two mounted soldiers brought up the rear of the small group. The sister expected to reach Huldenburg within ten days, stopping overnight at convents along the way, or in the manor houses of Carloman's noblemen if there were no convent. A week after the group left Lerchfeld, Sister Magdelen stopped over night with some old friends. During dinner they told her about the terrible pestilence that was raging in Huldenburg.

"The people say there is a witch in Guldenbrand's castle, who brought the plague down on them."

Sister Magdelen jumped to her feet in disgust. "That is complete nonsense!" she cried. "Our Savior told us to love one another, so the silly townspeople blame their misfortune on an innocent girl."

"I don't know," said her host, "but there seems to be evidence that she really is a witch. Many have seen her two huge sheep that actually growl and bite, and she has a lynx that follows her about, as tame as a cat, they say. The physician Maguerus swears he has seen her practice her demonology at midnight. There must be some truth in their stories."

Sister Magdelen stood in horrified silence, as she realized the 'witch' they were talking about had to be Almos' Ilka.

Sister Magdelen left her friends that same night and rode as fast as she could toward Huldenburg. The group reached the town late at night, three days later. They slept outside of the plague infested place and rose at dawn to cross through to Guldebrand's castle. The two guards refused to enter the pestilence and witch haunted town, so the three nuns rode alone toward the castle. Suddenly one of the lay sisters reined her mule to a stop.

"Hark, Mother Magdelen, the church bells are ringing an alarm, and I thought I heard a drum beating."

The nun listened to the bells, and then moved ahead at a fast trot. "Hurry my sisters! Something is happening, and our help may be needed!"

The outskirts of Huldenburg were deserted, and the hoof beats of the mules echoed loudly in the deserted streets. They turned a corner and stopped, uncertain of which direction to take. Sister Magdelen listened, and then the cry of an angry crowd rose and hushed, then sounded again. The good woman hit her astonished mule and sent him galloping awkwardly in the direction from which the angry shouts has come. The animal dashed into the square, through the startled people, who moved aside to let him pass. Then the crowd hushed in amazement as they saw a nun leap to the scaffold, brandishing her little crucifix toward them.

Ilka regained consciousness, and an agonizing pain shot through her right arm. She tried to move, but she could not. Her fever-distorted vision saw thousands of mask-like faces below. She heard voices shouting,

"Burn the witch!"

"Burn her quick, before the Devil rescues her!" "Burn the witch !"

"Burn the witch!" The voices came from all sides, repeating the awful phrase.

The girl felt the pain in her arm, everywhere, and her head felt as if it would split from the terrible throbbing. She felt someone supporting her, and, for a moment, she thought it was Almos, then she realized that her support came from chains that cut her flesh and bound her to a scaffold.

"Oh, Hadur, let me die with courage," she mumbled, and then her voice rose, trembling and scarcely audible, in the pagan chant for the dead.

Someone struck her across the face, but she went on singing. She saw a man in an executioners garb raise a flaming torch above his head, but she no longer cared. Suddenly she saw a white-robed nun jump in front of the man and push the torch aside. Then the girl realized that someone had come to help her, and she wanted to live again. She saw two other nuns mount the scaffold to stand beside the first, whose voice rang clear as she told the people about Hulderich, and of what Ilka had done for him. Some of the older people, who knew Sister Magdelen as a child, listened to her, saying that perhaps the sister was right, but most of the people muttered angrily, still wanting the 'witch' to be burned.

Suddenly Maguerus, the physician, pushed through the crowd to the feet of the nuns.

"These women are possessed by the devil. The witch has even cast her spell on these nuns. Don't listen to them, I tell you. They are bewitched. Let the witch be burned!"

The physician's sallow face bearing signs of the last stage of the plague, trembled, and saliva drooled from his distorted mouth. Then his body convulsed in violent spasms, and he fell to the ground, dead. His twisted mind, warped by his hatred for Ilka, and he had spent his last energy in trying to destroy her. The towns people stared at the dead man, and began to scream again.

"The witch killed him!"

"Burn her before she kills us!" "Burn her and the false sisters too!" "They are all possessed by the devil!"

The mass of people began to push forward toward the helpless women. Then the bugles of the castle sounded the alarm.

When the ladies of the court started to morning mass, they noticed that Ilka was missing, and they immediately reported her absence to Guldebrand and his wife. The whole castle was searched, but the girl could not be found.

"We won't tell Almos just now." Guldebrand told Lady Goldekind, "It would just upset him, and I know she must be here somewhere."

They searched the girl's wardrobe and found that her old hunting costume was gone.

"Find out if anyone else is missing." Guldebrand told the captain of the guards. "Call all the servants together in the main hall and check them!"

When the servants were all gathered, Lady Goldekind immediately noticed the absence of the maid, Rony. The kitchen master told them, trembling with fear, that his wife had been behaving strangely of late.

"Forgive me, M'Lord," he said, "but I did not have the heart to tell on her. She must have known a way out of the castle, for she left many nights, when she thought I was asleep, and did not return until dawn. Her shoes always had red clay on them, and there is no red clay within the palace grounds."

Guldebrand was horror stricken, for he knew that if Ilka had left the castle, Rony had probably turned her over to the townspeople to be burned.

"Sound the alarm! Sound the alarm!" he cried.

Guldebrand kept only a small guard of fifty men at the castle during peace time. In the event of war the army was recruited from the peasants who worked the vast lands of the feudal lord, so he had to do the best he could with the small troop. The guards lined up in a hurried formation, while Guldebrand told them what they were to do. Almos was forgotten in the confusion resulting from the disappearance of Ilka. He had gone down to the stable to try to make friends with the suspicious Jegyes. He fed her grain and talked to her until she accepted him, then he had decided to take her up on the second story bastion in the castle, that looked down over the draw bridge.

Almos coaxed the mare up the flight of stairs with a handful of grain, laughing at Jegyes' anger at having to go to such trouble for her reward.

"Maybe if Ilka sees you up here," he said to the horse, "it will put her in a good humor again. She's like you Jegyes; she rebells against any restraint. I will have a hard task trying to tame her after we are married."

As Almos looked out over the moat, he could see clearly the whole town and the church square, where the people were gathered. He saw the scaffold, and it looked as if someone were bound to it.

"They are going to burn some poor devil," he thought, "and they've already got him tied to the scaffold."

The shouts of the crowd drifted up to the castle, and Jegyes began to move restlessly, her ears laid back, as she sensed that something was wrong.

"All right," Almos said, "I'll take you back to the stable if you're going to act that way. Here you can't jump over the moat!"

Almos caught hold of the mare's bridle, as she started for the edge of the parapet. Then he heard the alarm bells ring out, and he turned quickly to find some of the ladies of the court coming toward him.

"Where's Ilka?" he cried.

The tear-stained faces of the women seemed an indistinct blur, as one of them answered him. "Ilka is gone. Guldebrand says that they have her in the town square, and they will burn her if we don't get to her soon.

The horrified voice of a guard sounded from the main gate. "The drawbridge is stuck! Someone must have broken the mechanism. We could never fix it before they burn the girl!"

Almos wheeled and flung himself on Jegyes' back.

"I've got to get to her," he thought, ignoring the impossibility of doing so.

He snatched his light sword from his side and hit Jegyes hard, with the flat of the blade. The frenzied mare bolted in the direction of the moat, then shot out over the water, attempting the impossible jump to the other side. The women watched in terror as the horse leaped into space, then gasped in amazement as she landed, with a slide that almost threw her off her feet, but safely on the other side of the moat. She recovered instantly and galloped on toward the square. In less than a minute Almos was riding through the crowd, cutting a path with his sword. Jegyes helped him by bitting and kicking savagely at the people who stood in her way. Before the dumbfounded citizens could recover their wits,

Almos had reached the scaffold. He tore the flaming torch from the executioners hands and flung it into the midst of the crowd. One of the women's skirts caught fire, and she ran shrieking in blind terror setting many others ablaze as she went. The people were bewildered by this sudden turn of events, and they milled about helplessly, not knowing what to do.

A group of fanatic witch-burners attacked the little group on the scaffold, and Almos leaped from Jegyes' back to defend them. The mare was left alone, and a crazed man slashed at her with a hunting knife.

"I'll kill you, you soul-eating devil-horse."

Jegyes' head snaked out so fast that the man had no time to draw back. Her teeth crunched on his arm, and he screamed in pain. From then on the enraged horse fought off the people who pressed near the scaffold, and they backed away in fear from her flying hoofs.

Then Guldebrand and his soldiers thundered down into the square, scattering the rest of the crowd. The people ran home in panic from the avenging swords of Ilka's rescuers, and a still hush enfolded the place.

Only Jegyes still moved restlessly in her anger, then Ilka's low voice called, "Ne, Jegyes, ne. Stop it! It's all right now."

The mare snorted and stopped short as she recognized her mistress' voice.

"I thought," said Guldebrand weakly, "that we would never get that draw bridge fixed!"

Almos quickly untied Ilka and carried her gently down from the scaffold. She would not lie down, and she could not stand on her trembling legs, so she sat, giving Sister Magdelen directions as to how to set her broken hand.

"This is a lucky break," she said to Almos, who stood beside her, his face ashen as he realized how close Ilka had come to death.

"Why do you say that, darling?" he asked.

"It's a lucky break for you," Ilka said smiling, in spite of the pain, "because if my wrist weren't broken I would hit you over the head for jumping poor Jegyes over the moat. You might have killed her, and yourself too. Sometimes I wonder if there isn't some truth in what these Christians call a miracle."

"Well then, we are even," Almos said, "because if I weren't so exhausted from fighting off those insane witch-hunters, I would certainly beat you for leaving the castle. I knew you were stubborn, but I didn't know you were stupid too." Both Ilka and Almos burst out laughing at that.

"You are right," the girl said, "we're even, so we can start all over again." Carloman and his court arrived a few days later. The King gave Almos and Ilka permission to go back to Etel to be married and live there as rulers of the Magyars. The two nations lived peacefully after that, and even old Tokos softened. He was completely happy in being able to breed his beloved horses again, and Jegyes gave him many beautiful colts. The Magyars flourished and spread out on the rich lands, thinking that perhaps Hadur had meant this to be their new home after all. Hulderich and Juliana came often to visit Etel, and Almos and Ilka returned to Lerchfeld many times. And King Carloman sat happily on his throne, thinking to himself, that he had handled the situation very well indeed.

* * * * * *

Of the many children of Almos and Ilka, one became very famous in Hungarian history. This was the legendary hero, Arpad, who led the Magyars further westward into what is now Hungary. They gradually occupied all of the fertile middle Danube valley and became a stable, agricultural people. At the end of the tenth century, Christian missionaries entered the country, and under the first Hungarian king, St. Stephen, who was crowned in 1000, the religion of western Christianity was accepted. Stephen was crowned by a representative of the Pope, and during his reign of forty-three years, Hungary was influenced greatly by the western civilization and made rapid progress toward becoming an important European power. It was just before the coronation of Stephen that our next story occurred.

Mez

HE name Mez, meaning honey, exactly suited the little filly, who was out of a great granddaughter of Jegyes. The colt's sire was a white Turkish stallion from the stables of the ruler of the Byzantine empire. When Mez was born she was the pale gold of honey, which gradually turned a creamy butter color, and, by the time the mare was five years old, she was pure white. Her pink nose bore, very faintly, the slate blue mark of the clover. She belonged to Margit, who was the last child and only daughter of Gyula, a Hungarian Chieftain, who was related to Almos' family. Margit adored her little mare, and, to her mother's dismay, preferred to play with Mez rather than the children of the court. With the help of a little Moorish slave, whom her father had given her to be her groom, the child taught her filly many tricks. Mez could stand on her hind legs, lie down, bow, and kneel. She would perform only for her mistress or her little groom, and, try as they would, no one else could get her to move. She would stand firmly planted, her four legs wide apart and her ears laid back, if anyone else gave her an order. If they tried her patience too far, she would lash out with her tiny hoofs in anger.

When Margit was eight years old, her happy life was interrupted by a sudden tragedy. Stephanus, the Christianized great grandson of Arpad, was to be crowned King of Hungary by an emissary of the Pope, but his coronation depended upon his settling the Hungarians peacefully and converting them to Christianity. Stephanus argued with and threatened Gyula and a few other chieftains, but they refused to give up their pagan gods. Finally, in desperation, he had all the people who refused to adopt Christianity, executed. He kept the orphaned children of his dead noblemen in his court, and educated them in the Christian faith. Margit's father and older brothers were killed, and the little girl was taken to Stephanus' palace in Buda, where every thing possible was done for her, and the other children, to make up for their loss. Margit was given slaves, new clothes, and even a little grey monkey as a pet, but the child cried night and day. The only thing Margit loved after the death of her family was Mez, and they had taken the dainty cream-colored filly from her too.

Stephanus knew that the famous clover horses were symbolic to the Hungarians of their former nomadic and pagan life. He thought that the only way to make them forget the old life was to destroy everything that reminded them of it, so he had all the horses bearing the mark of clover destroyed. His soldiers corralled all the mares, foals, and stallions together, then built a great circling fire around them to burn them alive. A few of the screaming, tortured animals jumped over the fence and galloped away like huge torches. The silent crowd of new Christians saw them disappear into the marshlands, then turned back with helpless anger to watch the rest of their beloved horses being devoured by the fire. Heavily armed guards stood around the fire to prevent the Magyars from saving any of burning animals. These soldiers wore on their cassocks the sign of the God of love and understanding, the sign of the cross. When all the horses were dead, one of the guards turned to his captain.

"Shall we find the ones that escaped, sir, and destroy them?

"No," the captain answered, "They were too badly burned to live very long. It won't be necessary to go after them. Come on, let's get away from here. I can't stand to look at the faces of these people any longer!"

The captain was wrong in his belief that the escaped horses had died. A few of the Magyars, who preferred to live in the marshes as outlaws than bend to Stephanus' religion, found the dying animals and carefully nursed them back to health. These Hungarians were hunted and a price was set on their heads. They gradually moved eastward to escape persecution, taking the clover horses with them. They later intermarried with the pagan Cumanians, or Kuns, and lived in exile, far from threat of death that had followed them in Hungary.

Margit soon heard what had happened to the horses, and she was inconsolable. She refused to eat or play with the other children, and no one could find out what was the matter with her. Finally Stephanus' exasperated wife, Gizella, ordered her to go riding with the other children. Margit was the only child who had not adjusted to her new life, and the Queen was at her wit's end as to what she could do about it.

"If I force Margit to join in the activities," she thought, "perhaps she will be all right in a few days."

Margit obeyed, but it was a listless and unhappy child who walked down to the stables with her companions. As the little girl entered the stable, she was astonished to find her Moorish groom waiting for her.

The little black slave grinned broadly, and beckoned to his mistress to follow him away from the others to the end of the barn.

"I waiting for you come, little Mistress, I keep surprise for you. Come where others not hear!

The groom ran to the last stall and pointed to it, still smiling as if his face would split in two. Margit followed him and looked into the stall. The pale honey colored filly, who stood there, whinnied in joyful recognition. "Oh Mez, my Mez, how did you get here?" The little girl flung open the door and wrapped her arms around the mare's neck. "Moro, what happened? How did she escape," Margit whispered.

Moro shrugged his shoulders. "I not know, little Mistress. Men kill other horses with red flower, but go pass Mez's stall. They look. They say 'this one all Oriental,' then they go. Later men bring us here. I wait for you."

Margit understood immediately why her mare had escaped death. Mez, with her white color and lovely head, looked like her sire, rather than the clover horse who was her dam. The mark of the clover was so faint and so small on Mez's nose, that the soldiers had overlooked it, and so the mare had been brought to Buda along with her father's other pure Oriental horses, for her own use. When Margit returned from her ride that evening, she was laughing and running with the other children. Queen Gizella was astonished at the change in her young charge, and congratulated herself upon using the right method to cure Margit of her lethargy.

The next few weeks were happy ones for the little girl as she played with Mez in the castle gardens or rode the mare over the grassy plains. The day of Stephanus' coronation was nearing, and, in the confusion of preparation, Margit was left to herself to do as she pleased. One day as she rode into the stable yard on Mez, Moro ran out to meet her, his usually smiling face twisted with terror.

"Princess, Princess," he cried, "I hear awful thing! Wilbur, who is groom to King, tell me Mez be killed in market place, after King crowned. He say Master Irtoban, your father's old friend want to get in King's favor, so he tell him that Mez is clover horse. King himself come to see this morning before you ride." The little groom choked on his words and tried to brush the tears away, that streamed down his face. "I hide in stall next to Mez, and hear King say he kill her same day he crowned. He say too, he brand Master Irtoban for telling on old friend, but horse must die as warning to any who keep what he call pagan things. I not understand, little Mistress, you do something!" Margit leaped down from Mez's back, took the groom by the shoulders and shook him.

"You're lying, Moro," she cried, "you made it all up. It's not true, or else you misunderstood, didn't you?"

Moro started crying harder. "N-n-no, little Mistress. I not lie! I hear King say this thing. I not lie!"

Margit knew the little slave would never lie to her, but she couldn't make her self believe that Stephanus would really kill Mez. She handed the reins to the bewildered Moro, and without another word, walked slowly back to the palace.

The week before the coronation, Margit spent all her time with Mez. She cried day and night, and she avoided everyone she possibly could. One day as he was walking in the royal gardens, the Bishop, who had been sent by the Pope to crown Stephanus, noticed a lovely little princess weeping, as she stood patting a cream-colored mare. He walked over to the girl and spoke gently to her.

"Can I help you, my child?"

Margit turned and, seeing the Bishop, dropped to her knees to kiss his ring.

The good priest took her hands and raised her to her feet. "What is it, child? What is your sorrow?"

"My horse, your Eminence. They are going to kill her."

"I'm sorry, but perhaps she is sick. It is better than letting her suffer." Margit shook her head, unable to answer as the sobs rose again in her throat. "Then, why will your pet be killed?"

"Because she is a pagan," Margit answered.

The surprised Bishop could not suppress a smile. "Don't cry any more, my child," he said, "perhaps we can convert her." He patted Margit's head and went on his way, leaving the little girl to wonder what he had meant.

Several days later, Stephanus and the Bishop sat talking together in the huge formal hall, that looked out onto the wide blue river below them. Beyond the plains, on the opposite side of the river, the purple mountains rose high into the clouds, as still and clear on this sunny day, as a detailed painting.

"You have done wonderful work in bringing Christianity to your people, Stephanus," the Bishop said, "but did you have to use such cruel methods. Our Lord taught us that much more is accomplished by love and understanding. If you would only use gentleness, and lead by example, the results would be much better. You were not like this when we were young." Stephanus and the Bishop Odovar had been pages together in the court of Henry. They had been best friends since childhood, and Gizella, Stephanus' wife, was a cousin of the Bishop's. The Bishop was astonished at the old and tired expression on Stephanus' face, as he raised his head to answer his old friend.

"Do you think, Odovar, that I like to murder my kin? Torture my best chieftains? I had to use force to get my country unified. My court is full of orphans because of me, and I cannot look at them without sorrow. Even Margit, the daughter of my cousin Gyula is here. He was the finest and bravest of my noblemen, but he stood in the way of progress of Hungary. I didn't want to execute him, but I had to. There is another child. . . "

The Bishop lifted his hand. "Stop, Stephanus, before I forget. There is some thing I want to ask you. I saw little Margit today, crying heart-brokenly over her white mare, whom she says you are going to kill. Don't tell me you are destroying horses to establish the Christian faith."

"Yes, unfortunately I must," Stephanus said sadly. "The breed of horses that Margit's mare comes from has been established as the symbol of the old pagan ways. There are innumerable legends about them, stories of their extraordinary deeds, that always remind my people of the old gods, the fighting, nomadic life. The mere existence of these animals, called the clover horses, did more harm to Christianity than a thousand pagan priests. Besides they are worthless. Now we need heavier horses for the tournaments, or gentle animals to pull the plow. These little devil-horses are fast and ill-tempered fighters. I admit that Margit's mare, who is the only one still alive, looks more like an Oriental horse, but if the people find out that there is still a horse who bears the mark of the clover, the trouble will start all over again. I must destroy the horse."

The Bishop jumped to his feet angrily. "You are a fine example of a good Christian. The whole business is ridiculous, and will only serve to make the little girl unhappy. All right, go your way, but if you don't let Margit keep her white mare, there will be no coronation. . . at least not until you get another Bishop to put the Apostolic Crown on your stubborn head."

The two men stared at each other in fury, then Odovar started to smile, and both began to roar with laughter.

"Aren't we a couple of old fools," said Stephanus, brushing the tears from his eyes, "All right, you win as usual. The child may keep her mare, and if anyone dares to notice the clover sign on her nose, I'll put them in the dungeon until they forget it."

"Well, that's more like you, Stephanus," the Bishop said, "Now how about some dinner, or I'll be too weak to lift the crown on your head tomorrow."

The next day the town of Buda was covered with flowers and green wreathes decorated every gate. Oriental rugs and rich brocades were hung from the windows and balconies. The wealth of the Hungarian nobility and of the visiting princes was on display. The peasants dressed in their best costumes lined the main street, waiting for a glimpse of their new King. Then the brazen fanfare from the shining trumpets rang through the town, and Stephanus, King of Hungary, left the church, the heavy golden crown upon his head. He mounted his white charger and rode slowly past his cheering people to take part in the coronation festivities at the palace. Multicolored flowers were strewn in his path as he went, and the flags of Hungary and the Arpad dynasty waved in the air over his head. Behind the King came his family and the noblemen of the land, then the holy sisters and the Bishop, who walked slowly under canopy and blessed the crowd that kneeled as he passed.

As the procession passed by the back entrance of the palace, the gates opened, and a little girl, her golden crown slightly askew on her brown curls, hurried out leading a lovely white mare. The startled people moved aside to let her through, and Princess Margit's finger clutched at the richly embroidered sleeves of the Bishop's robe. The priest stopped and tried to free his arm, then he saw Margit fall to her knees, and beside her knelt a little white mare. Bishop Odovar smiled, then he raised his hand over the kneeling pair and gave the blessing for hunter's horses and the chargers used in war. Mez stayed obediently on her knees, but her ears were laid back and her eyes were rolling to show her impatience at having to keep such an uncomfortable position for so long.

The Bishop finished the blessing and the procession moved on. Margit leaped onto Mez's back and galloped back through the gates. "Did you see, Moro, did you see?" the girl cried as she entered the stable yard. "The Bishop blessed Mez! Now no one can kill her. I'll have her forever! She is a Christian!"

* * * * * *

After King Stephen or Stephanus' successful forty-three year reign which ended in 1043 with his death, Hungary continued to flourish and expand. Stephen's successors acquired more territory, including Croatia and parts of Dalmatia. Under the able rule of Ladislaus at the end of the eleventh century, there were internal difficulties, which he successfully overcame. In the twelfth century a powerful landed aristocracy grew up, and procured from King Andrew II the Golden Bull, a charter which was the basis for the privileges of the nobility. The centuries from the time of Stephen to 1300 were years of development and expansion for the Hungarians. In the thirteenth century King László IV, called Kun-László, caused a great deal of unrest among his people by spending much of his time among his mother's people, the Kuns. He ignored his Italian wife, a political marriage, and married a Kun woman in a pagan ceremony. With the King away from his capital so much, there was the danger of a governmental upset, so the Church set out to get him back to Buda for good. Our next story is about this struggle and László's daughter, Beatrix.

ℭlover

HE endless expanse of marshes stretched out in a barren monotony of brown colors, from the pale gold of the sandy patches to the dark sepia of the low scrubby brush. The shrill cry of the waterfowl and the occasional bellow of a bullfrog broke the incessant chanting of thousands of little frogs. A flock of geese flew overhead, silhouetted against the purple of the sunset sky. The leader uttered its questioning cry, and from the rear of the perfect V-formation came the answering call.

A little girl and boy were riding side by side on the plains. The girl looked up unhappily.

"Geza, the geese came early this year. We will be going soon!"

The boy scowled and did not answer. He kicked the sides of his bay gelding viciously and sent the startled animal flying over the boggy land. The girl laughed and let her grey mare gallop after the boy. The falcon, perched on her right wrist, gave a worried squawk.

"Stop, you silly," the child called, "Silver Wing will catch up with your Csimbok anyway!"

The boy turned to watch the fleet little mare running close behind him. "Come and catch me then," he cried and turned his horse into a treacherous part of the marsh.

"Stop, stop, Geza!" the girl cried in panic, "My mare cannot go in there! She will fall!"

She tried to steady her frightened mount, who was accustomed to firm sand and rocky deserts, but the little horse plunged into the marsh. Immediately her small, narrow hoofs began to sink deep into the soft earth, and she fought her mistress frantically. The child was further handicapped by the falcon that clung nervously to her wrist.

"Geza," the girl called again, "we have to turn back. Silver is terrified, and anyway if we don't, we will be punished for having strayed so far from the other hunters!"

The boy turned to look at his struggling companion then pulled his gelding to a halt.

The two children turned their horses' heads westward and started home at a walk.

"Why don't you get a good horse that won't stumble at every step, Bea," the boy teased, "Those fancy Oriental horses are good for nothing but to stand in their stalls and look pretty."

The girl tossed her curls. "You're just jealous. Why, Silver could. . . What was that?"

The girl reined her mare to a stop, and, as the two listened, the eerie wailing of a wolf rose above the peaceful sounds of the moors. Another wolf answered, and then the cry of the pack howled through the oncoming darkness.

"They came down from the hills early this year, just like the geese," Geza said, "but, Beatrix, listen! They're chasing something!"

"The girl turned her horse in the direction of the wolves. "I have my bow and arrows, and you have yours. Let's go. Wouldn't it be wonderful if we could take a wolf hide or two home with us!"

The boy nodded his consent and put his horse into a gallop with Beatrix close behind him.

The howl of the wolves broke into a series of staccato barks and growls. The grey mist of the autumn evening enveloped the children as they rode silently in the direction of the sound of the pack. Soon they heard sounds of pain and rage mingled with the cries of attack.

"They must have cornered a stag," said the girl.

"Nonsense," answered Geza, "They could never catch up with a stag on the moors."

They pushed the horses through a stretch of high grass and came upon a strange and tragic scene. A small mare was kicking and biting for her life in the midst of five huge grey wolves. Blood was spurting profusely from a wound in her throat, and she was near death, but her heroic fight had cost the wolves dearly. Several were crushed by her flying hoofs, and were trying to drag themselves away from her fury.

"I wonder how they caught her," muttered Geza as he fitted an arrow into his bow, "she could have easily outrun them.

The answer was immediately clear, for at the mare's feet, half hidden by the tall grass, was a tiny newborn foal. It was still wet and was trying to struggle to its feet.

"It must have been born just before the wolves found the mare's scent," Geza said as he drew back his bow and shot one of the snarling animals.

Beatrix was struggling with her frightened mare, and, hampered also by the falcon, she was just a spectator. Geza shot again and wounded the leader of the pack, who, recognizing defeat, slunk off into the dusk with his battered companions. The girl dismounted quickly and ran toward the foal.

"Look out!" Geza cried.

The girl leapt back just in time, as the dying mare, thinking the child was some new tormentor, struck out with one last effort in defense of her foal. Exhausted by this final attempt, the little horse collapsed with a groan. The foal got to her feet and pushed at her fallen mother with a puzzled look in her eyes. At this the mare lifted her bloody head and called softly to her baby. The tiny filly answered happily with a shrill whinny, but this time she got no reply. The brave mare was dead. With tears in her eyes, Beatrix knelt down beside the filly and put her arms around her. The foal nuzzled the girl and gave its second inquiring whinny.

CLOVER

Look, Geza," the little girl cried, "she has the lucky Lohere mark on her nose, the mark of clover."

"You cannot take that filly," the lady-in-waiting said firmly. This stubborn ten-year old charge of hers was almost too much to handle at times. It was hard to be patient even with a princess.

"Oh, yes, I can. . . and I will," the child replied angrily.

"His Majesty will not permit it," the lady-in-waiting insisted. "Oh, yes, he will", the girl said stamping her foot.

"Oh, no, he won't!" A handsome young man pulled aside the heavy carpet that covered the entrance to the luxurious tent. "No, Beatrix, I cannot permit you to take that ugly runt back with us," the King of Hungary continued. "The filly comes from a vicious breed. Her mother was a killer, and it is only just that the wolves got her. She killed your step-mother's brother when he tried to capture her years ago. Your great-great-great-great uncle, Chieftain Arpad bred these animals, descended from a mare called Jegyes, 400 years ago in the 9th century, to be used as fighting horses. He valued them highly for their golden color and their great speed, and he found their ugly temperament an asset on the battle field. For this reason he encouraged it, but now they run wild and only cause trouble. I cannot let you endanger your life by having one of this breed."

"But, Father, please!" cried the little girl, "this little filly is golden too, but she isn't a bit mean . . . and she has the most beautiful clover mark on her nose." The King sighed.

The child was so like him, that it was difficult to refuse her anything, but he remained firm. "No, Beatrix, no! The filly must be destroyed today. She is completely useless." He sat down and took the little girl on his lap. "Don't cry, Beatrix, that is not the way a royal princess behaves, Kurdasdan says that he will buy you a snow white Oriental filly to make up for this one, and I will give you the emerald green saddle that you have wanted for so long."

Beatrix pushed herself away from his lap and faced him defiantly. "No, no, no!" she shrieked, "I won't have any other horse but Clover! Please don't kill her! She is only a month old, and she can't hurt anybody. . . and I love her better than any thing in the whole world!" Her anger spent, the little girl stood weeping before her father.

The boy, Geza, who had been standing there the whole time stepped forward, and, with as much poise as his thirteen years would allow, addressed the King.

"I beg your pardon, Your Majesty, but couldn't I keep Clover?", he asked.

Beatrix stopped crying and looked at her father hopefully. The King gazed at the two children for a moment. He was anxious to have the scene over, and this seemed an excellent way out.

"All right," he said, "but Queen Edua is not to know of this. That filly is dead, and dead to everybody. It is Queen Edua's wish to avenge the death of her brother, and she wants to get her revenge by taking the life of that miserable foal."

The King looked disgusted and unhappy over the situation, but there was nothing he could do. The Queen was capable of making things very unpleasant for any one, including the King, who went against her wishes. But Beatrix was happy. If she could not have the filly, the next best person was Geza. She ran to her father and kissed him gratefully.

"Your Majesty's orders will be obeyed," said Geza, "no one will know the foal remains alive."

The Court was in an uproar. King László IV, who was hard pressed by his Western entourage, had promised to stay in Buda and obey the wishes of the Archbishop. For the good of Hungary, the Archbishop wanted the King to be reconciled with his first wife, the legitimate queen, who was a sweet, listless little person. Further, to force the Kuns to return to Christianity, the Archbishop wished the King to renounce his second wife, Queen Edua, the daughter of a Kun Chieftain, and to forget his wild life with the Kuns. For political reasons, he also wanted László to promise his daughter, Beatrix, in marriage to an important German Prince. The King, who had abided by these wishes for six years, suddenly changed his mind. He gave orders to his intimate friends and his hunters to prepare to visit the Kuns.

On a sudden impulse he took Beatrix, who was then a lovely girl of sixteen, out of the convent on the Nyul-Sziget. For the last six years the girl had been carefully taught by the nuns and her aunt, Princess Margaret, who was the Abbess of the convent. The good sisters had a hard time making a dignified, well-educated Princess out of the stubborn, wild little girl, but now, as they watched the graceful, stately young woman leave the convent with her father, they were proud of the work they had accomplished. Beatrix was beside herself with joy that she was at last free of the convent. The King loved his daughter, occasionally spoiled her, but mostly forgot her in the busy routine of ruling a large Kingdom. As a result Beatrix was often lonely, and nothing could have made her happier than this journey to the country she had loved as a child.

King László hurried the preparations for the trip so that in a week's time they were on their way eastward. The King rode his huge black hunter, and the Princess, who rode at his side, sat upon a snow-white Oriental mare. She was a very different person from the little girl who had hunted in the marshes before. Her secluded scholarly life and the strict routine of the convent had robbed her cheeks of their bright color, and the tan of outdoor life had vanished long since. Her flawless white skin contrasted strikingly with the flaming gold of her abundant curls. She was small, and slender, and very sedate as she sat upon her lovely mare. Only the excitement in her brown eyes betrayed the happiness and anticipation she felt as they neared the plains of the Kuns where she could hunt and ride. . . where she could be free again.

One thought kept repeating itself over and over in Beatrix's mind. "Will I see Clover and Geza again?"

Geza's father was the Hungarian nobleman, Gara, the King's first hunter, who owned property near the Kun country. Beatrix glanced behind her at the train of ladies-in-waiting who followed on horseback or, the older ones, in carts with the servants.

"They are so proper and horrid about what a princess should or should not do that they will make it difficult for me to hunt with Geza as we did in the old days," thought Beatrix, and she felt a most unprincess-like urge to stick her tongue out at those pompous ladies.

It was a long and colorful, but dusty, cavalcade that was greeted by the Kuns with a great display of eastern pageantry and pagan rites. Beatrix found Geza in the crowd that received them almost immediately.

"He has grown so tall. . . and so handsome," she thought. She had forgotten that he would change too, in the years since she had last seen him. "A few years ago I would have jumped down and rushed to greet him, and now I cannot. We are like strangers. . . I suppose we have both grown up." Then Geza's eyes met hers and he smiled. Beatrix knew then that she was partly wrong. They had grown up, yes, but they were not strangers.

She sat happily beside her father, smiling and poised, waiting for the time to pass that was wasted, she thought, in the tedious formalities and festivities that the Kuns had arranged for the arrival of the King and herself.

Queen Edua received the King and his daughter with great joy. She had waited a long time for Kaszlo to return, and she was prepared to do everything in her power to keep him there. In her eagerness to be left alone with the King, so that she could persuade him to stay with her, she suggested that Beatrix have her own suite of young people.

"She can have young Geza as her first hunter, as Gara is ours. The boy is sensible and knows as much about hunting as his father. . . and Beatrix likes him. Besides she would only be bored in the company of the older people of the court. Let the young people have a good time too."

Edua finished her speech and waited for the King's answer. The Kun chieftain's daughter was a reckless woman, goaded by ambition. She knew that the King's first marriage was valid in the eyes of the world, and that her position based on a pagan marriage ceremony was very precarious. It depended upon László's staying with her, and she had decided that this time she would somehow get the King so under her influence that he would not want to return to his Western Kingdom. Her words made sense to the King, and he decided that Beatrix would be happier with her own company of young people, so he readily gave his consent to the plan.

Before long the Princess got her suite made up of young members of the Kun nobility, and led by Geza. Through Queen Edua's scheming Beatrix's ladies-in-waiting were sent back home one by one, and Kun women of noble birth were assigned to her instead. Beatrix was astonished but happy over the change, for it meant that she was free to do as she pleased. Her first meeting with Geza was at a formal reception, and they had no time to talk. Only a brief, whispered exchange reminded Beatrix of their former friendship.

"What had become of Clover?", she asked.

"She is an excellent hunter now. You will see her soon," Geza answered.

The days and weeks passed in complete happiness for Beatrix. She hunted, rode, held tournaments, and danced with the large group of young people that made up her own court. One day as they were hunting near Geza's home, the Princess decided that this would be a good time for her to see Clover.

"Geza," she whispered to the young man beside her, "let's slip away from the others and go visit Clover. . . they are much too intent on catching that stag to miss us."

Geza grinned; this was more like the Bea he used to know, not the sophisticated young princess, and he consented willingly. The two reined in their horses and let the other hunters go by. Then they turned their mounts toward the Gara estate and galloped the short distance to the stables. Geza's father loved good horses and his barn was full of lovely animals that he had bought from the Turks. These horses were much finer than the small coarse animals native to the country of the Kuns, and Gara was very proud of them. At the far end of the stable a small horse stood in a huge box stall. The mare looked completely out of place in the midst of the highly bred Turkish animals. Geza opened her stall door. "This is Clover," he said.

Beatrix could not keep her look of disappointment concealed. The mare had a large head that only her dark, spirited eyes saved from complete homeliness. She was well built and in beautiful condition, but her over-sized head gave her an unbalanced appearance. Beatrix put out her hand to pat the mare. Immediately Clover's ears flattened against her head and she snapped viciously at the girl. Geza moved quickly to the mare's side.

"No, Clover, you behave yourself!", he said gently. At his words the little horse's ears came up, and she allowed the girl to pat her.

"Let me see your nose, Clover," Beatrix said and pulled the mare's head around to face her. "Look Geza, she does have the mark of Arpad's horses, the mark of the clover." The slate blue mark was vivid against the pink of the mare's nose. "But, poor thing," Beatrix added, I do think you are ugly!"

Geza laughed. "Don't be so critical, Bea. Your fancy horses are always beaten by ours in races over the moors. Clover is the smartest, safest horse I have ever known. When she was a yearling two wolves cornered her in our back pasture, and she fought them just as her mother fought the day Clover was born. By the time I got to her she had mangled both of the wolves to a pulp. I imagine that is what she would do to your yapping western hounds too," he added, "and I don't blame her, either. They just get in the way. Hunting with a falcon or a bow and arrow, is the only way to do it."

"But, Geza, you hunt boar with your hounds. What does Clover do about them?", Beatrix asked. "I don't hunt boar on a horse," he answered, "I wouldn't want to risk the life of my horse with an angry, charging beast around. It is a man's sport, and I hunt alone with three or four mongrel hounds to corner, but not to wound, the boar."

An idea began to form in the girl's head. It would be fun to hunt boar with Geza. She had never done it and he would be the perfect one to take her.

"Geza, I know what we will do. I will sneak away from the others, and you can take me with you when you go after the boar. I have always wanted to go, and now is an excellent time."

The young man shook his head. "No, Princess," he said formally, "it cannot be done. You are a royal princess, engaged to marry an important German prince. You will be Queen one day, and I cannot be responsible for letting you endanger your life just because you have a sudden whim to hunt boar."

"Geza, don't be silly," Beatrix laughed, "I won't get hurt, and I might as well learn how to hunt them before I'm Queen, for I will certainly do so then. . . and you will always be my greatest friend. Why, I will make you my first hunter when I am Queen."

Geza's face hardened. "No, you won't," he said angrily. "I will probably stick your husband instead of the boar if you do!"

The girl looked up at Geza, startled by the new tone that came into his voice, and her smile faded. She was silent, her cheeks flushed, and a frightened feeling rose in her at the thought of her coming marriage to the German Prince whom she had never seen. She forced the thought out of her mind and struggled to regain her composure.

"All right, Geza," she said, "now I will give orders, and they are that you will take me on a boar hunt three days from now. . . and I will ride Clover."

The young man's face flushed darkly with anger at her commanding tone. "The princess's orders will be obeyed. . . but, Beatrix, you are a stubborn little goose," and he turned to stalk out of the stable.

His dignified exit was marred by a well-aimed blow from the girl's shoe, which she threw at him in a display of her childhood temper.

At the royal hunting lodge, where the King and Queen held court, the days were spent in feasting and drinking, but the atmosphere was tense and restless. Day after day messengers arrived from Buda, their faces dusty and worried, their horses exhausted from hard riding. Lászlo read the messages and listened to the tales of unrest in his capital, then he sent them home unheeded. He deliberately sought to forget his increasing apprehension in the festivities of the court, and in the nearness of his Queen, Edua. The Church went into action again, trying to bring the King to his senses, and even old Gara tried to make him return.

"The fate of the country and of the royal crown is at stake, Your Majesty," he said, "you must go back."

But the King only became angry and banished Gara to his estate, telling him to stay there and mind his own business.

Queen Edua did everything to keep Lászlo at her side, and she practiced every measure of intrigue to accomplish her aims. On several occasions she had messengers killed and their messages destroyed, fearing the influence of the western empire that had made him leave her many times before. Once she had taken these drastic steps, she had to be sure the King would stay, for, if he returned to Buda, he would discover that she had intercepted the messengers and punish her for her evil deeds.

Edua's confidant was her uncle, Torma, an old and crippled warrior, who was ever greedy for power. Through his spies, Torma learned that a large convoy of noblemen and the Archbishop himself were approaching Kun territory to persuade the King to return to his capital. The spies also reported that they had a small troop of armed soldiers with them. The Queen, upon hearing this, gave orders that every precaution be taken that the King should not hear of the approach of the caravan. She also told Torma to ready the Kun soldiers and get some Byzantine hirelings in order to prepare an ambush. Preparations were made in the utmost secrecy, and a few days later a large, well-organized regiment left with orders to destroy the Westerners in the moors where the bodies would soon sink, never to be found again. Upon the Queen's orders not one was to be left alive to tell what had happened.

The day came for the boar hunt ordered by Princess Beatrix, and she started off with her court as usual for a stag hunt. Not far from the Gara properties, Beatrix and Geza slipped away from the others and rode to the stables. There they changed horses. Beatrix mounted Clover, and Geza took a small, sturdy Mongolian horse. They both carried bows and arrows, and the Princess had a gourd and a feed bag attached to her saddle. Four mongrel hounds, their tails whipping the air happily in anticipation, brought up the rear.

Geza's misgivings faded as he looked at his sunburned companion, sitting easily astride the chestnut mare. He was alone with her so little, and it was such a beautiful day that he could not help being unreasonably happy.

"Why is it that everything is so right when I am with her. . . and so miserable when we are apart," he thought.

The young nobleman had been brought up to respect the difference between his class and that of royalty. It was so ingrained in his beliefs that he could not think any other way. For this reason he would not admit, even to himself, that he had fallen in love with the beautiful princess, but deep inside him he knew that this was true.

The underbrush got denser and taller as the two riders moved deeper into the moor where the boars were found. A branch caught in Beatrix' richly embroidered cap, tearing it off her head. Her hair fell like burnished gold about her shoulders, and Geza thought to himself that he had never seen anything so lovely in his life. Suddenly Beatrix turned in her saddle to face him.

"Today is my day, Geza," she said, "we will forget that I am Princess Beatrix. I am the Bea I was years ago when we used to run away from the other hunters, knowing all the while that we were sure to get a spanking if we were found out."

Geza nodded and smiled. "All right, Bea, but you must be careful when we find the boar, or you will get a spanking. . . from me!"

They rode on silently for a while, happy in each others company. Abruptly the spotted bitch put her nose up and sniffed the air, a tentative whine rose in her throat. The red dog beside her gave a low whimper, then disappeared into the low shrubs, his tail wagging furiously. Geza and Beatrix reined in their horses and watched intently. Then all four hounds dashed into the brush, whimpering and scuffling as they tried to locate the scent. They moved farther and farther away from the two riders, and a few minutes later the howl of the spotted leader came back to them. The other hounds chimed in chorus, and then the sound grew fainter as they moved off. They had found the scent.

"My, what a plebeian din those mongrels make in comparison to my purebred hounds," laughed the girl.

Geza turned to her angrily. "Don't be silly. My hounds are more than a match for yours. They will not be disemboweled because they go to near a raging boar and attack, as your senseless hounds do. . . and they will not tear up the coat of a good boar."

Beatrix flushed at the rebuke and started to make a stinging retort, but she smiled instead. It would not do to spoil their day by fighting.

"I'm sorry, Geza, she said meekly, "I was only joking. From the way they picked up the scent I can tell they are excellent hunters."

"That's all right," Geza said gruffly, and then he smiled too. "Come on, we're going to lose the hounds if we don't get started."

The two riders followed the sound of the barks and whimpers as fast as they could; but the woods were dense, and their advance was slow and perilous. The little horses picked their way steadily with astonishing intelligence and skill, but soon the cry of the hounds faded in the distance. As soon as the ground became more open Geza turned to the girl.

"Now, Bea, we will have to move fast if we don't want to lose our pack. I saw you jump the other day, and you really looked lovely, . . . but don't use that western style here or you'll get knocked off your horse by the low branches. Crouch down forward Kun-fashion, and trust Clover."

Beatrix laughed. "Just watch me," she called and kicked Clover's round sides.

The mare, startled by this unaccustomed action, for Geza had never kicked her, gave a vicious plunge, then shot forward at a tremendous speed.

"Steady, Bea, steady", Geza yelled, as the girl fought to regain control of her bolting mount.

The Princess was an excellent horsewoman and a fearless one, and she soon brought the mare to a halt.

Geza cantered up to her.

"You don't have to kick her, Bea, just a light touch is enough."

"I know that now," the girl said breathlessly. . . "but I didn't think little Clover had that much speed in her!"

Geza grinned. "She didn't use half her speed. That little mare is the fastest horse I've ever known! She can beat any horse in this country. . . but let's catch up with those hounds or we'll lose our boar. We'll have to jump that fallen tree in the path. . . Ready?"

The girl nodded, and they turned the horses toward the tree. Both animals jumped well and cleared the obstacle with no difficulty.

"Oh, she's wonderful," cried Beatrix as they cantered on. "I can see now why you think Clover is such a grand mare. I've never ridden a horse that jumps like she does!"

"She can jump anything," Geza answered, "only she doesn't jump, she flies!" The young man suddenly halted his horse.

"Hold on, Bea, Listen! We've almost caught up with the hounds. They must have cornered a boar. . . They haven't moved on since we stopped. We'd better walk the rest of the way so there won't be too much noise."

As they got nearer the hunters could distinguish the yapping of the hounds and the furious grunting of the boar.

"Let's go around behind that shrub over there, Bea," Geza said, "we can see the boar from there. We're going to dismount, and I'll let you hold my horse, but watch out for Clover. She's never seen a boar, and she hates dogs, so there may be trouble."

The two hunters jumped to the ground, and Geza, taking a short spear in his hand, started off in the direction of the boar. Beatrix took the reins of the two horses and followed close behind him. Soon Geza stopped and pointed silently. Through an opening in the bushes the girl saw their quarry, a huge animal with long sharp tusks. The boar pivoted, charged, and tried to drive his tusks into the barking hounds, as they cautiously held the furious animal at bay. Beatrix was amazed at the agility of the mongrels. They jumped easily away from the boar, so that the enraged charge of the animal resulted in a dive into the empty space where a dog had been just a second before. The spotted bitch, who had led the chase, sank her teeth into the hind quarters of the frantic boar, but before he could turn on her, she had leapt away and was barking canine insults at him from a safe distance.

Wherever the boar turned his tormentors blocked his way, barking furiously. The animal trembled with rage, and tore up the ground in front of him, his small bloodshot eyes gleaming desperately. In his anger he uprooted a small tree, ignoring the two hounds that immediately began to worry his hindquarters. When he turned to charge them, they were already out of reach, but suddenly the boar forgot the dogs as he recognized the presence of another, more dangerous enemy. He caught the hated scent of man. He stood frozen for a moment, a statue of hate, and, with the bristles standing high on his back, his eyes focused on his new foe. With a snarl and a squeal of rage, he charged at the young man, who stepped out of the bushes to meet him, and then he went down with a spear through his heart, carrying Geza with him in the terrible five-hundred pound impact of his desperate rush. The blood spurted from the fatal spear wound, and then the hounds, yapping happily, closed in upon the still quivering form of the boar.

Geza pulled himself from under the heavy body and smiled as he beat the hounds away so that they would not tear up the hide.

"Look, Bea, he's a beauty. We can skin. . . "

He stopped and turned quickly as he became aware of the sounds of conflict going on behind him. The girl was struggling with a frightened, plunging Clover. The smell of blood was too much for the already maddened mare. She snapped at Beatrix, reared, and broke free, then dived forward biting and kicking savagely at the yelping mongrels around the still form of the boar. The hounds jumped aside, and the mare turned on the dead animal at her feet, trampling it wildly. She had mangled the boar badly before Geza was able to catch the ends of her reins and, with jerks of his powerful arms and soothing words, bring the mare back to her senses. Seeing that the horse was under control, the hounds sat down and began licking their wounds resentfully, and Beatrix ran quickly to Geza, trying to keep back her tears of distress, as words of apology tumbled from her lips.

"Oh, Geza, I am so sorry. You did such a beautiful job, and I messed up everything by letting Clover get away!"

Geza smiled and patted her shoulder. "Don't worry, Bea, there are lots of boars. . . we'll catch one another day. It's my fault anyway. I shouldn't have brought Clover so close. I might have known she'd act that way. After her experiences with the wolves, the combination of the dogs, which she thinks are another kind of wolf, and blood from the boar was too much for her. You mustn't feel bad. No one could hold her when she's that upset. Here take her back in the bushes with my gelding so she can't see this anymore, and I'll see what I can salvage from the boar."

Beatrix obediently led the mare away, happy that Geza was not angry with her. The young man knelt down beside the boar and cut out the trophies, the exceptionally fine tusks that the flying hoofs of Clover had fortunately missed. Then he got up and took them to the girl, who stood with her back to him concentrating on the horses. He sneaked up quietly from behind to surprise her with the tusks, but she sensed his presence and turned quickly. Geza forgot his boyish prank as he found the lovely face of the girl just a few inches from his own.

In the excitement of the hunt all rules had been forgotten, and they were just two ordinary people. Now the temptation was too great, and Geza felt all his love for the girl welling up in him until it was too much to bear. The foolish tusks dropped to the ground, as he closed his arms around her and kissed her. She responded purely and passionately, as a girl would kiss the man she loves. Beatrix still held Clover's reins, and a jerk of the mare's head, as she reached for some grass, brought the two back to reality. They broke apart and stared at each other in surprise and wonder.

"Geza, what are we going to do now?", the girl asked.

The young man looked pensive, almost sullen. "Princess,. . . ", he began formally.

"Hush!" The girl put her hand over his mouth to stop the words. "There is no princess for you, and there never was! I am Beatrix, and you are Geza and Beatrix and Geza belong together."

"Don't be ridiculous," he yelled at her angrily "that was your doing! I told you this hunt was madness!"

"But you didn't give this as your reason," she answered tartly.

"I know, darling. I'm sorry I yelled at you, but it's all so hopeless." Geza sat down on a rock, his head between his hands. "Now, here we are. In a few days you will return to Buda, and within a year you will be the wife of the German Prince. . . and I? I will roam the plains on Clover, wasting my life in wanting something that I cannot have."

The girl looked down at him sadly. "We will find a way, Geza, the Good Lord will help us."

Prayers that she had learned in the convent came back to her, but she did not say them now for she knew the boy would not listen. Instead she silently uttered a little prayer to St. Joseph, whom the good sisters had said could make the impossible possible.

"Well," Geza said, as he stood up, "I guess I'd better go wash the blood and dirt off in the creek. The boar really messed me up. Wait here with the horses. . . I'll be back in a few minutes."

After Geza had left, Beatrix tied the horses to a tree and started to build a fire. She gathered some dry brush and cut a green branch for the spit, then she decided to see if she could shoot a fat, tender bird with her bow and arrow to surprise Geza, before she lighted the fire with her flint.

She had not gone far when she remembered the boar.

"His hide is ruined anyway," she thought, "I can cut a few steaks out of him and cook them."

She turned to go back to the camp when she heard something. It was a sound that did not belong to the woods, and she instinctively stepped into a dense thicket out of sight.

"Perhaps it's only my imagination. . . no, there it is again!"

The clatter of many horse's hoofs came nearer and nearer, and soon she could hear human voices mingled with the rattle and creak of armour.

"It is probably the King's hunting party," she thought, "I'd better stay out of sight. If Father finds out I've been hunting boar alone with Geza, he will be terribly angry."

She peered through an opening in the thicket and saw a troop of mounted Kuns riding swiftly toward her. She stood motionless, afraid of being seen by the horsemen, who passed a few feet from her hiding place. Then she heard the voice of old Torma.

"We'll catch them in the red marshes by 'The Devils Gate', and then chase them into the quicksands without any risk of our men."

One of the Kun officers laughed. "No need to bury their saintly bones! The Christian dogs will be buried deep enough in the sands of death!"

Then Torma spoke again. "Our King and Queen will no longer be bothered by the troublesome Archbishop, and the King will remain here. Of course, we will all mourn the good, holy man and his company who 'lost' their way and wandered into the quick sands."

The two men laughed at Torma's joke, and the troop moved on out of Beatrix' hearing.

Beatrix was terrified that they might find the camp with Geza and the horses.

She waited until the Kuns had all gone by, and then ran as fast as she could back to Geza. She burst into the camp a few minutes later, and relief flooded her being, as she saw that the soldiers had taken another trail, by-passing the camp by at least a mile. Geza had skinned the boar and was cutting out big chunks of meat which he threw to the hounds as a reward.

"Hey, Bitang, stop that!", he called as the yellow mongrel jumped on one of his companions. "Come Fules, here's a piece for you. . . there's no need to fight over it."

Hearing Beatrix' step, Geza turned and smiled at her. "Where has Princess Lazybones been all this time?" I thought you would have a fire. What is it, darling?"

He rose quickly and went to her side as he saw the strained expression on her face. "Why you're all out of breath. What has happened?"

Beatrix grasped his arms. The horror of the situation began to sink in and she was frantic with worry. "Geza, we must do something. Old Torma and a tremendous number of soldiers passed me a few minutes ago. I heard them talking. They're on their way to trap the Archbishop and his caravan in the quick sands. It is Queen Edua's plan. Torma said so. Somehow she has kept the news of their arrival from Father. I knew she didn't want us to return to Buda, but I never thought she'd do a terrible thing like this. She has been so good to me. . . she even. . . but there's no time for that. We've got to warn the Archbishop!"

Geza cursed under his breath and took two pieces of meat from a leather pouch that hung from his saddle. "Here, Beatrix, take this and eat it." The girl frowned and started to protest. "Eat it, Beatrix," the boy insisted, "you will need all your strength. You will have to ride as you have never ridden before. The meat will help you."

Beatrix watched her companion gulp the meat down, and then obediently ate hers.

"Now, here is a knife," Geza continued, "cut off all that surplus skirt and wrap some of the boar meet in the rags. . . then get on your horse."

Beatrix sat down on the ground and began to chop mercilessly at her dress. Women had gone blind in working the minute embroidery that decorated the hunting costume, and the King had paid a load of gold to the traders for the material brought from Byzantium. When she had finished she wrapped up the meat and placed it in the leather bag that was attached to her saddle. Then she mounted Clover and waited for Geza's orders.

"My Beatrix," he said, "we are riding to save not only lives, but a Kingdom, and, most important, Christianity. Ride carefully, Bea. . . ride the way the east taught you, to save the west." Then Beatrix led the way to the spot where she had seen the Kuns.

Geza studied the direction in which the tracks of the Kun horses led. Beatrix frowned, "Oh yes, they plan to trap the caravan by 'Devils Gate', old Torma said so. . . I just remembered."

Geza turned to the girl. "Then I know the way they will take. That means that the caravan will be coming by the red moors. We must take the short cut that goes through our lands, but you will have to use all your skill to make it, Bea. Clover has the courage to do it, and she knows the way. We have been through there together, but never at the speed it will take to reach the Archbishop in time. With God's help we will make it though. Are you ready?" The girl nodded silently, and crouched down in her saddle. Geza smiled. "That's the way! Let's go!"

The boy took the lead and sent his horse flying down a stony gorge with Clover close behind. They galloped on amid the flying stones and rubble toward the plains. After a half hour of hard riding they came to a stretch of woods. There was a trail, but it had not been cleared in a long time, and many fallen logs lay across the path. For a while the horses jumped well, clearing the obstacles with skill. Soon, however Geza's gelding began to tire, and he had trouble taking the high jumps. The boy did all he could to support the winded animal, but it was obvious that the horse could not go much farther. He pulled to a halt and turned to Beatrix.

"My horse is winded. We'll have to detour about a mile to the stables so I can get a fresh horse."

Beatrix nodded and patted Clover. The little mare had come the whole way at a steady gallop and showed no signs of being even slightly tired.

"Now you see why I value Clover so highly," Geza said, "her strength and endurance are far beyond that of an ordinary horse, but come along I must change horses in a hurry." As they turned their horses toward the Gara stables they saw great billowing clouds of smoke and flames shooting up in the sky above Geza's home.

"Our house is burning," the boy cried, "those devils must have set it on fire." They practically flew the remaining distance. Geza's gelding, as tired as it was, was making a gallant effort, with Clover running easily beside him. At Udvar disaster greeted them. Only the smoking ruins of the spacious home remained, and old Gara, Geza's father, lay on the ground beside the house, dead. Beside him lay Geza's aunt, her blood-stained "Fokos", a long handled axe-like instrument, still clutched firmly in her hand. There was a large cut on her head, and the blood clotted in her white hair made a curious pattern around her face. Gara's servants and the hirelings of Torma were scattered, slain, on the ground around them. No one was left alive. Geza stared at the scene, his jaw set in an ugly line.

"Father must have found out about the Queen's evil plan, and they silenced him in the only way possible. Our elders put up a good fight. We must try to follow their example."

Beatrix knelt beside the prostrate forms. "Uncle Gara, Uncle Gara," she cried, the tears streaming down her face.

"Hush, Beatrix, we cannot help them with tears. Pray for them while I find a fresh horse, if those heathens left anything alive. Your's is the praying and mine the revenge," he muttered as he turned away.

After a while Geza came back with a frightened bay horse. "Mount Clover, Bea, God is with us. Torma chased off the horses hopping to make their heinous crime look like the work of the wild tribes that sometimes come out of the hills to rob and destroy, but Csillag wandered back home. He's our best horse, next to Clover."

Beatrix and Geza mounted in silence and disappeared into the fog caused by the clouds of smoke that hung low to the earth in the heavy atmosphere of the afternoon. The dust and soot covered them with an earthen-gray color. They rode on without speaking, gliding through the gathering mist like the riders of the Apocalypse.

The Archbishop's weary group of travelers anxiously watched the darkening sky.

"We will soon have a storm, Your Eminence. Shouldn't we make camp before it breaks?", one of the little pages said.

The Churchman's eyes held an amused twinkle. "So, you are anxious to rest and eat the fine meal that our hunters will kill for us, are you? No, no, my little friend, we have to hurry! What is your opinion Sister Agata and Sister Maria?" He turned to the two young sisters riding the two white mules next to his own powerful, black Spanish mule. "Aren't you anxious to get back your white dove who seems to have turned into a hunting hawk, if the rumors are correct?"

The sisters nodded in agreement. "It's not that we don't trust the Princess' judgment," Sister Maria said, "but we don't think such a long visit in a heathen household will do her any good."

"Anyway," said Sister Agata, "we will rest when we cannot go on! Perhaps if we keep on we can reach the royal camp tomorrow."

An elderly woman on a fat little chestnut mare rode up beside the Archbishop. "I am exhausted, Your Eminence," she whimpered, "I cannot stand to ride in those jolting carts, and my seat gets sore on horseback. Please, can't we stop and rest for a while."

The Archbishop eyed the rotund figure of the Duchess. "Your horse should complain, not you, Duchess. It was your idea to come on this mission, and persuade your cousin, the King, to return with your 'eloquence'. I tried to dissuade you, but now that you are here, you must go on with the rest of us."

The disgruntled Duchess fell back with her group of ladies-in-waiting, wiping the tears of self-pity from her eyes.

The caravan plodded on wearily. One of the little pages said to the Archbishop.

"That cloud looks very strange to me. It looks almost like smoke, and with the wind blowing in our direction I think I can smell it too."

Before the Archbishop could answer, the commander of the guards broke in. "I have been watching that cloud for some time. I'm sure it's smoke, but we have been in danger ever since we left Buda. If we listened to all the warnings we would not have left home in the first place. I have sent scouts to reconnoiter the only wide, passable trail between the quicksands. They saw nothing up ahead, so there is no reason to be alarmed."

The Archbishop nodded. "That was a very wise move, Captain. I'm glad you're with us. I would never think of these things my. . . "

The cry of the guards up ahead interrupted him, and the caravan stopped, the frightened, tense people muttering nervously among themselves. The guards came out of the woods just ahead escorting two mud-caked, dirty riders mounted on equally filthy horses.

"Your Eminence, we found. . . ", one of the guards began, but the young man he had captured stopped him.

"Alarm your men and prepare for a fight. The Kuns will be here in no time to attack you!" He yelled at the captain.

"Don't be ridiculous my son, the King would never permit such a thing," said the Archbishop. "He knows we are coming, and he has probably sent a troop out to welcome us and escort us safely to his camp. Who are you anyway? Where did you come from?"

The girl beside the young man exploded with anger.

"All right, your Eminence, go ahead and get killed. The King knows nothing about this. It is a plot organized by Queen Edua. . . and would we ride ourselves nearly to death just to play games."

"And who are you?", asked the commander of the guard.

"I am Princess Beatrix, and this is my first hunter, Geza, son of Gara, and I order you to prepare to fight."

The answer came with such dignity and authority from the dirty little figure, that the Archbishop rode up for a closer look at her.

"Why, it is the Princess," he said in surprise.

"Of course, it's 'the Princess', I told you that," Beatrix retorted, "now, please, do something before it's too late."

"Yes, of course, but the Captain must take charge now. Tell him all you know, and let him organize the company to fight."

"They plan to take you by surprise and drive you into the quicksands instead of fighting," Geza said, "we must stay here and resist them. They outnumber us, but they are superstitious men at heart, and they don't like to have their plans upset. This way we have a chance."

"All right," said the Captain, "you know more about the Kun tactics than I do. Tell me how to place my men, and I will do it."

Geza swiftly outlined a plan for the officer, and order was quickly restored. A few minutes later they heard the battle cry of the attacking Kuns. The two sisters ran to Beatrix to get her back to comparative safety with the women.

"Come with us, Princess," said Sister Maria, "It will be safer."

Beatrix pulled away from them. "You'd better come with me and help on the line, Sisters. It's stupid to wait like a flock of sheep for the Kuns to come get you!"

The sisters looked horrified and turned to the Archbishop for help.

"The Princess is right," said the good man, ignoring their pleas, "and I myself will break the head of every pagan I meet with the sign of the Lord, whom they will not accept!", and he brandished his crozier above his head. "You who cannot fight pray for their souls, and ours," he said, and then the Kuns were upon them.

The fight was short, furious, and bloody. The Kuns, led by Torma, tried and failed to push the valiant little company into the quicksands. They died fighting. Even the fat Duchess worked uncomplainingly, carrying water to the wounded, until she fell, struck by an arrow.

A few minutes after the Duchess fell, an arrow struck the Archbishop, and he was badly wounded. Then Geza decided on a desperate move. He put the Archbishop's Mitre and robe on, mounted Clover, and, waving the crozier above his head, gave a wild yell that sent the mare flying through the enemy lines. The little golden horse with her ears flattened viciously against her head so surprised the Kuns that they fell back out of her way, and it was a few moments before they sufficiently recovered their wits to give chase. When they mounted and flew after Clover, they left an unguarded spot in the line through which Beatrix and an old warrior escaped with the Archbishop.

Beatrix knew the country as she had often hunted there, and she guided the soldier, who carried the Archbishop, to a secluded spot where she could bandage the Holy man's wounds with cloth torn from her underskirts. Then she sat down and tried to concentrate on praying, but her thoughts were with Geza.

"Come here, Child, and talk to me," said the Archbishop, "it will make the time pass more quickly until I go to my Lord. In my youth I, too, loved to hunt on these beautiful plains. The Lord is good to let me die here on the lands that I used to love so much."

Beatrix answered him absently. She tried to talk to the dying man, but her thoughts of Geza kept interfering, and she could not keep her attention on what she was saying. "Oh, God, let him reach the King safely," she prayed.

The old Archbishop was very wise in the ways of the young, and he looked at her with great sympathy. "Listen, my child, there is no use in trying to fool me. It was not hard to see that you and that brave boy are in love with each other. Come, we will pray together for Geza and his valiant little mare." When he had finished the prayer, he said. "God will take care of them now. Tell me about your life here, about you and Geza.

The girl smiled, and, as the hours passed, she told him all that had happened since she had left Buda, but mostly she talked of Geza.

Clover was showing signs of weariness at last, and, knowing that the Kuns were gaining ground, Geza guided the mare to a place where a strip of solid ground ran narrowly between water and treacherous quicksand. The path was winding, and a tremendous stretch of water had to be jumped. The water was not deep, but quicksand lay under it so it could not be forded. Geza knew the little mare was exhausted, but there was no other solution than to trust Clover's fantastic jumping power and her courageous heart. He heard the yells of the Kuns as they came nearer, and a few arrows whizzed over his head. Fortunately they were screened by the tall marsh grass, and the Kuns could not see to aim correctly. A clear stretch lay before him, and then the wide expanse of water Clover had to jump. He thought of Beatrix for a second and then gave another wild yell that sent the mare flying toward the water. The Kuns yelled too, in triumph, certain that their cornered prey could not escape them. Then the miracle happened. They saw a golden horse rise over the water,

caught in a single shaft of afternoon sunlight that shot down suddenly through the clouds; and on her back the Archbishop sat, his crozier raised triumphantly above his head. Some stopped, paralyzed with fear by the sight, but most were galloping on too fast and were swallowed by the muddy water. The survivors turned back in fear, and rode to tell others of the strange wonder they had seen.

A few hundred yards after the jump Geza pulled Clover to a halt. The little mare was trembling with exhaustion, but she had accomplished the impossible. They were out of the quicksand now, so he took off her saddle and let her drink a little water, then roll deliciously in the grass of the plain. Geza took off the cumbersome robes of the Archbishop and threw himself down on the ground to rest for a moment. He was trying to figure out how to reach the King. He knew that this massacre and the murder of his father were unknown to László. It was all the work of Queen Edua and Torma.

"The King's life will be in danger too, particularly if Torma gets to the Queen and reports that the Archbishop escaped," Geza thought, "I've got to get to the King somehow."

He got up stiffly from the ground, and mounted Clover without the saddle in order to take a little more weight off her back. The mare was still tired, but the short rest had helped her recover some of her strength. Geza knew that if he tried to get through the gates of the hunting lodge, where the King and Queen were staying, he would probably be shot down. Old Torma was sure to have reported to the Queen by the time he got there, and they would stop at nothing now. The only chance was to jump Clover over the high wooden wall at the back of the lodge. He urged the mare into a canter, and, as he neared the camp, the sounds of battle reached his ears.

The Kun warriors, upon their return from the fight with the Archbishop's caravan, found King László lying in the courtyard dead, slain by one of Torma's Byzantine hirelings. The Kuns were a wild tribe, but they hated treachery; and they loved their generous, fun-loving King. The Queen had sent them to stop the Westerners from taking their King from them, and this task they gladly performed. When they returned and found the King, for whom they had fought, murdered, they rose up in riot against the Queen. By the time Geza got there they were fighting the Byzantine guards and had slain Torma. Now they were searching for the Queen.

Queen Edua, realizing too late that she had gone too far, ran toward the back gate with a few of her followers, hoping to escape while the Kuns were fighting at the front and searching for her in the lodge. Suddenly she stopped, frozen with fright, as she saw a golden horse fly over the fence, the red glow of the setting sun coloring the revengeful figure on its back with a strange light. Edua uttered a terrified scream as the spectral horse landed in front of her, and she lifted her arm to strike a deadly blow with her fokos. The horse reared and knocked the Queen to the ground. Edua's followers rushed to her defense, but the Kun soldiers, upon hearing her scream and the sounds of commotion, ran into the back court and quickly slew the Queen's defenders. A strange sight met their eyes when they turned back to the Queen. A maddened horse was trampling and biting the shrieking woman savagely. They looked for the horse's owner and saw Geza, the son of Gara, standing quietly to one side by the body of the dead King, making no effort to stop the horrible destruction. Finally the mare stopped pawing the body of the dead Queen and stood still, her eyes rolling wildly. Geza stepped over to the mare and patted her wet neck.

"As you took the life of my father through the hand of another, I have taken your's by another. We are even, Queen Edua!", Geza muttered to himself.

Then he turned to the Kuns and told them to organize a rescue party with horses, food, water, and a stretcher for the Archbishop. The Kuns, finding themselves without a leader for the first time in their lives, obeyed, relieved to have someone with authority tell them what to do.

It was dark when Geza finally located the little group of survivors by the light of the small fire Beatrix had built. A few soldiers and most of the women had escaped death at the hands of the Kuns, and now they huddled around the fire waiting for Geza to return. A long line of Kun people, men, women, and children, followed the young noble man to the Archbishop, for the soldiers' story of the miracle had spread in those few hours. They told how the Bishop had flown over the impassable moors on a great golden horse. The tale grew in color and magnificence as it passed from person to person among the Kuns. To those superstitious people it was a sign that they were to forget their pagan ways and follow the Christian faith. They came now to the Archbishop to be christened and to receive his blessing. Geza kept the truth of the matter to himself, for it had been his father's, and his own, greatest wish to bring Christianity to these wild, simple people.

As he entered the camp Beatrix jumped up to meet him, and then stopped short when she saw the Kun soldiers behind him.

"It's all right, Darling," Geza said, and then he explained the events of the last few hours to Beatrix and the Archbishop. He told them of the conversion of the Kuns and how it had happened, and as gently as possible he broke the news of the death of the King to them.

"An unhappy and a great man!", said the Archbishop, "by his death, he accomplished what he longed, and failed, to do in life. He brought about the conversion of these people. Don't cry Beatrix. He turned to the girl, silently weeping by his side. "Your father would be happy to know that his death helped this great cause. He is with the Lord now, and he would not want you to be sad."

Then, though he was growing continually weaker, the Archbishop sat up and called the Kun people around him. He told them of the great strength and beauty of Christianity. He spoke of how it gave meaning to life, and of how the Son of God died for all people, themselves included. He told them of the miracle of the resurrection, and the hope of everlasting life that it brought. He told them briefly, for his time was short, of all these things, and as he spoke, his voice grew steady and strong in the great love he bore his Faith. So strong was the Christian love that flowed from him, and so great was the truth of his words that the Kuns, gathered around him, began to accept this new faith in its own right and not only because of the story of the miracle they had been told. Finally the Archbishop welcomed them into the Christian faith, and blessed them.

When he had finished blessing the people, the Archbishop turned to Geza. "Do you love Beatrix, Geza, as she loves you?", he asked in his usual blunt and gruff manner.

The young man was startled by the unexpected question, but he answered immediately, smiling at Beatrix. "I love her far more than I could ever express."

"Then stand by her and take her hand, my son," the old Churchman said. And so, Geza, the son of Gara, was married to Beatrix, the royal princess and great-great great-great-grandniece of the Chieftain Arpad; and that is how the Kuns turned to Christianity and lived peacefully ever after. The good Archbishop, his work done, died blessing the crowd.

Geza and his Princess lived many years and raised a large family that became a prominent part of the Hungarian nobility in the centuries that followed. The golden horse, Clover, was cherished and spoiled for the rest of her life, and, when she died, she was buried in the family graveyard. Her children and grandchildren were carefully bred by the Gara family, on through the centuries, and three hundred years later a grey stallion was born, bearing the mark of the clover on his nose, but that is another story.

* * * * * * *

The extinction of the Arpad dynasty came during the fourteenth century, and the House of Anjou gained control of the throne. Near the end of the fourteenth century the thrones of Hungary and Poland were united, during the reign of the wise ruler, Louis the Great. Louis was succeeded by his son-in-law, Sigismund, who became Emperor of the Holy Roman Empire at the beginning of the fourteenth century. Unfortunately Sigismund neglected Hungary in favor of imperialism which left his country open to the threat of Turkish invasion. In the fourteenth century the Turks had entered Asia Minor and had conquered Macedonia. From there they invaded Serbia and Bulgaria, and, were approaching Croatia and Dalmatia which were next door to Hungary. Fearing that they would invade his country, Sigismund fought them in 1396 and lost the battle. It was only because Tamerlane was attacking the Turks at home, and they had to withdraw to defend themselves there, that they did not enter Hungary then.

After Sigismund's death, his son-in-law, Albert of Austria was crowned King of Hungary in 1438, but he died the same year, fighting the Turks, who had returned. Ladislaus IV of Poland then became King, but he, too, died in battle against the Turks in 1444. The young son of Albert was, then a boy, made King. Meanwhile John Hunyadi, Hungary's national hero, acted as regent and won many battles against the Turks. Hunyadi died in 1456, and the death of Albert's son, Ladislaus V, followed soon after. Hunyadi's son, Matthias Corvinus, then was made King, and his reign was one of the most brilliant and successful in the history of Hungary. Under his wise leadership Hungary became an outstanding European nation, and the Turks were successfully held off. But this prosperity was short lived, for when László II, of the House of Jagiello, came to the throne, factional strife developed, and Hungary was once more open to the Turkish threat. With the death of King Louis II on the field of Mohacs, the Turks, under Suleyman the Magnificent, began to overrun the whole country in the sixteenth century. It is during this time that the story of 'Bayram' takes place.

Bayram

THREE hundred years passed and the descendants of Clover remained in the Gara family. They came to be known as brilliant hunters famed for their speed and endurance. They were bred to Oriental horses that were either bought or looted from the Turks. Unfortunately there is very little about them either in the old family papers or the carefully preserved studbooks, except an exact record of their breeding and an occasional reference to reoccurring coarse heads and fighting temperaments, characteristics inherited from Clover.

There was only one mare who was actually described in these records. Her name was "Barsony" which means "velvet". Her lovely head was like that of the Oriental horses, her eyes were large, and her disposition, gentle. She was so fast that it was said that she could outrun the west wind. Barsony had only one foal, a silver grey colt who bore on his nose a vivid slate blue clover design. The horse was given, as a yearling, to a six year old girl. The child's name was "Bori", short for Borbala, and she was the last of the noble feudal family of Gara.

Bori and her colt were inseparable. She called him "Bayram", and when they romped together in the formal gardens of the castle they were like two young wild things from an enchanted land. The little girl would run laughing beneath the trees, her skirts held high, her blonde hair tangled into a golden crown around her head by the wind, and close behind her the grey cold danced, the little silver bell he wore around his neck gaily echoing Bori's laughter. Guests were often surprised to see the daughter of their host skipping merrily up the wide stone steps into the castle with a handsome grey colt, picking his way carefully behind her. They went everywhere together, down into the damp cellar to investigate the prisoner's cells, which had been empty for years, or into the warm kitchen to beg a treat from the cook. The horse became a beloved companion for the lonely little girl.

When Borbala was sixteen she became engaged to a handsome young noble man, Peter Bary. The two were married a year later, and the couple became known throughout the country for their great beauty. At first they were very much in love and very happy together, but their happiness was short lived, for both Bori and Peter were hot-tempered individualists, and their intense quarrels were frequent. At this time, also, Hungary was threatened by the Turks, and Peter was called to the defense of his country. And so, torn apart by the conflict between anger and love, the two were further separated by war. It is here that our story begins.

Borbala stared unbelievingly at the scroll of parchment in her hands, her eyes wide with horror and pain. The little page who stood beside her, his face pale and drawn with suffering, was the only thing that gave reality to this impossible situation. It was inconceivable that Peter, who had been with her only ten days before, should have so suddenly and violently gone out of her life. She felt a sickening wrench in the pit of her stomach. It was as if all the love and meaning in life had been torn from her with Peter. She turned quickly to the boy, struggling for control.

"Are you certain? Surely some must have escaped? Perhaps my husband was among them. Some did escape, didn't they?"

The page stared at the patterns on the marble floor unable to face the great faith that shone in the girl's face.

"They were all killed, m'lady. They all died. I saw the Turks close in on them from where I stood hidden behind a tree. I waited until those heathens left, and went to find Count Peter, but they had taken some of the bodies with them, and I couldn't find him. Then I came to you as quickly as I could. It was hard, m'lady, but I came." The youth's voice trembled and the tears began to run down his face. Ashamed, he brushed them away quickly.

Bori walked away from him and looked out of the window seeing nothing, her face contorted into a tight mask. There was something wrong with the boy's story. Why would they take Peter away dead? Perhaps they knew she would ransom his body for a Christian burial, yes, that was it! "Thank you", she said, "the servants will see to your needs. Wait outside, someone will come for you." She pulled the bell rope, and waited for the page to leave.

"I'm sorry, M'lady", he said, and hurried to the door relieved that this part of his terrible mission was over.

"What am I to do now", Bori said aloud to the empty room. "I must think. There is no one to decide for me". She sat down on a hard wooden chair, surprised to find that her legs would no longer support her. "I can't give in to this. They all depend on me now." She looked about the bare uncomfortable room in which she sat, and felt a sudden longing for her own familiar apartments. "Well, I should be glad to have this," she thought. She remembered the terrifying confusion of the day she had been forced to flee her home, Parno, and take refuge in this old fortified castle. It had been hopeless from the start, she had known that. With only herself and a group of men, women, and children, who were either too old or too young to fight the Turks on the battlefields, their valiant defense had been no more than a ridiculous burlesque.

"At least we are still alive which is more than poor Peter is", she said to herself, and, at the thought, a sob rose like a burning knot uncontrollably in her throat. "At least I won't have to tell Peter that I have failed, that I have lost Parno and all the family treasures to save my own skin," she thought with an odd feeling of relief. Suddenly the realization that Peter was dead, gone from her forever, came over her with a paralyzing shock. Unable to restrain her tears she flung herself on the bed, put her head down on her arms, and cried as if her heart would break. Finally, exhausted by the violence of her grief Bori fell asleep.

"A horse is coming", the voice of an old woman screamed into Bori's consciousness. She turned over in the great bed and wondered for a moment what she was doing there fully dressed in the middle of the day. Then she remembered. "Peter is dead, really dead, I can't believe it!", and the tears began to well up in her eyes again.

"A horse is coming", the old woman cried again.

"The Devil himself must be riding it, it comes so fast", another one yelled.

Bori sat up and listened. The voices came from the northern ramparts where the old women were boiling tar and water in readiness to greet the Turks when they attacked.

"Let down the drawbridge! Let down the drawbridge!" The call of the guard came clear and strong from his position near the front gate.

Bori leapt from her bed, ran out into the hall, and down to the ladder that led up to the turret overlooking the courtyard. The guard, formally the old head gardener at Parno, touched his cap and moved aside to let her look down.

The servants gathered quickly near the gate, their voices rising up to Bori in a confusion of excited murmurs. Slowly the great wooden barrier creaked down and struck the earth on the opposite side of the moat with a heavy thud. Just as the gate touched the ground, as if in perfect timing, a magnificent grey stallion galloped head long on to the drawbridge, into the courtyard; then, seeing the awed huddle of servants, he swerved to a sudden stop. For a minute no one moved. They stared at the huge animal who stood trembling before them, his sides heaving, his coat black with sweat and caked with dirt. A small figure was crouched motionless on his back. Bori felt her throat contract and her heart began to beat abnormally.

"It's Bayram!", she cried.

Bori wheeled around from the sight and started down the ladder as fast as she could, mentally cursing the long, cumbersome skirts that impeded her progress. Her first thought as she hurried down the hall was, "he has brought Peter back to me", but she knew immediately that the tiny figure huddled on the great horse's back could not be Peter.

Abruptly the girl stopped in the middle of the great entrance hall. The startling appearance of Bayram made her remember the bitter and furious quarrel between Peter and herself the day he had left to fight the Turks. Peter had insisted upon taking the stallion with him into battle, and she had opposed his wishes because she wanted to use the beautiful animal for breeding. She had wanted him left at home for another reason also. She could not bear the thought of her beloved pet being killed, and Peter had known that. She remembered his last words, his bantering tone, as he tried to conceal how deeply she had hurt him by so curtly refusing him the horse.

He had said, "Which do you love best, Bori, your husband or your horse?"

She had turned her back on him in silent fury as he galloped away on Bayram without another word.

"I wish I could tell you how sorry I am, Peter", she said out loud. And then, shaking her head, as if to clear it of her unpleasant memories, she hurried out into the courtyard.

The servants respectfully moved aside as their young mistress came running toward them. An old groom held the nervous Bayram, trying to quiet him by crooning low meaningless words, but the stallion still moved uneasily, pawing the ground, and looking wild-eyed at the people around him. Bori walked up to him and put her arms around his massive neck.

"Bayram", she said softly.

The girl stood with her arms around her horse for a few minutes, and then she turned to the groom. "He'll be all right now. Take good care of him.

"Yes, M'lady," said the groom, and he led Bayram toward the stables. Bori watched her horse disappear around the corner. "I wonder where you left Peter, Bayram", she thought, and again she felt the ridiculous tears welling up in her eyes. "I must stop this!" Suddenly she turned to the group of servants. "Bayram's rider! Who is he? Has he any message?"

"He is my son, M'lady", said a voice, "he's alive, thank God."

Bori looked down at the wife of the head groom who sat on the cobblestones of the courtyard with the head of a bloody, half-unconscious boy in her lap. The boy was Peter's groom.

Bori knelt down beside the youth. "He's wounded but not badly", she said, "bring him to my apartments. We'll wash him and feed him. Perhaps when he's rested he'll have news for us." As she stood up to lead the way Bori said to herself, "Oh God, let it be good news!"

The young groom was more dead than alive when they carried him into his mistresses apartments, but from exhaustion and fright rather than from his wounds. In a few hours after he had been washed and fed, and had slept a little he sat up ready to tell Borbala and the old servants all he knew about what had happened to Peter.

"Where is your master, boy," said Bori, "we must bring him home to bury him, or is it possible that he. . . "

"Bury him? But he is not dead," the boy interrupted, "The Turks took him prisoner. I know because I was there."

"Oh thank God", Bori cried and this time she did not brush away the tears of joy that sprang to her eyes. "The messenger this morning said they all were killed, but I knew somehow that Peter could not be dead."

"No, M'lady, the Turks took many prisoners, but they knocked them unconscious first, so perhaps that is why your messenger thought they were dead. And you should have seen Bayram, M'lady, you would have been very proud of him. The Turks tried to take him too, but he bit and kicked so viciously that no number of those heathens could capture him. While they were trying to catch Bayram, I saw some of the soldiers tie Count Peter on another horse and take him away. Then Bayram broke away and started galloping homewards. I called to him as he came near my hiding place, and he stopped for me. Of course the Turks saw him stop and saw me climb on, and some of them chased me. That's when I was wounded by their arrows, but no one could keep up with the great Bayram, and...", the boy hesitated, "but I am talking too much, M'lady."

"No, no", said Bori excitedly, "keep on, tell me everything!"

The lad smiled shyly, "I guess that's really all, M'lady, I rode to Parno, and when I saw it had been pillaged, I came here as was planned before Count Peter and I left. But you must prepare the ransom, M'lady. They will surely let the Count go if you send the ransom in time. Please send the ransom, M'Lady." The exhausted boy's head sank back on the pillows as sleep began to overcome him.

Bori smiled down at him. "You have done well, and Count Peter will be proud of you when he comes home. I will get the ransom off immediately, don't worry."

The boy tried to smile back to her. "Yes, M'Lady", he muttered and then he was asleep.

Bori turned to his mother, "Let him sleep here tonight, and take good care of him. He will be well enough to move to your quarters tomorrow. You have a fine son, and he has proved himself well."

Then, after she had dismissed the servants, Bori walked to her room and sat down on the bed exhausted. It had been a very long day. "Oh Peter, forgive me. If you hadn't taken Bayram I would never have known you were alive and needed my help", the girl said; and though she knew her husband couldn't hear her she felt suddenly better, as if Peter knew, wherever he was, that she was thinking of him, loving him more than she ever had before.

Someone tapped softly on the door breaking into Bori's reverie. "Come in", she said. The door opened and Erzsebet, Bori's childhood nurse, entered bearing a tray of food.

"It has been an exciting day for you, my child, and you have eaten nothing since morning," the old woman scolded. "You should eat or you will be sick. You must save your strength for much depends on you now. Count Peter's life is in your hands."

"Oh Erzsebet", the girl cried, "what am I to do? The ransom will be terribly high, and I lost all my jewels, money, and silver when we were forced to flee from Parno. The Turks killed my animals, plundered my corn and hay, and burned my houses to the ground. My properties are all in their hands, and I have nothing left to sell. Even if I did, who would buy in these terrible times? I am defeated before I start."

The old woman frowned at the girl. "This does not sound like you, my Borbala", she said softly, "you will find a way. Don't forget your kin in the west who are still holding out against the enemy. You must go to them, and they will help you."

Bori looked up, her eyes shining. "You're right, Erzsebet," she cried, "my Uncle Miklos will help me. I must get to him somehow."

"Yes, my child, Miklos Zrinyi, the great warrior will stand you by. He is very wealthy, and he would want you to come to him in your great need. Now eat your food and get some sleep. You must save your strength for it will not be easy to reach your uncle." The old nurse reached down and touched the girls bright head. "God protect you, Borbala, you will need His help."

After Erzsebet had gone Bori sat, barely touching her food. There was so much to do. "How can I leave my people here?", she thought. "They all depend on me, and yet I must go." She wished for a moment that her father whom she had adored was there to help her, but he had died fighting the Turks. Only her mother, who had grown so old after the death of her husband, and an aged aunt, who had been the abbess of a convent before the enemy had pillaged it, were left. The girl jumped up and ran down the hall to her mother's apartments. "I must ask her what I am to do", Bori thought. She knocked on the door and entered to find her mother and aunt sitting up as if they were waiting for her. Bori looked at her mother for a moment. The woman's face still held traces of beauty, but now it was lined by grief and by a painful disease that was slowly destroying her. "How can I complain when she has suffered so much." Bori thought. Then she ran over and kissed her mother's cheek. "Mother,. . . " she began.

"Greet your aunt, Borbala," her mother interrupted gently.

"Good evening, Aunt", Bori said hurriedly, and turned back to her mother.

But before Bori could explain her mission her mother stopped her again. "We are so happy that Peter is alive, my daughter. You must go and take the ransom to free him immediately."

"I am going to Uncle Miklos for help, Mother," said the girl, "I know you would understand . . . but will you be all right if I go?"

The older woman smiled, remembering her handsome brother, and how, as a child, Bori had idolized him. "Go ahead, Borbala. We have no man in the fort so you must go out and take the place of one until you have brought Peter back. Don't worry, God will give me the strength to take command, and I know He will let me live until you and Peter come back. It is a long trip to your Uncle Miklos, but if you go alone on horseback you won't arouse the enemy's suspicion. With only Bayram as a companion there will be no one to betray you, and you can move faster than the armed troops." Bori's mother stopped and smiled at her daughter. As for me it's been years since I felt so young. I won't fail you. Good luck, Borbala. God protect you".

A strikingly handsome man gazed out of a small window of the huge fortress in which he stood. The low thick walls of the arch forced him to bend down to look out on the thousands of brightly colored tents of the besieging Turkish army camped outside the walls of the castle. His eyes were sad as he turned away from the scene and sat down at a table. There was no escape but death now, and Miklos Zrinyi suddenly felt very tired. All the forts around his, but one, had been captured, and his own was running dangerously short of food. They had killed most of the horses and eaten them. Only a minimum number had been kept, and these were nothing but skin and bones. "Even so", Miklos thought ruefully, "those wretched animals are in better condition than my poor soldiers who have so bravely defended Szigetvar. And for what reason? It is only a matter of days now!" He picked up a pen and tried to write, but the lines that used to come so easily to him seemed to have left him now. His mind was filled with the horror of the days behind him, and the certain tragedy that lay before him. Miklos turned back to the window. The early morning sky was splashed with red by the sun as it came up over the mountains. "How appropriate", thought Miklos sarcastically, "even the sky is attuned to our catastrophe." He stared down at the Turkish camp and felt a helpless rage fill his heart. Then as he watched he saw a horse move slowly away from the enemy ranks toward the main entrance of the fortress. As it came closer he could distinguish a figure on a big grey horse brandishing a white flag in his hand. "What in the name of God are they up to now", Miklos muttered aloud. "It's ridiculous that the Turks would send a peace emissary now." They know the fort is badly damaged, and that the soldiers are nearly dead from lack of food. They themselves had cut off the food supply weeks ago." The emissary stopped in front of the drawbridge and waved the flag. "It is some of their heathen trickery," Miklos said to himself, and turned to hurry down the steps to the courtyard.

As he descended the steps Miklos met one of his soldiers coming to tell him of the Turkish emissary's arrival.

"Captain Zrinyi", the soldier began.

"I know, I know", Miklos said impatiently, "I'll go down to him myself", and he hurried away leaving the puzzled soldier on the steps.

As he entered the courtyard Miklos saw a mud-caked, tired Turkish youth standing before him. Something was wrong. The Turks would never have sent an emissary in this condition.

"What are you doing here, boy," he barked.

The boy's face underwent strange contortions, and then with a muffled voice he stuttered something in bad Turkish.

Miklos Zrinyi was in no mood for diplomacy. He grabbed the boy's shoulders and shook him, but with strange results. The "emissary" felt very small and slim in his hands, and it was obvious that he was shaking with suppressed laughter. Miklos lifted the boy higher, his eyes level with two grey pools of gaiety that could have belonged to only two people, his sister and her daughter, Borbala.

"So, you are a Turkish emissary now", he laughed, depositing a resounding kiss on Bori's dirty face to the complete astonishment of the soldiers surrounding them, eager for news. They retreated quickly to tell the rest of the troop that their captain was certainly losing his mind for he had kissed the Turkish emissary, or was it possible, they mused hopefully, that the boy had brought them good news.

Later after she had washed off the dirt gathered on her long journey, Bori sat with her beloved uncle hardly able to believe her good luck that she had at last reached him safely.

Miklos touched at his niece's shaved head. "Your lovely hair, Bori, how I wish you hadn't had to lose it", You played your part well though, and I am very proud of you."

Bori smiled, "I still have one piece left", she said, touching the one remaining lock that grew from the middle of her head in an exact replica of the Turkish youths hair style. "And the rest will grow back soon. The important thing right now is to get Peter back. That's why I came to you." Then Bori told Miklos of the danger Peter was in and of her desperate need for the ransom money.

Miklos sat silently for a long time after the girl finished her story, a hopeless look on his handsome face. "Bori, child", he said finally, "I could give enough money to ransom three Peters, but you would never get out of the fort alive with it." The girl opened her mouth to protest, but Miklos stopped her.

"Yes, I know you got through their lines once, and you are a very lucky girl. The Turks aren't stupid, Bori, don't underestimate them. You may have fooled them, but they probably let you through just to find out what you were up to. They will certainly pick you up if you try to leave, and torture you for information." Miklos took the girl's hand in his own. "I'm sorry, Bori, but there's nothing I can do just now.

"Oh, Uncle Miklos," Bori cried, "you don't understand! I have to go to Peter!

They might kill him if I don't get there in time.

The tall man just shook his head helplessly. He would have given his life for his adored niece, but now they could only wait.

Suddenly Bori smiled up at him. "Well then, if I must stay here, I must. But I'm going to look around your gloomy pile of rocks anyway, and see if I can find a way out. . . and please", she said, her eyes rested upon him pleadingly, "do you have some feed for Bayram. We came such a long way. He is very tired and hungry."

Miklos laughed. "So, you little devil, you kept Bayram from your husband after all. The story of your stubborn refusal to let Peter take your horse into battle even reached my fort. I think you need a good spanking."

"Oh no," cried Bori, "Peter took Bayram, but when they were captured Bayram got free, and Peter's little groom brought back the news of his capture. If it hadn't been for Bayram I would never have known Peter was alive. I am so ashamed that I tried to make him take another horse. I would not be here if it weren't for Bayram. He gave me the courage to come somehow."

"The legend of Clover", said the Captain, half to himself, "it is a strange thing." He smiled at his niece, "Of course your brave stallion will be fed. We slaughtered two more horses to feed the soldiers today. He shall have their rations, scanty though they are."

Two weeks passed, and the Turks still waited patiently for the surrender of the helpless fortress. Meanwhile Borbala and her uncle searched feverishly for a secret passage out of the huge castle. Everyday Bori carefully covered the catacombs, passages, and tunnels that ran for miles under the earth, but the few hidden exits had been found by the Turks either through spies or ruthless questioning of prisoners. Because of this Miklos had walled up the doors securely weeks before. There seemed to be no way out except into the arms of the waiting Turks.

The emotional and physical strain began to weaken Bori. She lost weight, her face became unnaturally white and sallow, and the diet of moldy bread and horse meat that she shared with the ghostly thin soldiers kept her constantly ill.

Miklos watched his niece with helpless concern. "If she dies it will be my fault", he thought, "and yet I can't do anything to help her." His soldiers troubled him too. They were hungry and frightened. The constant waiting for the end, they knew must come soon, made them unnaturally nervous and irritable.

"Let's attack the pagan fiends and be done with it. We are dying anyway", they muttered as day after day they carried their comrades to the cemetery. They considered the dead lucky to have been relieved of the torture of living.

The cemetery ground was hard and rocky, and the work of burying their dead was almost too much for the wasted men. Miklos watched the vultures, attracted by the stench of the rotting corpses, settle on the ramparts over the graveyard where the men were digging the shallow graves. He sighed and turned away from the sight. "How much better it would be if we could let the vultures take care of that business altogether," he thought. "At least they do a thorough job. . . better than a burial a few inches below the surface. The air is polluted now. It won't be long before the plague attacks us too." Miklos sat down at the table near the window from which he had first seen Borbala riding up to the drawbridge, and put his head down in his hands. "Oh God, how long is this going to go on", he thought.

Nearly a month after the gates of the fortress closed behind Borbala was attracted by a strange light. As she walked along the walls of the castle she noticed some thing moving on the surface of the moat. The water was low from lack of rain, and as the girl watched she saw hundreds of rats, their ugly bodies half submerged in the slimy water and their naked tails beating around them as they tried to keep their balance on something just below the surface. The girl leaned over the stone parapet, nearly losing her balance, as she tried to see then she noticed beams, like part of an invisible bridge half submerged by the moat and covered with moss. The foul smell was nauseating, but she was used to such odors since she had been in the make-shift hospital rooms where she nursed and administered last rites to the sick and dying, since the chaplain himself had been buried beside his children in the little cemetery.

The bridge-like structure emerged from an opening that connected or had connected something with the other side of the moat, the side where the Turkish troops, well fed and well-groomed, camped around the gates to the fortress in their bright tents, with the horse and half moon insignia emblazoned on them, a constant eyesore to Captain Zrinyi's starving soldiers.

Bori turned quickly and ran up to her Uncle's rooms. The rich beauty of the wide staircase, carved long before by Italian craftsmen, that wound up the upper galleries filled with priceless treasures, was in strange contrast to the poverty and misery of the castle's inhabitants. Heavy gold goblets and huge oriental rugs filled the rooms. Velvet and gold brocades were strewn between giant bearskins that covered the dusky red of the marble floors. For a moment Bori saw Szigetvar as it had been in her childhood with the tournaments, the magnificent display of color and pageantry. She remembered riding Bayram's mother, her falcon perched on her wrist as they galloped over the drawbridge onto the marshy plains where the aigrettes were found. Her falcon had caught three of the lovely birds, and she had given Miklos the feathers for his sable trimmed cap. But there was no time for remembering now, and she hurried toward her uncle's study.

Miklos stood at his writing desk staring down at a small piece of white silk next to the large sheets of parchment. The silk was a message he had unwound from the leg of his last passenger pigeon. The soldiers knew the essential need for these birds, but in the agony of their hunger, they had killed and eaten all but this one. The bird had reached Miklos, but it's message brought only another note of despair. It read, "Last fort surrendered. Don't hope for help."

He looked up as Bori entered the room. "I hate for you to read this, Borbala, but. . .", he hesitated.

The girl came quickly to his side, and silently reached out her hand for the piece of silk. She read the message, and then said dispassionately, "I never thought it could have ended any other way, but Hungary will recover even if we die. The parent trees may be cut to the ground, but their seeds always fall, and new life begins again. We are just unlucky that we are the trees that are to be made into fire wood." Then the girl smiled. "But we are not kindling yet, Uncle Miklos, I have found something that may mean our escape. I think I have found an underground bridge that looks as if it comes out on the far side of the fort, out of sight of the Turks."

Miklos looked with pity at his niece. "No one knows this castle better than I", he thought, "the poor child is so confident that she will find a way to her Peter that she is imagining her 'bridge'. If it were there I would surely know about it. Still it is possible, and it won't hurt to look. Women see things that men are too blind to notice."

"What is it, Uncle Miklos?", the girl said, alarmed by his long silence. "Nothing, Borbala," he said, "I was just thinking that we must explore your discovery tonight. If there really is a way out, it's better for the soldiers not to know yet. The wretches are half insane with hunger and suspense, and they would probably riot if they thought they had a chance of getting free. They are so close to death now that discipline means little to them. You understand?"

Bori nodded. "Of course! I will meet you here at midnight."

As the castle guard was changing at midnight twelve, Bori and Miklos quietly descended the steps into the huge dungeon of the fortress. Their way was lit only by dim lanterns so that they would not attract the attention of the sleepless soldiers who wandered aimlessly around the fort, staring with unseeing eyes at nothing as they senselessly used up what little strength they had left. As they passed the prison cells Bori was thankful that they had been emptied long since. Prisoners were always the most underfed, the first to die in case of a siege. She thought of Peter, cold and hungry, in some enemy prison and shivered unconsciously.

"At least we are not torturing some poor human as you are tortured, Peter", she thought.

They went lower and lower, passing the walled in, heavily barricaded secret passages. Finally they came to a large underground tunnel that was part of the castle sewer. It's rocky ceiling was supported by rough hewn, but incredibly powerful columns. In the dim light of the lanterns it was difficult to distinguish the height or length of the corridor, but it was obviously tremendous.

"This was built. . . God knows when. . . before Roman times probably", thought Bori. "How I would have loved to have explored this. . . well, someone else will have to do the exploring, I'm afraid."

"Well, Bori, if your bridge exists it should be somewhere around here", said Miklos.

They saw the dim glimmer at the end of the tunnel where the light of the moon was reflected on the water of the moat. Bori was not squeamish, but it took all her will power to keep on walking over the army of cockroaches, centipedes, and thousands of other insects that ran blindly to the unaccustomed light of the lanterns. She felt the sickening crunch, or the soft squash of their bodies as her foot skidded over them. The huge water rats brushed against her too, and she heard her uncle cursing under his breath in the rich and varied manner that only a soldier can master. Somehow it braced her more than if he had spoken words of comfort. They moved ahead until they came to a spot where the water of the sewer fell like a filthy ribbon in many little rivulets that trickled along the moss covered stones into the moat. Even the appearance of Borbala and Miklos did not disturb the hundreds of rats who were fighting to keep their footing on something submerged beneath the water, something that showed above the surface at intervals, the brownish moss that covered it in line with the dark figures of the rats.

"My God, Bori, you were right", exclaimed Miklos. "There is, or was, a well or bridge here. But where could it lead? Perhaps you have found a way for us to escape!"

"But suppose the supports are rotten, eaten by the rats. The bridge hasn't been used for hundreds of years", said the girl.

"No, Bori, look at these columns in the tunnel." Miklos turned to shine his lantern back into the room behind them. "I shouldn't be surprised if the bridge weren't supported by stone pillars. Look farther out the line of rats. See how wide it is. It may be thousands of years old, but that bridge is made of stone. Now, that's enough for tonight. Let's get some sleep."

"Oh no, Uncle Miklos", cried the girl, "we can't turn back now. Please, we must go on until we find out where it leads."

"We have to go back, Bori, we aren't dressed to go into that water, and the rats will bite. We have to have protection from them. But we'll come back tomorrow night, and find the end of your mysterious bridge even if it leads us to hell." Miklos put his arm around the girl's shoulder and together they went back through the dark passages to their rooms.

The next night Bori entered her uncle's study, and found him bending over a bundle of clothing that contained heavy leather leggings with a light cover of chain armour over them. They were cumbersome, but Miklos knew they would prevent the rats from inflicting any wounds. Hearing the girl's step Zrinyi turned, a pair of the leather pants in his hand.

"Hello, Bori," he said, "put these on and we'll get started." Bori took the outfit from him.

"Uncle Miklos, they're so heavy. We'll never be able to swim if we fall in the water."

"I've taken care of that too. See this piece of rope? I will go first and if I fall you can pull me out of the water with it. Now run into the bedroom and get dressed." Miklos smiled and patted his niece on the shoulder.

"All right", said Bori dubiously, and she hurried into the next room to change her clothes.

When she returned the two again took their lanterns and made their way down to the tunnel where they had found the bridge.

As they approached the hidden tunnel Bori turned to her uncle.

"Why don't you let me go first. It will be much easier for you to pull me out of the water, and besides I'd hate to sit on the wall with the rats biting my face. If, after all this trouble, I reach Peter, I don't think he'd welcome a pug-nosed wife." They both laughed, and the laughter echoed weirdly, sounding strange and out of place in the dark tunnel.

"All right, my girl, go ahead", Miklos smiled, "we must make the most of this chance to get you to Peter."

Bori looked at her uncle, a puzzled expression on her face. "And you, Uncle Miklos?", she said softly, "You're coming too, aren't you?"

Miklos handed her one end of the rope, avoiding her bewildered eyes. "Don't be silly, Borbala", he said roughly, "I am a soldier and my duty is here. I cannot run away, you know that. Now then, let's go."

Bori turned from him quickly so that he would not see the tears in her eyes and stepped out on the rat-covered path. She struck out at the snarling animals as they jumped out of her way into the water, their furious eyes shining up at her in the darkness. Some climbed back as soon as she had thrust them away, and a few even tried to fight her. Bori was frightened, but she moved steadily on step by step. After a few yards her stick slipped on the moss covered stone, and she almost fell into the water as her support skidded from under her. As the stick plunged into the water it hit on something solid a few inches below the surface, and Bori quickly regained her balance.

"I think I've found it", she cried.

Miklos came up close behind her, and they began to fathom the ground next to the rat besieged wall. It was solid stone. They had found the bridge. Then, very slowly, they began to move forward, testing the floor of the bridge as they went. Miklos waded waste deep in the water along the span, which was about the width of a drawbridge and strong enough for the heaviest cart to go over. Bori continued along the wall which was a few feet under water so she no longer had any rats to impede her progress.

Finally they found the underground opening at the end of the bridge. It was lower than the castle sewer, and reeking from the stagnant water that flowed down into it. Miklos took Bori on his shoulders to keep her out of the water as they entered the dim tunnel. The stench was unbearable and decaying corpses floated on the surface near the entrance. Bori had to control herself to keep from being sick at the sight.

Soon Miklos was able to put Bori down as they came up on solid ground, and they progressed quickly as the corridor started to mount upward. The tunnel was high and the path clean, even the air began to get fresh, and the two explorers wondered, if they had at last found the exit that would mean freedom for Bori. Then they came to a heavy door. By the light of the lanterns it looked frightening and solid, but upon closer inspection they found it was rotten with age. Miklos rammed it with his shoulder and it gave way immediately. About two hundred yards farther on the tunnel began to rise sharply, and curious clefts were cut into the rock base of the floor as if to give horses a good grip as they went up or down with heavy loads.

Miklos stopped and turned to his niece. "We'll have to be very quiet from now on, Bori", he said, "I'm afraid this comes out in the middle of the Turkish camp, or close to it anyway."

Bori looked up at him, horrified. "Oh Uncle Miklos", she said, "it can't!" But Miklos theory proved to be doubly right. The tunnel gave a sharp circular turn, and the two heard the rush of water overhead.

"Let's sit down a minute, Bori", Miklos said, "I have to get my bearings." They sat down on the floor, and with some primitive, but efficient calculations, Miklos came to a quick conclusion. He knew where they were.

"Bori", he said, "This tunnel comes out under a waterfall that cascades over some tremendous rocks that hide the entrance. I know the place very well, although I never knew until now what it hid. I remember when I was very young I used to meet my first love here out of sight of the castle. She was the daughter of father's first hunts man, and we thought that we would never recover from our hopeless love." Miklos smiled remembering. Then he looked at Bori's expectant face. "I have bad news for you, my child," he said, "The waterfall is right in the middle of the Turkish tents. It is from there that they get their water. Let's go back now, Bori," he said softly, "there is nothing else we can do."

Bori tried to smile at him, fighting to keep the tears from her eyes. She had prayed so hard that this old sunken bridge would mean the road to freedom and to Peter.

After a depressing morning nursing the sick, Bori spent the afternoon with Bayram. The disappointment of the findings of the previous night hung over the girl like a great weight, and she sought to relieve her depression by playing with the grey stallion as she had in her childhood days.

"Bayram, come", she called softly, and the twelve year old stallion followed her up the steps to the wide wall that ran around the castle picking his way carefully and stopping from time to time as if to say, "There is a limit to my patience, and I've had enough of this."

But to the girl's low pitched, "No, Bayram, come", he would start after her again, his ears flattened against his head, to show his disapproval of the whole procedure.

The sick, dirty soldiers sat on the ground below them, the lazy flies buzzing around their open sores, unnoticed, and smiled for the first time in weeks to see the antics of the girl who had become their adored angel of mercy. Miklos stepped out into the courtyard unnoticed and smiled too. Then his face became serious as he watched the stallion follow

Bori in places where no ordinary horse would go. An insane idea began to form in his year; yet it was not insane in these times. Miklos turned and hurried back to his rooms.

———————————————————————

Peter sat staring blankly at the horizon. Weeks had passed since he had been knocked unconscious from Bayram. The despair of being a prisoner had blurred with the passage of time, and even the hope of being ransomed had taken on a dream-like quality. He had become conscious of his own being and the things that went on around him indistinctly, and life, being no longer real to him, did not matter very much. It was like a horrible nightmare that could be thrown off and forgotten with the coming of morning, but morning was slow in rising.

Peter was not alone in this situation. There were many Hungarian noblemen, members of wealthy families, that the Turks had not killed in order to get high ransoms, or to exchange for their own captured officers. But now the chances for either exchanging or ransoming the imprisoned Hungarians were slim, for it was the Hungarian army that lost by far the most men as the Turks little by little overran the whole country, and with their occupation the lands and money that would have served as ransom were confiscated. The Hungarian feudal lords realized too late that only their cooperation could have saved their country from the conqueror's oppression. Through old family feuds and intrigues they had dissipated the Hungarian forces, and destruction was upon them before they had time to unite their efforts against the enemy.

From the little news that had reached him by recently captured prisoners Peter knew that Szigetvar was one of the last forts still standing. His wife's uncle was holding out against impossible odds much to everyone's surprise. Miklos Zrinyi in peacetime was a ruthless landlord, and his great fortune had been amassed by making the most of the feudal system. Though he treated his peasants fairly, according to the standards of the times, he took everything he could get from them. In spite of this he was a brilliant soldier, capable of inspiring great loyalty in his men. Peter knew that it was only this loyalty, this blind faith in their leader, that had enabled the starving handful of men to hold out so long, although they knew defeat and death to be inevitable.

Since the ransom that would have freed him had not arrived, Peter was nearly frantic with worry about Bori. The long imprisonment had dulled his senses it was true, but his love for his wife was still passionately alive. He eagerly questioned each of his fellow prisoners as they arrived, but every time he was turned away with no answer. No one seemed to know what had happened to the girl. A month earlier a fellow officer whom Peter had known since childhood had been brought in by the Turks. The man had heard that Bori had fled from Parno to a nearby fortification, and soon after had gone on from there alone, leaving the fort in her mother's hands. Where she had gone he did not know. From this sketchy piece of news Peter realized that all their properties had probably been burned or ravaged, and he knew that his stubborn little Bori would not have left Parno until the last possible chance of saving it had been exhausted. For this reason her flight must have been hurried with no chance of escaping with any large amount of money. It was clear then to Peter why he had not been ransomed, but the question of Bori's whereabouts was yet another matter. The uncertainty of not knowing whether she was dead or alive, or, even worse, suffering as a captive in the hands of the ruthless Turks tortured him day and night.

"If only I could get free and help her wherever she is," he thought, but he knew that any attempt at escape would mean certain death, for the Turks guarded their prisoners carefully and well. "Certainly my death, however courageous and colorful, would not do her any good", he said sarcastically to himself, immediately ashamed of his false heroics.

There was another matter that tormented Peter also. He knew that it was very possible that he might never see Bori again, and the fact that they had parted with a violent quarrel filled him with bitter regret. He remembered it vividly now, for time had failed him in its task of blurring the pain of unpleasant memories. He and Bori had loved one another so intensely, perhaps that was why they were capable of hurting each other so deeply. The memory of the quarrel became more and more real to Peter as he thought about it. The monotony of prison life often plays strange tricks upon the mind of an ordinarily active man, and, as the reality of the remembered situation burst upon Peter, he suddenly cried aloud, "I wish I'd never taken the damned horse, Bori !"

Peter's fellow prisoners turned to stare at him, surprised at this violent, senseless exclamation from their usually silent companion, but Peter, if he saw them, paid no attention.

"Poor Bayram was probably killed", he thought, "that horse would never let a stranger touch him, so those heathens probably had to destroy him to capture him. Still, he carries the mark of the Clover, and if the legend is true he is probably safe somewhere. He was a great horse though, and I can't blame Bori for loving her grey stallion. . . but it was ridiculous to fight over a mere animal." He remembered the girl's face, white with rage, as he jerked Bayram's bridle from her hands with the angry words, "I'll take your God-forsaken beast, and I'll come back on him. . . if for no other reason than to give you the spanking you deserve. I'd do it right now if the servants weren't here, but since you are left as head of the family I can't very well disgrace you in front of them."

She had turned her back on him then in silent anger, too enraged to speak, and with a jeering comment he had spurred Bayram savagely, unnecessarily, and galloped off.

Peter's mind came abruptly back to the present. "I wonder if she ever thinks of me with anything but bitterness," he said to himself. "This I do know though, I can trust Bori's loyalty, and I know that somehow, if she's still alive she'll find a way to get that ransom money and come to me. . . if for no other reason than to prove, with her old bravado, that she could do it!

The sudden clatter of hoofs and wooden wheels over the hard ground sounded into Peter's consciousness, and he looked up to see the Turkish transport wagons being halted near the prisoners. A guard called roughly to them to fall in line, and Peter struggled stiffly to his feet with the others. They were marched into the bullock-drawn wagons, and there the heavy chains, bolted at one end to the seats, were fastened around the legs of each of the captives. They were moving again. Peter didn't know where, and he didn't particularly care.

After he returned to his room to consider it, the crazy plan that had occurred to Miklos Zrinyi as he watched Bayram follow Borbala along the castle walls, began to take shape.

"It's ridiculously simple, and perhaps that is why it may be successful", thought Miklos. "It all depends on Bori and the swiftness of her grey stallion." He hurried to the door and ordered the page, who waited outside, to bring Borbala to him immediately.

A few minutes later Bori came into the room, her face showing her deep concern over the unexpected summons.

"What is it, Uncle Miklos?", she said anxiously, "has something happened?" The man rose from his chair and led her to a seat near the window.

"No, Bori, nothing has happened, but something is about to, and it concerns you and Bayram."

Startled, Bori looked up at her uncle and waited for him to explain.

"I think you may escape after all," he continued, and, as the girl started to interrupt, he raised his hand to stop her. "Wait a minute, my child, we haven't got much time", he said, "my plan must be carried out tonight, in just a few hours, so let me finish. "I watched Bayram follow you around the castle walls today. He followed you where an ordinary horse could not be beaten into going. Because of this I believe he would go with you down into that tunnel if you asked him, foul-smelling and dark though it is. Once you come out by the waterfall your escape will depend on surprising the Turks, as they certainly don't expect anyone to come out of the ground right in the middle of their camp, and it will depend on Bayram's great speed, for once you get started, there is no horse that can catch him. Do you want to try it?" Miklos Zrinyi stopped and waited for his niece's answer. It came immediately with no hesitation.

"Oh, Uncle Miklos," she cried, "Of course I'll go, and Bayram and I will make it too."

Miklos looked at Bori's shining face. She was more alive than he had seen her in all the dreary weeks she had been in the fort. "Oh, God, let me do the right thing", he thought, "if she dies I could never forgive myself." But the decision had been made, and Miklos knew he must abide by it.

"Besides", he thought, "it is better for her to have this chance at least than to sit here and wait until the Turks lose patience and attack us. There will be no chance for anyone then." Then Miklos turned to Bori. "All right, Borbala," he said quietly, "meet me at midnight, with Bayram, by the entrance to the cellar. I will go down with you to the waterfall. From then on you are on your own, and may God be with you."

At midnight Bori took Bayram into the castle and met her uncle by the stairs leading down into the sewers. Then the three, guided only by the dim light of a single lantern, silently began to follow the long winding passages down to the underground tunnel. Bayram picked his way slowly but steadily behind his mistress, snorting softly now and again at the foul odors which pricked his sensitive nostrils. In spite of the rats and insects that plagued him as he went, he still followed Bori obediently, his ears laid back in his old way to show his disgust over the whole affair.

It took them nearly an hour to reach the exit hidden by great boulders and the waterfall. At one time there had been a trap door, but it had crumbled away long before, and now only briers and shrubs covered the large dark hole. As they reached the spot Miklos turned around to face Bori. He took his short hunting knife from its sheath, and handed it to her. "Take this, Borbala, if you should fall into Turkish hands. . . " He could not go on, but Bori understood. She nodded silently and stuck the knife in her belt.

They moved as quietly as possible up to the opening and looked out through the dark pattern of leaves at the sleeping Turkish camp. A flag, with the emblem of the Turkish high command faintly visible upon it in the darkness, fluttered in the breeze atop a tent not more than a hundred yards from them. "Get ready, Bori," Miklos whispered. The girl turned to bring Bayram up to the opening, when Zrinyi's voice stopped her.

"Wait!", he said, "Look at this!"

Bori came swiftly to his side and peered out at the camp. She saw guards jump to attention as several high ranking officers and Sultan Suleyman the Magnificent himself, ruler of the Turkish empire, approached the tent near the hidden opening. Beyond the tent dark, swiftly moving shapes were assembling in formation.

"Good Lord, they're gathering for the attack", hissed Miklos, and, as he spoke, the wall-breaking machines and ladders used to scale enemy walls were drawn by horses into background. "Quick, let's get back and warn the fort," Miklos said. And so by a strange twist of fate Bori's chance to escape was destroyed.

It took them less than an hour to get back and sound the alarm. The soldiers awoke from their restless sleep immediately, and soon the courtyard that had been silent for so long was filled with the clatter of arms, the cursing of the men, and even laughter could be heard. They welcomed the approaching battle. Anything was better than waiting for starvation or the plague to end their lives. Even the sick voluntarily left their beds to help, and certainly every hand was needed. Bori went to work too, preparing bandages for the wounded, filling the cauldrons of the tar-hurlers with dry tar to be boiled, and getting the reserve troops organized. In spite of this preparation the fort had little chance for survival. Nearly all the officers were dead, and not one in ten of the men was left alive. There was no food and scarcely any equipment to back up these pitiful forces. There was but one factor in their favor. The Turks had expected to surprise Miklos Zrinyi and his men, but now the element of surprise was on the side of the Hungarians.

Miklos had thought that the reason why the Turks were attacking was that they were tired of waiting for the fort to surrender. This was partly correct, but only partly. The old, fat, and choleric Sultan had been feeling ill that week. His doctors had treated him with various herbs and then had warned him not to go into battle or the excitement would surely kill him. The Sultan was a spoiled, stubborn, and perverse man for, though he often asked for advice, he would never take it. For that matter he usually went against it just to prove that no one was wiser than he. This time the Sultan followed his usual pattern. He became enraged at his physicians, and threatened to execute them if they did not retract

their stupid diagnosis, which the frightened men immediately did. The Sultan was known as a man of his word when it came to executions. Placated by their denial of the original diagnosis, Sultan Suleyman assured them that he suffered from nothing more than indigestion and then dismissed them, in order to plan a surprise attack on Szigetvar with his officers.

"I am tired of rotting here", he told them, "It is time we finished those Christian dogs off anyway."

Now, several days later, his face purple with exertion, the Sultan mounted his horse at the head of his troops in order to direct the attack.

"We will certainly shatter their mangy forces in no time catching them unaware like this", he said to an officer near him, and then chuckled to himself at the thought. The he turned to his men and gave the command to attack, and with a terrible shout the Turks converged upon the castle.

When the ladders were set up against the walls of Szigetvar and the first line of Turkish soldiers began to mount them, they were met with a torrent of boiling tar and scalding water. The Sultan was insane with rage. He screamed at his soldiers to attack again, but once more the burning mass poured down upon them, forcing them to turn back. The Sultan was beside himself with anger by this time. His carefully planned surprise attack had been spoiled, and the Sultan was not accustomed to having his plans upset.

"The Christian infidels must have smuggled new forces into the fort somehow", Suleyman thought, "and some dog of a spy on my staff must have warned the fort of my proposed attack".

His face got even more purple at the thought that anyone might dare betray him, and if it was possible for him to become any more enraged he did so then. He stormed at the officers near him threatening to have them all drawn, quartered, and impaled if the traitor among them did not confess at once to a pact with the Christian dogs. The officers stared back at him in amazement wondering from what source the Sultan had got this information, but they were used to his unreasonable accusations of his so they turned back to direct their men into the attack. The ungovernable temper of their ruler was something to be dealt with at another time.

A messenger rode up to Suleiman, being careful to keep a good distance between them for he had bad news, and he did not want the wrath of the Sultan to fall upon him.

"Sultan, I regret to report the death of your valiant and courageous royal nephew", he said, inching his horse a few steps farther away from Suleyman.

The loss of his best officer, the man in whose ability he trusted most, was too much for Suleyman. Since he couldn't reach the messenger he brought his crop down hard between his horses ears for lack of anything else to take his rage out upon. By the time he had brought the frenzied animal to a halt the Sultan's face was blue, and his blood-shot eyes seemed to pop out of his head. He reeled in his saddle, gave a stifled croak, and fell to the ground dead.

The frantic Turkish officers looked at each other in despair as they quickly surrounded the fallen figure of their ruler. In spite of his faults, the Sultan was a brave and cunning, if ruthless leader. He had built a tremendous empire in his life time. The remaining officers knew that if the Turkish soldiers found out that the Sultan was dead they would be completely demoralized. Suleyman's chief aid made a sudden decision.

"We must tie the Sultan to the back of his horse so the soldiers can see him", he said, "then they will think he is still alive!"

The other officers quickly agreed, and they tied the body to the saddle. Then, marshaled by two of the officers, one on either side of the horse, the bobbing figure of the dead Sultan rode forward still in command of the troops.

Inside the fort the sick and starving Hungarian soldiers found new strength in the job of battle. The fact that they were repelling the Turkish attack brought them to a high pitch of excitement, and they fought as if they were fresh troops not dying men. Not one of those soldiers thought that he might survive the attack, but each sought to die well, taking more than his share of the heathen Turks with him. Miklos Zrinyi's passionate nature served him well in battle. In peace he was ruthless in business and the conduct of his estates, but in war he was magnificent. All the wealth he had gained from his overworked serfs and his estates had gone to defend Christianity and to preserve Hungary for the children of succeeding generations. Miklos was a hard man, of a physical rather than a philosophical nature, but he would have given everything he had, including his life, without hesitation for his religion and his beloved Hungary.

Szigetvar was Zrinyi's last fortress, and the men who manned it were his last men. He knew this would be his last fight and so he entered whole-heartedly, almost joyfully into the battle. He drew his sword from the body of a Turk who had managed to mount the wall and looked around to see if Bori was all right. He saw his dirty niece, red with the blood of the wounded whom she had been attending, moving among the dying men with comforting words. When the cauldrons were empty she helped fill them with scalding water or tar that were then poured on the attacking Turks who clung to the ladders, scalded and blind, then fell screaming with rage and pain into the moat. Several more Turks managed to climb over the wall, and Miklos turned from Bori, brandishing his sword above his head, to dispatch them.

Borbala saw that the tar supplies were nearly exhausted, and as she looked over the parapet to see how many Turks were left, hoping that the supply could be stretched, she saw several Turkish corpses caught on the bastion below her. Suddenly one of the bodies moved and began to crawl into the castle by the way of the sewers. Bori felt an awful fear paralyze her for a moment.

"All our men are up here," she thought, "If that man gets into the castle he can lower the drawbridge, and the rest of the Turks can walk into the fort unhindered."

She caught up a bow and arrow and took careful aim. The man must have instinctively felt the danger for he turned and looked straight up at the figure on the wall above him. Then with an awkward gesture he threw back his shoulders and spread out his arms giving Bori a perfect immobile target. The girl lowered the bow.

"I cannot kill an unarmed, wounded man", she said softly.

They stood there looking at each other for a long time while Bori desperately sought for a solution. Then she noticed a ladder-work of hooks descending down to the bastion.

"I will go down and take him prisoner", she thought, "as if a dying fort had any use for prisoners, but there seems to be nothing else to do".

She looked around to see if she could descend without being noticed by the Turks. The sight that met her eyes was absolutely unbelievable. The Turks were retreating, gathering up their dead and wounded as they went. Bori had to clutch the edge of the wall to keep from falling, she was so dizzy from happiness and relief. All around her Zrinyi's soldiers were laughing and shouting with joy. They had accomplished the impossible!

"Oh Lord, St. Joseph, my patron, it is so beautiful to live", whispered Bori.

Then Bori climbed over the wall and began to descend slowly by way of the hooks down to the bastion. As she went down she began to sing a little song that she and Peter had loved. She felt senselessly, drunkenly happy, and she kept turning to watch the retreating Turks to make sure it was really happening. Suddenly she heard a weak baritone voice echoing her song.

"Now I am going crazy", she thought, "that sounded like Peter".

She jumped down the short distance to the bastion, and took her sword from its place at her side, ready to defend herself if the prisoner should show signs of attacking her. The soldier was there all right, standing with his back up against the wall and supporting himself with difficulty. There was a crazy look in his eyes, a crazy look of happiness. Then he sang the second verse of the song very softly.

"Peter" was all that Bori could utter. . . "Peter", and the world started to spin around her again. She leaned against the outer wall of the bastion opposite her husband and her sword clattered unnoticed to the ground.

"Why are we bracing the walls of the castle like a couple of fools?" The familiar jesting tone of Peter's voice penetrated her stunned mind. "Come here, Darling", he said softly, and there was no jest in his voice this time.

Bori ran the short distance to him, unable to speak. Peter's hands reached out to take her to him, and the two stood there, their arms around each other, for a long time.

Finally Peter lifted his wife's face from his shoulders and kissed her gently. "I promised you a spanking the last time I saw you. Remember, Bori? But I suppose I will have to save it until later. I'm too weak right now."

Bori smiled at him. "Yes, and I told you I would bash in your head if you lost Bayram, didn't I, but "Peter interrupted her, his voice contrite. "I'm sorry, Borbala, I was a stubborn fool to take your horse. I lost him the day I was captured. The Turks must have killed him because they didn't bring him back to their camp, and they usually take over captured horses for their own men."

Bori laughed. "You may have lost Bayram, Peter, but he didn't lose you.

He is here in the fort with us, thin but alive."

Peter smiled again. "I might have known that horse would get back to you somehow. It would take a lot more than an army of Turks to stop him!" Bori covered Peter's mouth with her hand.

"That's enough talk for now," she said. "You're exhausted and wounded too. Put your arm around my shoulder for support. Once I get you cleaned up and fed you can tell me how you managed to get here."

The tired man nodded in agreement and put his arm around Bari's shoulder. Then together they started into the castle.

"You may not be an ideal wife, Darling, but you're just the right size for a perfect crutch," Peter said as they walked slowly through the halls. Even now he could not resist teasing her to see if she would still flare up at him angrily in her old way. He was not disappointed.

Bori's face darkened with rage. "Go back to your fat, sugar-fed Turkish women if you object to me! You. . . you. . . ."

Peter threw back his head and laughed. "Stop", he said, "what will Uncle Miklos think if you bring him your long-lost husband with such naughty words on your lips. Come along now . . . and smile. You know you love me."

Bori looked up at him frowning, but his smile was so infectious that, as always, she was unable to resist it. "War hasn't changed you a bit, my Peter, you're just as horrid as you always were. . . but you're right I do love you, though I couldn't possibly tell you why."

Miklos Zrinyi stood in the courtyard in the midst of his battered but happy group of soldiers. He was praising them for the fight they had won so bravely and well. The blood was running down his cheek from a slight head wound, but in the excitement he had not noticed it. Suddenly, out of the corner of his eye Miklos caught sight of his niece as she came toward him supporting a wounded Turkish soldier. The oddly matched couple were obviously blissfully happy.

"What the. . . ", Miklos yelled, and then he stopped short. "For the sake of all the gracious Saints in Heaven, it's Peter! Peter, you old so and so, how did you get here?" Without waiting for an answer Zrinyi ran to the young man and enveloped him in a bear-like hug.

"Don't ask him any questions now, Uncle," Bori said, "he's about to drop from exhaustion now, and I must take care of that leg wound. . . and your's too. I'll bet you haven't even noticed it, even with all that blood on your face."

Miklos touched his cheek in surprise and then grinned at Peter. "That's quite a woman you've married, my friend. If you don't start beating her regularly she'll be the boss in no time at all."

Bori and Peter looked at each other and laughed. "Come on, Uncle Miklos", the girl said, "Help me get Peter in bed. This is one time you both need bossing".

Grumbling something about all women being alike, Miklos obediently took his place at Peter's side, and the three moved slowly into the castle. "I'm going to have to get you out of her, Bori", Miklos said, "If you produce any more surprises I'll be a nervous wreck".

His tone was jesting, but Borbala knew that he was serious and for good reason. The Turks would come again, and Zrinyi was already planning what line of action he would take.

The dull monotonous atmosphere of the fort quickly returned in the days immediately following the battle. Miklos saw the Turks settling down again, and knew that they were certainly not going to leave the scene of their defeat. In a few short days they would attack again, and this time there was nothing to stop them.

In the fort, after a conference between Bori, Peter, and Miklos, preparations were being made. During their talk they discussed the now barely hidden sunken bridge. The drought had continued, and since there had been no rain in months the moat had dropped way below its usual level showing more and more of the bridge each day. Soon the Turks would see it and upon investigation find the secret tunnel that led on one side of the moat into the castle and on the other the opening by the waterfall. It was obvious then that if they waited much longer there would be no chance to escape. They had to face the fact, also, that the remaining men could not defend the fort successfully in the next attack. Food and supplies were almost completely gone. All that Miklos could do was to attract the

Turks' attention while Peter and Bori escaped, if the Turks had not already noticed the bridge because of the corpses that hung limply over the sunken parapets. Borbala and Peter tried again and again to persuade Miklos to go with them, but it was in vain. They knew that he would never leave his fort and the men who had suffered so much for him in its defense.

In the Turkish headquarters all was alerted for a new attack to destroy the fortress. In their stubborn refusal to meet defeat the soldiers of Szigetvar had outwitted the greatest Turkish soldier of that time, Suleyman the Magnificent, and had been instrumental of his death by the rage that their unexpected resistance had caused. The Turks knew that no new supplies had got to the Hungarians for many months, and that many of their men had been killed either in battle or by starvation. The Turkish officers could be safe in their assumption that this time the fortress would be destroyed once and for all.

Inside Szigetvar the soldiers were preparing for their last battle. There was almost an air of gaiety about the men as they went about their work. They accepted their fate with courageous resignation. While they polished their armour, the one remaining horse was slaughtered and prepared for eating, and the only cask of wine was dragged up from the cellars. Bayram was fed the last sack of oats as he watched the horse being led out of the stable to be slaughtered, his intelligent eyes worried and anxious. Then he was left alone in the stables.

After many hours of sleep Peter had recovered from his exhaustion; and his leg wound, under Bori's expert care, was healing quickly with no sign of infection. While the soldier's were going about their final preparations, Peter was giving Bori her second Turkish haircut just as her hair was beginning to get long again. She looked tearfully at her lovely hair scattered on the floor around her chair, but she remained silent.

"Oh, well, it will grow again", she thought, "as long as Peter can love me without hair I don't suppose it matters." Bori sat up straight in her chair. "Now I am being silly! The important thing is to escape."

She smiled at Peter who was engrossed in his job, a frown creasing his forehead as he stepped back now and again to appraise his handwork. Finally he finished, having cut all of Bori's hair off except the one lock that hung down from the middle of her skull.

They had decided earlier that they would have a better chance of escaping notice if they left singly rather than together. Peter was to go first, and Bori with Bayram a little later. Peter put the sharp knife with which he had cut his wife's hair back in his belt and prepared to leave, dressed in the Turkish uniform in which Bori had found him a few days before. He turned to bid farewell to Miklos, but he found he could not speak so great was his emotion. The two men shook hands silently, and Miklos smiled slightly, his eyes full of understanding.

"It's all right, Peter", he said, "This is just the way things have to be."

Peter nodded and smiled back at him, then he bent down and kissed Borbala goodbye. He turned and left the room swiftly to return to the Turkish camp by way of the sunken bridge.

When he reached the hidden opening by the waterfall Peter sat there for a long time watching the enemy's preparations for the new attack. As he waited for a chance to join the Turks unnoticed he began to think of his escape from the Turks a few weeks before. The whole thing had been a stroke of luck and even now it was hard to believe that the escape had actually been accomplished. After the bullock-drawn carts, to which he and the other prisoners had been chained, had gone a few miles from the Turkish camp, a small band of peasants had attacked them. There were many of these Hungarians who had banded together after their homes had been destroyed to practice guerrilla warfare upon the invaders. They were mostly older men, who were considered unfit for regular service, and women. Their weapons were few, usually rude clubs, but their surprise attacks on the enemy were frequently successful and destructive. This time they had easily overcome the small unit that guarded the convoy in which Peter was a prisoner. They then took their countrymen to their hideout, gave them what clothes and food they could scrape up, and set them on the roads to their homes. Many of the former prisoners stayed to join the band, however, their homes and regiments having been destroyed.

One of the members of the band was a blacksmith who struck the heavy chains, from Peter's legs. From this man, Peter learned of the thousands of homeless Hungarians who banded together in various parts of the country, living in caves in the woods or in huts in the vast marshes where the Turks did not dare to go. From these inaccessible spots they would strike back at the hated invaders whenever possible. The blacksmith also told Peter that one was the few remaining Hungarian fortresses was the nearby Szigetvar. Peter had immediately decided to go there for he knew the fort was under the command of Miklos Zrinyi, and perhaps Bori's uncle knew where she was.

Peter left his liberators the next day and covered the few miles to the Turkish camp surrounding Szigetvar in a few hours. He wore the uniform of one of the dead guards of the prison convoy from which he had just escaped, and his mastery of Turkish was sufficient for him to masquerade as one of the replacements who came almost every day. He had originally hoped to sneak into the fortress unnoticed, but he arrived at the camp on the night of the attack so he had joined the Turks hoping that in the confusion he might get inside. He had almost succeeded when Bori had caught him on the bastion. He had known that if he had tried to escape she would have shot him. His only hope was an attitude of complete surrender, and it had worked. Now, as he waited behind the waterfall for a chance to sneak out and wait for Bori at their appointed meeting place a few miles up the road at the hideout of the guerrilla band, he prayed that their luck would hold out just a little longer. Escape was so near, and yet a dangerous time lay between now and that moment when they would be free.

Abruptly Peter's attention was brought back to the activity in the camp. A limp form was carried out of the Sultan's tent and lifted with care onto the back of Suleyman's charger who shied violently as the dummy was tied to the saddle. Peter stared in astonishment as the horse moved off between his escort of high-ranking officers toward the battlefield. Before he had time to think about the meaning of this strange action a group of soldiers began to move into formation near the waterfall so Peter rose from his hiding place and joined them. He could break away later; the important thing was to get away from behind the waterfall unseen. What Peter didn't know was that Suleyman's officers had sent his body back to Constantinople, and were still deceiving the soldiers into thinking that their ruler was alive by placing a stuffed dummy, dressed in the Sulfan's clothes, on the back of his favorite charger.

Under cover of darkness Peter slipped away from the soldiers he had joined as they marched toward Szigetvar, and hurried toward the place where he was to meet Borbala. Meanwhile the Turks had scarcely taken their positions for the battle when they heard fanfares and loud battle cries from the fortress. As they watched in astonishment the drawbridge was lowered with slow dignity to the ground on the opposite side of the moat. Then Miklos Zrinyi, his gold-trimmed uniform gleaming richly and his golden-handled sword raised in a challenge to the Turkish warriors, marched firmly over the bridge followed by his small group of soldiers. Each was dressed in his finest uniform, and each wore a sable-trimmed cap ornamented by white aigrette feathers that tossed back and forth jauntily, bravely, as the men marched. The battle did not last very long. Soon the white feathers lay dirty and bloody in the mud beside their once proud owners. Not one of the defenders of Szigetvar was left alive, and the officers of Suleyman went back to their brightly colored tents congratulating one another on an excellent victory.

In the meantime Borbala, dressed as a Turkish groom, was coaxing Bayram through the castle tunnel that led to the bridge. The horse was saddled and bridled with the finest equipment, stolen the night before from a dead Turkish horse left on the battlefield, so that the girl could pass him off as a wealthy officer's mount if she were questioned once she reached the encampment. Snorting and shying with disgust, the stallion, in spite of his fear of the foul place, followed his mistress to the sunken bridge where Bori waited for the sound of the battle cry as Zrinyi took his men over the drawbridge. This was her signal to cross as they had counted on the attention of the Turks being focused on the battle.

The plan worked, and soon Bori reached the waterfall. She had just stepped from the opening with Bayram when a guard came from behind the Sultan's tent, and stared at her in surprise.

"I did not see you come here, boy," he said roughly, "how did you get here all of a sudden?"

Bori caught her breath, but she answered coolly, amazed to find her voice so steady. "You must have been dozing, Friend. I was watering the Pasha's stallion over there. . . I'd better take him along now, and you had better be more careful. The Sultan would have you drawn and quartered if he found you had been sleeping while on duty."

Bori caught Bayram's bridle and walked away not daring to look back. The girl had taken a dangerous chance, but she had been right. The guard had taken the opportunity of a short nap while most of the men had gone to the battlefield, and the camp was quiet.

Now as he watched her walk away, a puzzled expression on his face, he said to himself, "He has a strange accent, but I dare not make him angry or he might tell the Sultan that I was sleeping. Oh well, why worry about a mere child leading a horse around." He turned away, the matter forgotten, and went behind the Sultan's tent for another nap.

Borbala went through the rest of the camp undisturbed. She kept rechecking mentally the directions Peter had given her, afraid that she might take the wrong roads instead of the ones that led to the hideout of the peasants who had rescued Peter from the Turkish prison convoy. She did not lose her way, and before long she came to the little hut back in the woods where, through the open doorway, she saw Peter and several peasants huddled around a fire to escape the cold dampness of the night.

"Peter," she called softly and slid from Bayram's back to the ground. Peter looked up quickly, then jumped to his feet and ran to her side.

"Thank God you're safe, my darling," he whispered as he took her in his arms. Then he led her into the hut and introduced her to the men and women who nodded silently and made a place for her at the fire side. The old blacksmith looked up at Bori as she sat down and then turned to Peter.

"You'd needn't a' worried so much about her, young man. She's a good'un. . . brave to come all this way alone with just her horse. . . not so vain as t' spoil her chances either," he said perking a thumb at Bori's shaved head. "I guess you two'll make it all right," he finished. The blacksmith was not much of an orator, but he was a good judge of character.

In the silence that followed they realized that the sounds of battle were no longer heard from Szigetvar. Peter gently put his arm around his wife's shoulder, his eyes full of pity.

"Can we pray for them, Father?" Bori whispered to the little country priest who sat near her.

"Of course, my child," he said, and at his signal the bedraggled company got to their knees to pray for the brave defenders of Szigetvar and their valiant leader, Miklos Zrinyi.

The next day Peter and Bori left with Bayram to find safety in Austria. As they made their way to Vienna they carried the news of the Sultan's death, bringing hope to the miserable Hungarians they met. The little guerrilla band near Szigetvar told them where to find other such groups who aided immeasurably in their escape. When they finally reached the emperor in Vienna, that good ruler gave Peter new lands in Austria. There Peter and Bori lived a long and happy life, spiced by frequent quarrels, for Peter never could resist teasing his wife. As for Bayram, he was retired to the luxurious life he so deserved, and sired many colts to carry on the line of the Clover family. None of them attained any importance, however, until a clover horse that was born three hundred years later. The life of this horse is recorded in our next story.

* * * * * * *

In those three hundred years, Hungary was a troubled country. By the middle of the sixteenth century the Turks had conquered all of the lower part of the country including the capital city, Buda, and the Turkish threat remained for a century and a half. So terrible was the invasion of the Turks that in one battle, on the field of Mohacs in the early sixteenth century, it is said that twenty thousand Hungarians were killed in an attack led by Sultan Suleyman, before he died on the battle field at Szigetvar.

The fateful battle of Mohacs became a symbol of disaster to the Hungarians, and one of their popular folk songs was based on the theme: "But what matter! More was lost at Mohacs field!" Eventually the Turks conquered upper Hungary also, but finally with the help of Austria they were driven out for good. But that was not to be the end of foreign domination for Hungary, for it then came under Austrian rule, and it was only after many bitter political and religious struggles that Hungary finally became an independent Kingdom again in the nineteenth century, the time in which the next story took place.

Rezust

LL the people of Szalanci crowded out into the street as a large wagon turned into the wide road that led up to the castle gates. They watched in awed silence as the padded doors were opened, and a carefully prepared gate was let down. A big rough hewn stallion looked out curiously at the villagers, then a small white goat appeared at his side. The goat walked down the platform with great dignity, followed by the horse. Then the local gypsy band struck up their music with a loud fanfare, which decidedly upset the billy-goat's nervous system. He rose in a graceful capriole, and butted his head right in the middle of the Priest's fat housekeeper's plumpest part. The housekeeper lost her balance and fell against the grocer's inquisitive wife, who, in turn, sat down on the old country doctor. Mr. Williams, the English groom, who was hired to stay with the great horse, let go of his charge and lunged at the offending goat. He missed his mark and fell on his face in the dirt road. The crowd cheered and roared with laughter, while the band started playing "God save the King." No one knew whether it was for Mr. Williams or the horse. When the noise subsided the Priest blessed the horse, and the procession passed under the gate of the stable yard, upon which hung a sign in large black letters saying, "Szalancz welcomes Kettledrum, the British Darby winner to his new home."

Kettledrum was led to his comfortable box stall, and Count Kálman Gacsy admiringly patted the head of his new horse, before he went back to his guests, who were assembled in honor of the arrival of the famous stallion. In the castle courtyard, huge wooden tables were loaded with barbecued steers, fouls, wild game, and wine. The gypsy band was playing loudly from a stand near the great barbecue pits, while the simple peasants and the noblemen of the county celebrated together. They talked together of farming, horses, the government, and the unusual drought, as if they were accustomed meeting each other on the same level everyday. There was a silence as Count Kálman rose to tell his guests why he had brought Kettledrum to Hungary "Our Hungarian horses are world famous," he said, "and I know we all want them to continue to be so. For this reason I decided to buy the best stallion I could find to help us preserve that reputation. The best is, of course, Kettledrum, the winner of the British Darby. I want you all to know that you may use my stallion for your good mares and there will be no stud fee whatsoever. With Kettledrum behind our colts, we will have the best horses in the country. I propose a toast to that great stallion!"

The count raised his glass and drained it, then he sat down among the cheers of the crowd.

In the meantime Kettledrum was munching his oats, while four interested young faces peered over the top of the door to his stall. Mr. Williams stood beside the children and proudly explained the fine conformation and great speed of the stallion. Istvan, Kálman, Lászlo, and Margaret, the four children of Count Kálman, listened eagerly to the groom and argued with one another over who would be the next to feed Kettle drum a carrot. Finally all was quiet, and even James, the goat, forgot his nervous condition after the shower of carrots the children gave him.

"I simply can't understand you, Kálman! Why don't you stop this ridiculous business of breeding those hideous horses? You get one ugly, useless foal after another from that strain. People from all over the country beg you, offer you fabulous sums of money, to get their mares bred to Kettledrum, and what do you do? You let the villagers, the servants, breed to him first, and then you use that magnificent animal to continue that horrible line of clover horses!"

The old countess glared at her husband, who sat with his back to her, putting the pedigrees of some new foals in his studbook.

"And why do you do it?" the countess continued, "Superstition, nothing but superstition . . . and sentimentality! You've bred those beasts to everything possible, Arabs, Barbs, and now a thoroughbred, and when you think you've finally got a decent horse, the next generation comes up with that ugly, oversized head and that mean streak. It's ridiculous, I tell you, utterly ridiculous!"

Count Kálman raised his head wearily. He had heard this argument countless times before, and it was hard to ignore his insistent wife.

"Stop it, Maria! We've been through all this before. Leave the horses to me, and pay attention to your children for a change. Istvan is running wild again in Vienna, trying to forget one or another case of puppy-love. He is having an affair with a vaudeville star at this point, and writes at least once a week for money. Something has to be done. We can't afford to have him go on living this kind of irresponsible life. And what about Margaret? Are you going to let her marry that old fool Paul Ziry, who is twice her age? As for Lázslo and Kálman, I certainly don't approve of their courting the Serey twins. They're both vain and stupid, just like the rest in that family. How can you bother about horses when all our children are either behaving like fools or rushing into bad marriages?"

The count tried to take his wife's mind off the clover horses, and, although he succeeded in changing the subject for a while, the countess soon got back to her pet discussion, to get the clover breed out of the stables.

Kálman met Istvan at the station, and the two brothers shook hands, their faces mirroring their happiness over seeing one another again.

"Well, what's come over you, Brother. I would never have expected you to come all this way to meet me," Istvan commented laughingly.

Kálman smiled. "I'll have to admit that it was Fanni's idea, Istvan. She's almost succeeded in reforming me. I'm a model husband with no bad habits. . . well, very few anyway. You haven't seen Fanni since before we were married, but you remember how proper she was ?"

Istvan nodded.

"Well, she hasn't changed a bit!" Kálman said sadly, and both men laughed. "She's even been worried about you," Kálman continued, "She doesn't approve of your chasing foxes in England or hunting tigers in India, and she is particularly against your running after girls in Paris. She says six years is more than enough time for a man to get the kinks out, and she thinks it's time you settled down. I'm glad you're home, Brother. Now she can concentrate on reforming you, while I have some fun again!"

"Oh, no," Istvan laughed, "No one's going to reform me. I like me just the way I am, and heaven help any woman that tries to change me. She'll live a life of complete frustration." Istvan clapped his brother on the back and turned to greet his old valet and secretary, Janos.

A fat bird dog crawled stiffly from under the carriage, tiredly wagging his tail. He sniffed the air and turned his opaque, sad eyes in the direction of Istvan.

"Good Lord, Is this Tref," Istvan exclaimed, "It's been a long time, old man. I guess we've both changed. How are you, János, it's good to see you again."

"I'm fine, thank you, sir," the valet answered, "We're glad to have you back with us."

"Thank you," Istvan said, and he turned to inspect the four light carriage horses. "These Juckers aren't bad. Mother used to like them better than any other breed for carriage horses, and she had some good ones." He turned back to his brother. "Come on, Kálman, I am anxious to get home!"

The luggage was loaded into a wagon drawn by workhorses. When all was ready, Suba, the coachman, called to the horses, and the four browns leapt forward, making the two brothers laugh as they were jerked back in their seats. The light carriage flew through the dusty streets of the village.

Istvan settled back on the cushions and grinned at his brother. "Something's on your mind, Kálman. Out with it; you might as well tell me now."

Kálman nodded and started his speech like a child reciting his lesson. "Well, as a matter of fact, Fanni did want me to talk to you. She's worried about your reputation, Istvan. You seem to have broken hearts everywhere you've been in Europe."

"And what's wrong with that?" Istvan laughed, "If I remember correctly, Fanni left quite a few young men with broken hearts when she married you. Besides, I continually run the risk of having the tables turned on me. What's the matter with you, Kálman? Are you suddenly becoming a Puritan?"

"Don't be ridiculous, Istvan! You know Fanni and I have no children. László married Klara, and they don't have any either. Margaret is only a girl, but all her children have been stillborn. You're twenty-six years old now, and frankly, we all want you to settle down and marry some nice girl. If you don't there will be no children to inherit the family title or the lands and villages. We must count on you, otherwise the Gacsy family will die out."

Istvan started to argue, but he realized it would be useless. He thought bitterly of the fight his mother and father had put up years before when his brothers announced that they were going to marry the Serey twins. The old count and his wife had argued and threatened. There had been twins in the Serey family for many generations, and it was a well-known fact that the twins in that family never had produced any offspring. The girls were educated, wealthy, and fine sportswomen, but they were cursed with barrenness.

"Since you have decided that it is up to me to correct the mistakes that you and László made, have you also chosen the future mother of my heirs?" Istvan's sarcastic tone made his brother redden with embarrassment.

"Oh no," Kálman exclaimed, "But we did think. . . " With this they reached the castle gates, and the cries of the welcoming crowd drowned out the end of his sentence.

Istvan entered the castle and met his brother, László, standing at the top of the stairs, his red, jovial face beaming in welcome. Behind László Istvan's two beautiful sisters-in-law stood side by side. They wore the same dresses and used the same kind of perfume, making a joke of their resemblance, which was astonishing, in spite of the fact that Klara had blonde hair, and Fanni had brown. Next to them Istvan saw Kata Drassy, a handsome, buxom girl whom he had known since childhood.

"A typical Drassy," he thought ruefully, "and just the kind of girl they would select to be the mother of the Gacsys that the Serey twins couldn't produce."

Istvan greeted his family first, then turned to the estate's officials and personnel. Among them he saw Mr. Williams, who had been promoted from groom to head trainer. The man stood on his short, bowed legs, his checkered cap in his hand and a welcoming smile on his face. Next to Williams was his wife, the former French governess of the Gacsy children. She ran to Istvan, who had been her favorite among the children. He enveloped her in one great movement of his arms, gave her a kiss, and deposited the laughing woman back beside her husband.

"Hey, ma belle Titinne. . . " he started, and then he saw a beautiful young girl with blue eyes and curly brown hair smiling at him. The Frenchwoman's smile faded as she noticed the expression on Istvan's face.

"No, Istvan," she said softly. "La petite jenne fille is not for you. Don't break the tears of the girls at home, mon Bonhomme, and especially not the heart of my daughter, Aline!"

The lovely young girl curtsied, her face dimpling in a roguish smile. Istvan felt a funny feeling welling up in him, a feeling similar to the one he felt when he picked up a fluffy little kitten and held it against his cheek, murmuring silly sounds of endearment. He shook his head to get rid of the idea.

"I am getting old and foolish," he thought, and he turned his attention to Kata. "If she is going to be my wife, I might as well get to know her better. I haven't seen her since we were children."

After the dinner and dancing were over, Istvan retired to his room as soon as he could get away. János followed at his heels, talking incessantly, as he tried to report in one evening what had happened to everyone in the family and the village during the years that the "young master" was absent. Finally Istvan sent the man away, and stretched out on the huge four-poster bed. He watched the embers in the fire that faced him drowsily. A pair of sparkling blue eyes seemed to stare at him in the dark, and the silly feeling of tenderness, that had overcome him when he first saw Aline, was the last sensation that he had before he fell into a deep sleep.

Istvan had returned home in June, and he had spent the summer months renewing old acquaintances and catching up on the business affairs of the estate. His brothers had not pressed his marriage to Kata, but they made it clear that they expected him to do something about it soon. Now it was a lovely autumn day, and Istvan was jogging homewards on his big bay hunter. "Kettledrum really sired some grand colts," he thought, "even if they weren't like the Juckers that mother loved, with small heads and delicate conformation. Juckers make good carriage horses or ladies' hacks with their bobbed tails and arched necks, but I much prefer the big rangy horses got from the Kettledrum-clover horse combination."

Istvan's bay gelding was sired by Kettledrum, and he was out of a clover mare called Mocskos. His low head carriage and flat extended gaits bore no resemblance to the flashy action of the Juckers. Istvan's mind wandered back to the legends of the Clover horses. He had never seen a golden colored one with the clover mark, only bays and brows. The color and the mark of clover seemed to have been bred out of them. Küzdö, the bay he was riding, was the only one they had left of the breed, and he was gelded. There was no mare or stallion left to carry on the breed that he knew of. He remembered the day, years before, when old Pribek, the stud master, had stood beside him, watching a group of the little clover horses.

"Little Master," the old man had said, If your mother has her way, and these horses leave your stables, the Gacsy family will be finished too. . . the Gacsy family will be finished too!" He repeated his words, as if he had to be sure the boy understood him. Istvan had been frightened by the old man's ominous words, and he had run away.

Now on the back of the bay gelding, Istvan seemed to hear old Pribek's voice. The strange fear that the stud master's words had aroused in him was still alive. After his father's death his mother had sold or given away all of the legendary breed, that she had hated so. A few days after the horses were taken away, the four brown Juckers, that the old Countess drove so well, had shied for some unknown reason at the castle gates. The light Eszterhazy carriage had turned over, and the countess had been killed instantly. Istvan shivered. Perhaps there was something in old Pribek's prophecy after all. "I'm acting like a superstitious fool!" Istvan thought. "The whole story is nothing but a legend. It was just a coincidence. Still all Margaret's children have been born dead, and the Serey twins will never produce. I had better marry Kata soon. All the Drassy's have dozens of healthy children, and Kata is intelligent and understanding. I'll ask her to marry me tomorrow. . . No, I won't. I'll take a trip to Vienna first, then I'll do it when I come back."

Istvan felt much better at the thought of going to Vienna, and he turned his horse into a lane with a four foot gate at the end of it. The big bay jumped it easily and started off in a steady gallop toward home. Suddenly Istvan felt Küzdö tense, and the man looked around to see what was the matter. He saw an ugly little horse, it's ears laid flat on it's large head, gallop past him. Two large gardener's basket's bounced and beat against the sides of the galloping pony. Carrots, beets, potatoes, and other vegetables flew crazily through the air. Istvan stared at the horse's rider as she went by him, her skirts flying up over her sunburned legs. It was Aline, and she was heading straight for a wide creek, that clearly was far too wide for the small, over burdened horse to jump.

"Stop!" he yelled. "Stop that horse! You'll never make it!"

"I would, sir! I would! But Rézust will not!" The girl laughed and pulled with all her strength on the rope attached to the pony's halter. The maddened Rézust ran on at an astonishing rate of speed for such a small horse, and rose over the water with a tremendous leap. Aline tumbled over her pony's head and landed with a splash in the muddy water. Rézust kicked up her heels, showering the remains of the vegetables over the ground, and galloped off in the direction of the stables.

Istvan jumped off his horse and ran to retrieve the soaked girl. He pulled her out of the water and carried her up to the bank of the stream. Her body was limp and her eyes were closed. For the first time in his life Istvan felt helpless with a woman. He tried to rub her hands and her body to bring her to. Finally, thinking that she had swallowed water, he took her by the waist and turned her upside down. The girl giggled, then gave him a stinging slap. Istvan was so surprised that he lost his balance and dropped the girl. Aline fell headlong back into the creek, from which she emerged a second later, laughing merrily. Istvan was so relieved that the girl was not hurt, that he immediately forgave her for fooling him with her assumed faint and joined in her laughter.

A little while later a frightened groom, leading Rézust, found Istvan and a very damp Aline sitting on the bank of the creek engrossed in conversation.

"There they sat," he reported to the servants that evening, "just as cozy as if they were sitting in the front parlor. No good will come of this. The young master should have better sense than to meddle with the daughter of one of his servants."

Weeks passed after Istvan fished Aline out of the creek. Istvan continued to postpone his engagement to Kata, and also his excursion to Vienna. The time of the races at Budapest was nearing, but, in spite of this, he stayed in Szalanc. All his interest was focused on teaching his basket-horse rider the correct way to handle a horse. At first Mr. and Mrs. Williams had opposed respectfully, but firmly, the riding lessons. Aline cried and argued with her father, but he was adamant.

"You will someday marry a modest official. No riding lessons for you, Aline. Work on your music and help your mother around the house. Behave as a nice girl should. Riding lessons! That's ridiculous!"

Titinne had gone immediately to the source of the trouble. She scolded Istvan in stinging French.

"You are being stupid, Istvan," she is only seventeen and just out of the convent. She doesn't understand a man like you, and I don't trust you, so let's forget about these idiotic riding lessons. No good will come of it."

Istvan laughed and coaxed his old governess back to her usual smiling good humor. He finally convinced her that the riding lessons would be just that and nothing more. The instruction started, and Aline proved to be an excellent pupil. Even Mr. Williams was overcome with pride when he saw his daughter sitting gracefully in the side saddle, as she cleared the jumps with ease.

"Ain't she looking just like a little butterfly now," he said, "that just lit on the back of that big brute of a horse."

Istvan surprised Aline with a lovely bay thoroughbred mare, but, to his astonishment, she refused the horse and asked to have Rézust as her mount.

Rézust can run faster and jump higher than any thoroughbred in your stables," she said.

Istvan laughed. "After her performance when she dumped you in the creek, I can believe that. All right, if you want that funny little pony, you can certainly have her."

Istvan ridiculed the little mare, but he had got interested in her, so he inquired about her pedigree. It turned out that her dame was one of the clover horses and her sire was

Kettledrum. The old countess had overlooked her when the other horses were sent away, because she was used by the gardener to haul vegetables and was not kept in the stables.

"That's quite a pedigree for a pack pony," Istvan laughed, when he told Aline what he had found.

From then on the girl used Rézust for everything and even hunted her. Through Istvan the girl received an invitation to the hunt ball, one of the most important social events of the season. The night of the ball the most coveted bachelor of the county danced most of the evening with "A British groom's" daughter, and the village gossips went to work spreading scandal. Fanni and Klara were horrified and immediately went to Kálman and László to tell them they had to do something about Istvan. Titinne was in tears, and old Williams cursed eloquently. Istvan was pressed from all sides to announce his engagement to Kata and stop all the rumors by so doing.

Aline was bewildered by all the excitement, and cried bitterly when her rides with her big friend were stopped. Rézust was her only consolation, and they often went for long rides together. The girl's favorite spot was a high plateau that overlooked a valley, which spread out for miles below it. The lazy river that wound through the plain looked like a narrow silver ribbon from the top of the precipice. One day Aline rode up to the plateau and left Rézust to graze in the shade. She sat on the edge of the cliff, her legs dangling over, completely unaware of the danger of the three-hundred and fifty foot drop to the valley below. She was thinking of her lost friendship with Istvan, and of the unhappy prospect of being sent to England for a year. She heard a twig snap behind her, and she turned, forgetting her precarious position. A pair of strong arms grabbed her and pulled her back from the edge of the precipice. Aline looked up at the face of Istvan, who stood before her white with anger and fright from the risk the girl had taken.

"Shall I spank you or kiss you, Aline," he asked in a strange, tight voice.

"By no means spank me!" the girl laughed, but a few seconds later she wished she had chosen the spanking. She struggled for a moment and then relaxed happily in Istvan's arms, but even in her youth and innocence she realized the hopelessness of the situation.

Istvan smiled and shook his head. "It will work out, darling. I will marry you! Wait and see."

"Don't be silly, my Istvan. Then a groom's daughter will be the mother of the heirs of the Gacsy title and estates. That's complete nonsense." In her way the young girl was strangely wiser than the handsome nobleman. She realized that his family would never forgive him, and the unhappiness that an estrangement from his brothers would bring would ruin their marriage.

The two stayed together on the plateau until dark. Aline mounted Rézust and prepared to start down the trail.

"I hate to see you go alone in the dark, Aline," Istvan said, "but, if any of the villagers see us together, we will both be in trouble."

"Don't worry," the girl answered, "Rézust knows all the trails, and she will take me home safely."

"Be careful, Darling. Will you meet me here in two days? We still have a great deal about before they send you away to England."

Aline nodded happily and turned her little mare toward home. Istvan and Aline met often on the high plateau, far from the prying eyes of the villagers. The next few weeks passed all too quickly for them, and the time came for the girl's departure. Aline went to England, and Istvan reluctantly announced his engagement to Kata.

Aline was very much of a young lady as she walked down the Sussex village street to the old thatch roofed post office. She hoped she would find a long envelope with Istvan's familiar scrawling hand writing on it. His frequent letters were her only consolation, for she could not get used to the puritan atmosphere, the dull diet of cold mutton, and the complete lack of color and gaiety in her father's family. She took her mail from the postmaster, but instead of a letter from Istvan, there was an envelope addressed to her in her mother's handwriting. She opened it hastily and was shocked to find that her father had died suddenly of a heart attack. Some money was included for her fare, with the words, "come home immediately." The prospect of returning to Szalanc made her so happy that she almost forgot her grief for her father, who had always been something of a stranger to her. She had been in a convent from the time she was seven years old until she was sixteen, so it was no wonder she had never felt close to him. She ran back to tell her aunt and uncle, with whom she was staying, what had happened, then she packed hastily so that she could leave for her beloved Hungary the next day.

Two days later after Aline arrived in Szalanc a servant from the Gacsy castle brought her a little dachshund puppy, who peered out of a big wicker basket covered with white orchids from the castle hothouse. A gold tag was attached to the puppy's leather collar with the dog's name and address inscribed on it. A card was attached to the basket which read, "Welcome home. My name is Kavecska, 'little coffee.'" Aline was delighted with the gift, but suddenly her mother appeared beside her.

"What is it?" Titinne asked, then she saw the puppy and the orchids. "I forbid you to either see or accept gifts from Count Istvan," she burst out hysterically. "He is to marry Countess Kata Drassy within the month, and I won't have him making a fool of you. Give me that dog."

Aline instinctively clutched the dachshund tighter in her arms, but Titinne tore the puppy from her and thrust it into the hands of the frightened boy who had brought it. "Here," she cried, "Take him back to your master and don't you dare bring him back, no matter what the Count says!" The lad took the dog and the basket of orchids and ran home as fast as he could to escape the old governess' rage.

From then on Aline's life was unhappy and tortured. Titinne was unbalanced by her husband's sudden death, and the gossip about her daughter only upset her further. She began to drink heavily, and she vented her rage on Aline. She whined endless reproaches at the girl, and often beat her. She even blamed Williams' death on the excitement caused by the scandal about his daughter. Aline was horror stricken at the change in her usually cheerful and understanding mother, but she was helpless to do anything about it. The girl's only escape from her abnormal life were her nightly rides on Rézust, who had been assigned to garden duties again. When Titinne fell into a drunken sleep, Aline would slip out and saddle her mare. Almost every night she rode up the steep trails to the high cliff overlooking the valley. She never saw Istvan there, although they had met in church. He sat in the family pew by the altar, and she sat in the employee's pew with her mother.

He had spoken to her politely as they entered the church, but Kata's smile was genuinely warm and friendly. Aline instantly liked the older girl, and she thought that if Istvan could not be hers, then the generous and understanding Kata would be the perfect wife for him. Aline said a prayer for their happiness as she knelt down in the pew. Suddenly her mother hissed in a loud whisper. "Regarde. He is so old and she. . . she is a vache, a cow. You'd better pray that Mr. Szabo, the druggist from Kassa, proposes to you. I will marry you off before the year is out, my girl, when the young men of this village finally realize that Istvan is out of the way for good!"

Aline blushed scarlet. She realized that the people in the pews around them must have heard her mother's very audible whispers, and it seemed to her that the stale smell of borowicko, a hard liquor, with which Titinne drowned her widow's sorrows, filled the church. After this Aline drove each Sunday to a church in a neighboring village. She drove Rézust in the little governess' cart that had been given her mother by the Gacsys.

One evening Aline rode Rézust up to the plateau, and was startled to find Istvan standing there, gazing out over the precipice. "I am eighteen now. I'm not a child, and I've got to act like a sensible person," she thought, but somehow the girl's attempt at calmness was not a success. When Istvan turned and smiled, then walked toward her, her mouth began to tremble, and her eyes dimmed with tears. She flung herself into his arms and clung to him sobbing. All the sorrow and injustice, that she had endured for the past year without breaking overcame her now, and she could not stop crying. Istvan sat down and rocked the girl in his lap, crooning softly to her. He rubbed his cheek against her soft face and dark curls, that smelled of clean hay and of youth somehow. They sat for a long time in the darkness until the girl was quiet again, then Istvan took some food out of his leather hunter's pouch and made her eat. It was nearly dawn when Aline happily mounted Rézust and started home. She was worried about her promise to Istvan to meet him there as often as she could get away, but her delight at the prospect of seeing him again soon dispelled all her doubts.

The large paneled library of the Gacsy castle was illuminated by the burning logs in the fireplace. The three brothers sat around the fire smoking. Suddenly Istvan jumped to his feet and strode to the far end of the room. He stood looking out of the window, his tall figure dim in the shadows. Lászlo and Kálman looked at him in surprise.

"What's the matter, Brother?" Kálman said quietly.

The flames from the knotted logs shot up suddenly and cast crazy patterns on the wall. For a moment Istvan's face was visible, his features seemed twisted grotesquely by the light. He looked like a tortured soul from Dante's Inferno. He moved slowly back to the fireplace and leaned against the mantelpiece, facing his brothers.

"I can't do it!" he said. "I just can't go through with it! Until I fell in love with Aline, I could have married Kata, or anyone else you had chosen, but now I simply cannot!"

Kálman and Lászlo looked up at their brother angrily.

"Istvan, we've been through all this before," Lászlo said. "The future of the Gacsy family depends upon your marriage. You cannot throw aside your loyalty and your duty to the family just because you imagine yourself in love with that little wench. How many times have you been in love before? Be sensible! Don't be a puppet in the hands of that scheming little. . . " László stopped, aware of the intense anger that showed in his brother's set face and glittering eyes.

"How can either one of you talk about duty to me," Istvan said, his voice ominously quiet, "you, who married your beautiful twins, when you knew all the time they would never give either one of you any heirs. Now I have to suffer for the mistake you deliberately made."

"At least our wives are ladies!" Kálman shouted.

Istvan leaped at his brother, but László caught his arms and held him back. "Stop acting like a bullock-driver! We can settle this without such stupidity. Now calm down!" László's contemptuous tone made Istvan feel ashamed of his inadvertent action, and he relaxed. "That's better," László said and let go of his brother's arms.

"If you would not be so hard-headed, Istvan, there would be no need for these unpleasant conversations," Kálman said. "But I will tell you this, and you'd better listen. I will not have my wife's name mentioned in the same breath with that girl. As for that cock and bull story about the twins in the Serey family, it's complete nonsense, just a superstition like the legends of the clover horses. It's purely coincidence that Fanni and Klara have not had any children."

Istvan's face was set in an ugly grin. "How do you know the story of the clover breed is just a superstition. The curse of those who sell the horses out of the family may be upon us now. Perhaps we can't keep the Gacsy family from dying out. But you did know Fanni couldn't have children. You had plenty of time before. . . "

"Be quiet!" Kálman shouted, "If you ever so much as intimate such a thing again, I'll kill you."

László stepped between his two brothers. His voice was quiet and cold. "Behave like gentlemen, please. After Istvan has married and produced an heir, you can settle the question by a fair duel, if you still feel it necessary. But now, I think we ought to retire."

From then on harmony was outwardly restored between the three brothers, but rumors of discord between them had spread through the village. Kata was distressed about it, and about the ugly stories that were being circulated about Istvan and Aline. Titinne was said to have beaten her daughter several times, and in her drunken stupor she had told her friends that she had often found only a bundle of covers in the girl's bed at night. The absence of Aline was quickly connected with Istvan's nightly rides, which had been reported to the villagers by a groom from the Gacsy stables. Although no one ever saw them together or knew where they went, the townspeople made up what knowledge they lacked. The women turned their heads away when Aline passed them on the streets, and the men smiled and joked behind her back.

About a week before her wedding Kata decided that she had to do something to help the unhappy girl. She ordered her carriage and drove down to the Williams' cottage on the edge of the village. The women ran to their windows and doors looking, with malicious curiosity, to see what Kata would do to humiliate the girl.

"I knew it would end badly," the vicar's wife said in her sterile, acid voice. "That conceited, low-born little foreigner thought she could become a great lady. Ha! Countess Kata will fix her! Riding in hunts, going to parties with the gentry. . . who does she think she is?" The woman pulled her lace curtain open wider so she would have a better view. A few minutes later Aline came out of the cottage with the foot man who had gone in to get her. She got in the lovely Victoria carriage beside Kata, and the four seal-brown Juckers whirled them away in a cloud of dust. The village women settled down by their windows and eagerly awaited the return of the two girls.

Almost an hour later the carriage pulled up beside the little cottage. To the villagers' surprise and disappointment, they saw Aline and Kata sitting side by side engrossed in a gay conversation. The woman, who a short time before had turned away from Aline, bowed to Kata and had to include the impishly smiling Aline in the salute. They did not realize what a serious discussion the two girls had engaged in. Kata understood the young girl's love for Istvan, and told her that the only remedy for it was time.

"I don't see why you have to stay here and suffer, Aline," she had said. "I'll tell you what we'll do. I will send you to a wonderful school I know of in Switzerland for three years. You can continue to study your music there, and after that I will give you a piece of property in France with enough to live on until you marry. You are young and completely innocent of these vile lies they tell about you. I can not let your life be ruined by permitting you to stay here. You will forget Istvan, darling, and, if you do not in all that time, we will see what can be done about it then. Come to the hunt breakfast with me tomorrow, and we will discuss the plans for your departure, before my marriage. If you stay it will only upset you more."

Through this whole speech Aline sat silent. She nodded in agreement to Kata's plans, not knowing what else to do, but she was bewildered by the girl's kindness to her.

Kata looked at her companion for a moment, her eyes sad. "Dear Aline, please understand that I would be happy to switch roles with you, to go abroad again and lead a carefree life, instead of having the burden of the Gacsy estate on my shoulders, plus an unhappy husband. You must understand that both Istvan and I are controlled by our duty to our families, and our lives are not our own. Do you think I like the idea of being a broodmare to fill the Gacsy stable's empty stalls with children again. Oh yes, I love Istvan, in my way, but mine will be an unhappy life. . . married to a man who loves you."

Aline looked at Kata, and smiled sadly. "I am so sorry for all of us," she said, "and I think you are the kindest person I ever met. I could never thank you for all that you are doing for me. I wish I could do something to help you."

Kata took the girl's hand and smiled. "You can. I want to surprise those evil-minded village women, who think I came to berate you for your supposed misdeeds. Start smiling and chatting when we reach the town. The shock will probably keep them quiet for a while."

Istvan waited a long time that night before he finally heard the beat of Rézust's hoofs coming us the steep trail. He lifted Aline off her mare and kissed her as he held her close. He immediately sensed that something had happened. She was quieter than usual, and somehow he felt that she was happier.

"Where have you been, Darling, I was worried when you were so late. Has anything happened?"

Aline nodded and told him about Kata's visit and the decision they had made. The knowledge that the girls were right, and that there was no escape from the ties that bound him, made Istvan angry. His tone was bitter as he spoke to the girl.

"How nice for you both. And didn't anyone think to consult me in this matter? After all I seem to be one of the central characters in this farce." He had never spoken to Aline with such harshness, and the girl was completely confused. She had thought he would be happy that they had found some sort of a solution. Istvan felt her shrink from him, and he was immediately contrite.

"I'm sorry, Darling" he said, "I guess I was upset. You and Kata are right, of course, but God knows, I would do anything to change the situation, if I could. Will you meet me here tomorrow night. There is a bear hunt all day, and I will be busy with that until evening."

Aline shook her head. "I cannot, Istvan. I promised Kata I would not see you alone again until I got back from school. I have to go back now and pack. I am leaving in about two days, and I will be busy helping at the hunt breakfast tomorrow. Good-by, Darling. God bless you!"

Istvan kissed the girl and bade her farewell, but his heart was full of bitterness. He felt as if he had been tricked somehow.

The group of drivers gathered around the huge bonfire that had been built to warm their numbed arms and legs. Gulyás and the spiced wine filled the huge cauldrons that hung on the cross poles over the fire. All around the fires people were laughing and talking, and near them the stretch from the morning's hunt was lined up in the snow. There were dozens of wild boars, three brown bears, two deer, and hundreds of hares. The ladies had come out after the hunt to serve the men, and they were red-cheeked from the cold weather winds that came with the first snow of the season. Kata had Aline with her, and the two laughed and talked together like old friends, to the great astonishment of the assembled guests. It was Aline's last day in Szalanc before she started on her trip to Geneva.

When the tired hunters had been served, the ladies went to the hot cauldrons to get their meal. Aline felt ill at ease as she offered a bowl of soup to Kálman's wife Fanni, who had walked up beside her. Fanni ignored the girl and stepped to dip the big silver ladle into the rich golden-brown gulyás herself. Aline was left standing, the tears welling up in her eyes and the bowl of soup in her trembling outstretched hand. Istvan was watching the scene, and he walked quietly up to Kálman.

"Tell Fanni to apologize to Aline," he said in a low voice.

"Tell her yourself," Kálman answered, "I'll have nothing to do with that groom's daughter."

The argument between the brothers attracted the attention of the guests, and Kata quickly came to the rescue. She spoke a few sharp words to Fanni, who was eager to please her future sister-in-law. Fanni ran over to the still tearful Aline and apologized.

"I am sorry, Aline, I just didn't see you offer me your bowl," she said. Then the bugles sounded to call the hunters for the afternoon drive.

Everyone hurried to his carriage and drove to his assigned stand. It was a colorful scene with the light carriages bouncing over the rough roads drawn by prancing Juckers.

When all the hunters had taken their stands, the signal was given, and the drivers began to head the game toward the canyon the hunters were in. A few distant shots echoed through the woods, and Istvan forgot his anger, his love, everything but the hunt, as the cry came down the gully. "Bear in the drive! Wounded bear in the drive!" A few moments later a huge bear came through the trees ambling clumsily toward Istvan's stand. The animal had a superficial wound in his shoulder, and his rumbling growl announced that he was enraged and ready to kill. Istvan raised his gun and took careful aim, then a shrill scream broke the stillness. A little boy crashed to the ground, still clinging to the broken branch that had given way with his weight. He landed almost at the feet of the startled bear. The boy jumped to his feet at the same time the bear rose up on his hind legs to strike. Istvan fired quickly, and then he heard the bullet ricochet off the rocky wall of the canyon opposite his stand. In his haste he had aimed high and missed his mark. The bear stood for a second, then charged at the boy, but Istvan's second bullet caught him. The great animal fell to the ground, churning the mud and snow convulsively with his huge paws, then he lay still. The little boy watched motionless, his eyes wide with terror, then he turned and scuttled away, fearing a spanking for the trouble his curiosity had caused.

Suddenly Istvan became aware of the voice of Kálman's hunter. The other members of the hunt had left their stands and were running toward the place where Kálman was. Then Istvan saw Kálman's hunter through the trees. The man was gesturing wildly.

"My Count has been shot! My Count has been shot!" he cried.

Istvan felt a cold horror almost paralyze him. "Oh my God, no! That ricocheting bullet!" Istvan heard his own voice cry out. It sounded cracked and strange, as if someone else had spoken. He ran to Kálman's stand and found his brother lying on the ground, trying to support himself on one elbow. His gun-bearer knelt beside him, wiping away the red foam that bubbled at Kálman's mouth with every breath he took. Dark blood was oozing out of a wound in the man's chest. The bullet had obviously gone through the man's lungs. Istvan dropped down beside his brother, and supported the wounded man in his arms. "Kálman, Kálman, forgive me." Istvan's voice rose in a cry of anguish. "Oh Lord, how could I have fought with him over that silly little goose?" he thought. He gently wiped the blood away from the count's lips. "What can I do?" he whispered hoarsely.

Kalman coughed, the pink foam spurting out of his mouth as he tried to speak.

Istvan had to bend close to hear his words.

"Don't worry. . . I was. . . no good any way with Fanni as my wife. . . Marry Kata. . . have children. Give my love to Fanni. You. . . were right, the horses. . . the hor. . . " Kálman tried to form the words, but the blood was choking him and he could not.

"It's all right, Brother." Istvan said. "It's all right. Don't try to talk anymore." Kálman shook his head and gestured, trying desperately to make Istvan understand him. He started up abruptly, then fell back, his eyes wide and staring. Istvan let his beloved brother gently down on the ground. László, who had been standing near, put his arm around Istvan's shoulders, but the grief-stricken man shook it off and walked away. László watched him with worried eyes, then turned back to hushed guests and told them to go home. Then he had the gun-bearers and drivers prepare a stretcher on which to carry Kálman back to Szalanc.

That night, half insane from grief and remorse at the thought of his quarrel with Kálman, Istvan walked out of the castle. He had no idea where he was going. He just wanted to flee from the sorrow that tortured him so unmercifully. Kálman's blood spattered form. . . Fanni's frozen face, as she gazed in unbelieving horror at her husband's dead body. . . Kata's sad, understanding eyes when she learned the terrible news: All these pictures were stamped on his mind. He couldn't shake them off. The silent grief that surrounded him at the castle was more than he could bear. He walked faster and faster, until he broke into a staggering run, as, if by actual physical movement, he could run away from the thing that tortured him. He must have walked and run for hours before he finally realized where he was. He had come to the high plateau where he and Aline used to meet. The lovely valley could be seen dimly in the faint pink light of the early dawn. Istvan saw a few lights twinkling from a far distant village below. It was quiet, so untroubled, it seemed to call to him. "Just one step," he thought, "and this nightmare will be over. I will see Kálman again." He moved forward, then he was conscious of a searing pain. Then there was nothing. His body fell from rock to rock, twisting in grotesque patterns as it went down.

The news of Count Kálman's death spread among the villagers, and with it the hideous rumors were loosed like furies riding the night. The people threw stones at the windows of the Williams cottage, where Aline sat, still and empty eyed. Titinne was sober, and she was terrified that her daughter would be harmed. She barricaded the doors and windows. She kept asking Aline to help her, but the girl did not seem to hear. She just sat, staring before her with unseeing eyes. She did not move when the door at last gave way, and the enraged crowd surged in to take her.

"She is the cause of all this trouble," a woman shouted.

"If it hadn't been for her Count Kálman would be alive!" another yelled. The cries were blurred in the roar of the hysterical mob. Titinne fought with all her strength for her child, but she was trampled down by the screaming women, led by the Vicar's wife, various farmer's wives, and some gypsies. The pack of infuriated women dragged the unresisting girl out of the house, raining blows on her head and shoulders as they went. A group of policemen tried to interfere, but they could not control the crowd and were pushed aside. Suddenly a woman's voice rose clearly over the confusion.

"Stop, you scum! Leave that girl alone," The authority of her command accomplished what the six policemen could never have done by force.

The mob of women slunk away, muttering angrily, but obedient. They left a bloody little heap on the street, that only a few minutes before had been the lovely Aline. Kata and her maid-servants carefully carried the girl back into the cottage. The furniture was smashed to bits, and Titinne was lying dead on the floor. Someone must have stepped on her windpipe with a heavy shoe when she was knocked down. Her face was a bloated, purple mass of horror.

"Take her back to my carriage," Kata said to the servants, "If she comes to this place and sees her mother, she will lose her mind."

Aline was carried out, and Kata placed the thin body of Titinne on the only piece of furniture that was left unbroken, the heavy dining room table. She covered the dead woman with a sheet and said a prayer for the soul of the old governess. She left the house and got into the carriage, then drove back to the castle. She put Aline to bed in her own apartments and called the family doctor.

It was not until the next morning that the disappearance of Istvan was noticed. Searching parties were sent out to find him, but they were unsuccessful. The villagers whispered the old superstitions about the clover horses to one another, and they began to imagine all the terrible things that might have happened to the young count. The senile old stud master, Pribek, who was now about a hundred years old, came out of his dirty cottage at the end of the stable yard and sat down on a bench. He listened to the stable help talking about the disappearance of Istvan. They heard his high shrill cackle and turned to listen to him.

"Hihihihihi. They had to sell my horses did they. Now they are killing each other. I warned them. . . I warned them, but no one listened. A curse is on the breed. When there are no more horses, I said, there will be no more Gacsys. His high cracked voice was like a child's treble, and his head shook with palsy. The stablemen stared at the ominous figure of the dirty old man, and, frightened by his words, they left him alone. "I warned them," old Pribek repeated. "Hihihi. . . hihihi." His cackling laugh echoed in the silent stable yard.

Night came, and the torches of the searching parties looked like giant fireflies, as they flickered on the hillsides and through the woods. Aline lay in bed. She was aware of all that was going on around her, but the strange apathy kept her still. She was paralyzed by fear and sorrow. She had the feeling she was completely out of the center of all this disaster. She kept thinking of the lovely plateau that had been the scene of so many happy hours with Istvan. Suddenly she sat up in the bed.

"What if Istvan went back there," She thought. "If only I could sneak away and get Rézust, I could go and look for him."

Kata was sitting beside the girl's bed, and when Aline started up so suddenly, she rose and gently pushed her back on the pillows.

"It's all right, Dear," she said. "I'm here, and I'll get you anything you want. Just lie back and rest."

Aline obeyed, still wondering how she could get away. A knock sounded on the door, and, at Kata's call a servant entered.

"The Countess wants to see you, Madam." the girl announced.

Kata turned to Aline. "I'll be right back," she said, "If you need anything, just pull the rope beside your bed. Fanni is still hysterical, and I'd better go to her."

When Kata left, Aline knew that this was her chance. She slipped out of bed and wrapped a heavy blanket around her. She found a pair of Kata's shoes and put them on, then she dropped from the ledge of the low window to the ground. She ran all the way home to get her clothes and saddle Rézust, her feet splattering in the slushy snow as she went.

The cottage was dark, and Aline climbed in through the window of her bedroom in the back of the house, as she used to do when she met Istvan. She didn't use the front door that faced the street for fear someone would see her. She ran to her wardrobe and took out some dark clothes and heavy boots. When she had dressed, she decided to take a small flask of brandy, in case she found Istvan alive. She opened the dining room door, and, by the dim light of the moon, she saw something bulky, covered by a white cloth, on the table. With trembling hands the girl pulled the cover back and gasped with horror, as she stared down at her mother's twisted, discolored face. She gently covered the body again and knelt down beside it to pray, but the familiar words of the prayers would not come. She heard herself repeating, "Murderer, murderer. I am responsible for all this. I am a murderer!" Finally the girl got up and hurried out to the stables. She thought if she didn't do something, concentrate on finding Istvan, she would lose her mind. She wanted to run through the streets screaming her hatred at the despised village women.

She went into the stable and put the curcingle, that usually had the vegetable baskets attached to it, on Rézust, who whinnied softly at her mistress' approach. Aline got blankets and ropes, then secured them to the mare's back. She mounted and trotted off in the dark. She felt better with the wise little mare under her. Rézust was warm and friendly. She would not desert her. She was her only real friend. Tears came to the girl's eyes, and she cried all the way up the steep trail to the plateau. When she got there, she felt much better, the tears had relieved the ache that had been inside her for so long. She left Rézust to graze and took her lantern to look for footprints. She saw where shrubs had been recently broken, and she found the distinct imprint of a man's boot that led up to the edge of the cliff. She knew immediately that Istvan was down there, three-hundred and fifty feet below her. In the back of her mind she had been sure this was what had happened, so the reality of the situation did not shock her. The fact that Istvan had returned to the place of their love gave her some consolation, painful as it was.

She started at the precarious, dark trail that ran down the side of the precipice. She knew it, for she had slid down it, with Rézust behind her, tobogganing on her end, to scare Istvan several times. How angry he had been! A little smile touched the girl's mouth at the memory. It was so incredible that he should be lying dead at the bottom of the gully. She wondered for a moment if Rézust would be able to make it at night, but there was no time to loose. She urged the worried mare to put her front feet on the steep trail. The path was slippery, and Rézust had to be coaxed to take her hind legs from the safe ground. It was very different from the daylight stunts to slide blindly downward in the darkness. The flint stones sparkled as they were hit by the mare's hoofs, and Aline felt Rézust lurch, as she nearly lost her balance. Finally the slope got more gradual, and the horse was able to walk instead of slide. It was getting lighter, as the late moon rose higher in the sky.

When they reached the bottom Aline mounted and rode her mare slowly toward the little creek that wound under the protruding cliff. She knew that, in this way, she would not miss the point where Istvan's body was. Rézust saw him before the girl did. The mare snorted and warned her. She jumped off the horse and put a trembling hand on the dim form. Istvan was warm and his heart was beating. She looked up at the high cliff, and saw, by the moonlight, fragments of garments hanging, like black crows, from the gnarled, stunted trees, that grew in twisted patterns out of the crevices in the rock. Istvan had caught on their branches as he fell, slowing his fall. He groaned when she tried to move him, and Aline knew that he must be badly broken up. She wrapped the unconscious man in blankets, then tugging and straining at the limp form, she rolled him up on a rock. She made Rézust stand beside the rock, that was nearly as high as the mare at the top, and hoisted Istvan up on the pony's back. When she had tied him on securely, she led the mare back to the steep trail they had just descended. It was the only way out of the canyon. Rézust struggled, blowing and slipping up the side of the cliff. With a final push, kneeling as she made it, the mare clambered to the top. There she stopped puffing with exhaustion. Aline sat down to rest, then Istvan's harsh voice cried out in the night.

"If it is you, Aline, who saved me, I prefer to be dead!" Then he lost consciousness again. The fact that Kálman was dead, and that he had quarreled with his brother over Aline were still torturing Istvan, and for some reason he blamed the girl.

Aline's face turned a chalky white at Istvan's words. She got up and went to Rézust. She pulled the blanket up higher over the unconscious man and tightened the rope around the horse, then she bent down and kissed Istvan's bruised, bloody face.

"I am sorry, Istvan," she said simply. Her voice sounded like a little girl's. She stroked Rézust's head for a moment, then gave the mare a slap that sent her jogging happily towards home. Aline turned back to the cliff, and walked slowly to the edge. She leaped out a little to be certain to miss the trees.

On a dreary winter morning a tired pony from the breed of Clover cautiously turned into the stable-yard at Szalanc castle, carrying the safely attached figure of Istvan on its back.

Istvan gradually recovered from the injuries he suffered in his terrible fall. His legs and several ribs were broken, and he had a brain concussion. Kata stood by him and nursed him through his long illness. When Istvan recovered, he and Kata were married. He was gloomy and irritable, and the words he had uttered, that had sent Aline to her death, haunted him for the rest of his life. Istvan and Kata stayed away from Szalanc, traveling through Europe, and it was only when Kata was expecting her first child, that they returned to the village. They wandered around the house and gardens, but Istvan refused to go near the stables as long as little Rézust was there. He could not bear to look at the mare. Finally Kata sent the horse to one of the Drassy estates, so that her husband would not be continually tortured by the presence of the mare. A few months later Kata died, giving birth to a stillborn baby girl. After this, Istvan closed himself up in the castle and lived as a recluse. Few people ever saw him again, except when he went out riding. The villagers would see his lonely figure galloping through the fields, but he spoke to no one. It was said he spent his time tinkering with old clocks in the great castle. Istvan never remarried, and the only child who remained to carry on the family was Margaret's daughter, who had two children, a girl and a boy, both of whom died tragically. The servants and the villagers at Szalanc believed firmly that the death of the Gacsy family was caused by the exodus of the last of the clover horses from the castle stables.

Sarga

A T the small Drassy estate in Olahpataka, Rézust was bred several times in the following years. Her colts were sired by Arabs, Lippizanos, and thoroughbreds, but they were all small, ugly horses and were sold to be used as hunting ponies in the mountains. Somehow one of Rézust's fillies came into my grandmother's hands. I have never been able to find out how it happened, but perhaps it was because the clover horses came into the Gacsy family from my grandmother's, which was related to their's by marriage. The mare's name was Gyopár, and she had only one foal before she died. This filly's name was Sarga, and she was sired by Warhorn, a very fine thoroughbred. Sarga was a pretty, yellow-chestnut mare with lovely gaits. She had a mushroom like mark on her nose that was almost a blurred clover sign. Viola, my stepsister, and I used to tease Uncle Pista, our oldest groom, into a rage about the mark on Sarga's nose.

"Look," he would say, "she has the mark of clover!"

"What!" we always exclaimed. "That's no clover! That's a mushroom!" Uncle Pista would redden with anger, then draw himself up very proudly.

"It is a three-leaf clover," he said "a four-leaf clover is not the real clover. It is like a calf with five legs. I like my calves with four legs and my clover with three leaves! It is no mushroom on that horse's nose."

We would argue with him until we thought he would surely explode, he got so enraged, then we would have to pacify him.

"Perhaps you are right, Uncle Pista," we would say at last, "It does resemble a three-leaf clover."

Then the old groom would smile and happily demonstrate Sarga's tricks for us.

As I remember her, she was usually fat and slightly potbellied from too much feed. Viola and I rode her often in the company of the groom, but she absolutely refused to let us mount when we tried to sneak a ride by ourselves. She was a friendly mare though and always greeted our arrival with a low whinny. I think it was the carrots we smuggled into the stable that caused this display of affection, but she could not be bribed. When one of us tried to mount her, her ears went back, and she side stepped quickly, so that we often fell flat on our faces.

When the first World War started, I was thirteen years old, a leggy thin, ungraceful child. It was at this time that Sarga was given to me, and I adored her. She was small, but her long swinging strides made her gaits delightful, and she had an extraordinary jumping power for such a little horse. She was well over ten years when she was trained to hack and jump, and only then because the war caused a shortage of horses. Uncle Pista loved Sarga, and he often amused us with the trick he had taught her. He would tie his big, blue handkerchief around the little mare's hind leg, and Sarga immediately twisted her head and plucked the offending cloth off. Then Uncle Pista would bring out a carrot, and the mare would come for it, the handkerchief in her mouth. The handkerchief and carrot exchanged owners, and we would laugh delightedly. We never grew tired of watching the old groom's antics with the horse.

Sarga couldn't stand to have a blanket on her back, and she attacked anyone who approached her with a stick. Uncle Pista, with a peasant's cunning and talent for theatrics, worked up an act with the mare, based on those two aversions of hers. I remember one day when it was announced that a circus was coming to town, and we were beside ourselves with excitement. Viola, and I ran to Grandmother and begged her to give us permission to go. We were not spoiled when I was a child, and an ice cream cone or a cup of hot chocolate in the small town's sweet shop was a rare treat. I remember how I loved my infrequent visits to that store, with it's wide imitation Rococo counter, upon which sat the wonderful pink and white confections and, in a glass case, the rich chocolate candies and pastries. But the thought of going to the circus was the most glorious thing that had ever happened to me. Grandmother looked at our excited faces and decided immediately that we could go.

The day of the circus finally came, and we stood on the main street of Rozsnyo with our nurses, who were instructed to keep us out of trouble, to watch the parade go by. What a wonderful sight it was for me. The blaring music was the most beautiful I'd ever heard, and the clowns, the bare-back riders, the trapeze artists, the huge elephants, the awkward camels, the red wagons containing wild animals of all kinds moved past me in a blur of brilliant color. I couldn't imagine anything better than the life of a circus performer. When the parade had gone by, we hurried to the big tent to our special box. The circus people always came to the castle to request food for themselves and their animals. They were loaded down with free supplies, and, consequently, a box of honor was always reserved for Grandmother and her household. It was inevitably lined with red plush and decorated with golden tassels and fringes. A red plush chair stood in the middle for Grandmother's special use, but she never went.

"I will feed them and their animals," she said, "but I will not feed their fleas." She was absolutely right, for the deep plush was a heaven for fleas. Our nurses and governess scolded us severely if we started to scratch, but we caught up with it when we got home. I often wondered how those prim ladies refrained from squirming when the pests must have been biting them too.

The performers, who came for the food, usually invited our farmhands to participate in the wrestling or to ride the bucking donkey, while they waited for the circus director, who was paying his respects to Grandmother. The director was a long winded man, and, though Grandmother was graciously helpful, she usually had to send him away very firmly in order to get rid of him. Because of the war, the circus was short of horses, and the horse acts were very popular in our small town. Uncle Pista knew this, and finally he asked to see Grandmother. He told her he wanted to show Sarga in the circus to help the people out, and also, I think, because he was inordinately proud of his pupil and their act. Grandmother consented, and she even went to "see the old idiot make a fool of himself."

Everyone in the town knew Uncle Pista and Sarga, and they watched for his act with great interest. When they saw it, they called for countless encores. Sarga, dressed in a bonnet and something representing a nightgown, came out into the ring trying angrily to tear her costume off. Uncle Pista, resplendent in top hat and tails, begged and pleaded with her not to do such things in public. He talked to the mare as if she were his wife. My sister and I thought it was terribly funny, although we didn't understand the coarse jokes that went with the act. Grandmother completely forgot the fleas and laughed until the tears rolled down her cheeks.

The crowd was so insistent, that Sarga was redressed and led back to perform again several times. Finally she lost her temper and snapped at Uncle Pista, then she pivoted around and gave him a farewell kick that sent him flying up in the air, as she galloped out of the arena. The audience roared with laughter, thinking that it was part of the act, and poor Uncle Pista, like a true showman, rose to his feet, smiling and bowing in spite of the pain caused by several broken ribs. Behind the scenes Sarga bit and kicked her way through the frightened performers, who scrambled out of her way. She galloped home to her comfortable stall and settled down to munch the oats, that Uncle Pista had put out for her before the performance. When the old groom returned home that night, literally "feeling no pain", and smelling strongly of whiskey, he went into Sarga's stall and patted her neck lovingly. "You were right, old girl," he said, "I shouldn't have made a fool of you in public." A stable boy, who had over heard this conversation, told us about it the next day when we went down to ride, and we teased Uncle Pista unmercifully about his cross "wife" for weeks.

A few months later my happy life was interrupted by a tragedy, at least it was to me at that time. Some of our carriage and farm horses were drafted, and Sarga was taken by a mountain regiment along with them. After the mare had gone, I cried myself to sleep in her stall. Uncle Pista sat by me, and from time to time I heard him sniffling in the gathering dusk of the autumn evening. A few hours later he woke me up and took me back to the castle. The next morning, when I went downstairs to breakfast, I saw that the serving maid had been crying and I didn't hear the usual chatter of the servants from the kitchen. I asked the girl what was wrong, and she told me that Uncle Pista had hung himself in Sarga's empty box stall.

At the end of the war, our little town, Rozsyno, was taken over by Czechoslovakia, and my grandmother's properties were confiscated. They left her only the big castle with no estate to support it. She sold it, and we never returned. Thus I lost my old home and the last traces of my little Sarga.

It was the summer of 1919. The First World War was over, and Hungary was in the hands of Bela Kun and other members of the Communist party. I fled with my family to Vienna, where the life was wildly gay and irresponsible. I was eighteen and had recently married a wonderful young man, named Paul. We had plenty of money and time, so Paul and I joined in the almost hysterical gaiety of the young crowd. We went to nightclubs, races, theatres, dances, and parties. We usually ended up, in the pale light of the early dawn, at the little pubs in Grinzing or Dobling, or we went to the Wurstl-Prater, an amusement park, where we rode the roller coaster and merry-go-round in our evening clothes. We were highly amused by the attention we attracted from the crowd of housemaids, coachmen, and other such people who came there. One of the attractions of the park was the "Hippodrome," a place where some old, broken-down horses could be ridden around a ring to the accompaniment of an organ-grinder's music.

We went there one evening and I noticed a new horse standing among the others. The animal drew my attention because of a heavy muzzle that covered half of its ugly head. It had drooping ears and a shaggy yellow coat. I started to turn away, but then for some reason the owner of the horses started beating the helpless animal, who tried pitifully to defend itself. I shouted at the man to stop, but he just kept on hitting the horse on the head. I grabbed the owner's arm, and tried to stop him.

"I'll beat my own horse when I please! Get away!" he yelled. "All right then, I'll buy it!" I retorted angrily.

The man turned and stared at me in amazement. "What?" he said. "You'll buy this worthless devil-horse? I won't guarantee her, you know."

He finally consented to sell her for an outrageous price, after a long argument. I did not know what I was going to do with the mare when I got her. The only thing I thought of was to get her way from the man, who treated her so cruelly.

There I stood in my gold evening dress and sable wrap, holding a rope with the lame, aged mare at the other end of it. The horse glared at me viciously from sunken eyes, that looked out over the top of the enormous muzzle. My friends had watched the whole scene with amusement, then they laughed and teased me, as I walked out of the ring with the yellow mare.

"And now, my tender-hearted one, what are you going to do with that monster?" Paul asked, smiling. "Are you going to take her to Bauer?"

Bauer was my Viennese coachman, who drove my standard-bred. trotters to the races and other sporting events. We used Lippizaners for formal occasions, but the trotters were used for all other events. Bauer was so proud of his lovely horses and beautifully kept stables, that I knew he would just ignore my note if I sent the ugly mare to him by one of the carnival men, who were eagerly offering to do so in hopes of a large tip. My companions were getting impatient.

"Oh, come on, Judith," one of them called, "Let the man take that horror to Bauer."

We were supposed to go up to Cobenzel mountain by car and have an early breakfast there, before getting home to bed, about seven in the morning.

I wanted to go, but I thought of Bauer's reception of the horse, so I told the others to leave without me. My friends left in the huge Maybach, amidst much laughter and hooting. Paul and I followed the horse back to the stables in a borrowed car. I wanted to take the heavy muzzle off the poor animal, but the man who led her home protested. He would not be able to control her, he told me, because she was so vicious. When we reached the stables, Bauer's reception was exactly what I had, imagined it would be. The shocked expression on his face was so amusing that both Paul and I burst out laughing.

"It was worth missing the breakfast to see this," Paul said, wiping the tears from his eyes.

I finally convinced Bauer that we were not playing a trick on him and really wanted to stable the horse there. The coachman pointed disdainfully at an empty box stall, but he did not offer to help me.

I led the mare into the stall and reached up to unbuckle the strap behind her ears, that held the muzzle on. The heavy contraption dropped to the floor, and I reached up to pat the old horse. The poor animal must have thought I was reaching up to hit her, for she jumped at me and missed my face by inches. I leapt back out of reach, and, as I did, I saw the startling mark on the mare's ugly nose. It was the funny mushroom shape, that we had teased Uncle Pista about so often. I knew then that I had found Sarga again.

The next day the maid came into my room about noon and woke me. She brought the terrible news that my companions of the night before had been killed. Coming down from Cobenzel, their car had got out of control and gone over the side of the mountain. I sat up in bed, numb with shock. All I could think of was the legend of the clover horses. They were always responsible in some way from saving their owners from death, and when they were sold out of the family, death came. Most people would say it was a coincidence, but I knew there was something else, too.

I didn't know what to do with Sarga. After the war we had lost most of our estates and were living in our town house in Vienna, so the mare was a definite problem. I could have kept her at our stables in the city, but it would have been foolish to do so. The old mare was completely broken down, and she could never be ridden again. She was so ugly anyway, that no one would have wanted to ride her. She was incurably vicious from cruel treatment, and stable boys were afraid to groom her. Finally I sent her to Langos, the estate of one of my cousins, to keep until I was in a position to take her back. My cousin had a stud farm, and he bred the old mare several times, at my request, before she died at the age of thirty. I was not going to let the clover family pass out of my hands if I could help it. Sarga had four lovely colts, and I could not wait for the day when I could have them.

My husband died in a tragic accident a few years later, and it was not until 1924, after my second marriage, that I was able to take Sarga's colts, two fillies and two geldings. I was in Ujszallas, our country estate, and I wrote my cousin to ship the mares to me. He wrote back and refused to send them. He told me he was using the two matched fillies and did not want to part with them. I wrote him an angry letter back, insisting that I had a right to the horses. Finally his reply came. He said that the carriage drawn by the two clover mares had been hit by a truck. The horses and the coachman had been killed.

I had a sense of foreboding that overshadowed my sorrow, when I finished reading my cousin's letter. There were no more clover horses in my stables, and they were gone from the plains of Hungary, where their ancestors had galloped thousands of years before. The legendary horses, with the mark of clover were all dead, and the fact that I had lost the last of the breed gave me a feeling of loneliness and of uneasiness.

Igezo

I was riding in the ring of the cavalry regiment near Ujszallas where we were jumping our horses in preparation for the international horse show at Luzern, Switzerland. After the ride, a group of officers and myself stood talking and criticizing each other. I was rather depressed because I had three horses entered in the show, and they were not going well. They were tired, nervous, and upset from the hard work of the early spring shows in Italy.

I complained to my companions about how hard it was to get new material in jumpers, thence even a very promising horse is all too often a flop. One of the officers laughed.

Well, if you want to see a good jumper, Countess, I will show you one. The horse is in the quarantine stables. She was brought in with the remounts a few days ago. That filly is small and ugly as the devil, but we can't keep her in the six feet high quarantine corral. She jumps out of it, and then we really have double trouble. Doxy, the vet. . . you know how conscientious he is. Well, he takes half of our soldiers to sprinkle disinfectant over the fort's grounds every time the mare gets loose. I don't know why he hasn't sprinkled the officers and the club with lysoform too! He sends the other half of the regiment to catch that four-legged demon. When she can't dodge the soldiers, she attacks them-bites, kicks. She's worse than a stallion. Since the old stable master died in Langos, the remounts we get from there have all been nervous and upset. The new man must handle the horses roughly."

"Don't tell me wild stories about your remounts, Captain Szücs," I laughed. "Countess, this is true. I am not joking," he assured me seriously.

"All right, then, show me your tiger," I said.

We gave our horses to the waiting grooms and went to the small quarantine stable. It was a brick building with concrete lined box stalls. Everything was washed and disinfected. The place reeked of cleanliness. It was feeding time, and the Hussars on duty were moving about carrying buckets of oats to the horses, who whinnied softly in happy expectation.

"Where is your monster, Captain?" I asked.

He pointed up to the last box stall. "There she is. They are just taking the feed to her. We can look in, and you will see the creature." He called to the strange procession of men, who stood by the last box stall. "Wait until we get to you!"

I was amused at the military precision of the way in which the four soldiers worked. One soldier went to the door, which he pulled back, for the doors slid on rollers. Two other soldiers stood beside him with pitchforks to meet the ugly mare that jumped toward them, her teeth bared, as she snapped at them. The soldiers used the pitchforks to force her back in the far corner of the box stall, where she stood, snorting and trembling with rage. The fourth soldier, in spite of the protection of the pitch forks, kept glancing at the mare warily as he poured the oats into her feeder. Then he jumped back, followed by the pitchfork holders, who covered his retreat.

The little mare charged at the oats, keeping her eye on us all the while. She started to gobble, her mouth foaming in her eager delight. The scene was so funny that all had to laugh. The Captain opened the side window inserted in the box stall's wall, through which we could watch the horse in safety. I immediately saw the beauty of her small but sturdy body, which was marred by the short neck and square, bony head. I even liked these faults of hers. She looked like a horse that could jump; she had the face of a jumper. As I looked I heard Captain Szücs' voice.

"Let's go along, Countess, and have a glass of beer at the officers' club." This was the custom after our morning ride.

"You seem to like my horse," the Captain said as we walked toward the club. "You're right," I answered, "that filly has charmed me." Captain Szücs burst out laughing. "Good Lord, Countess Judith, that ugly beast. Instead of beer we'll have champagne and a christening. This year remount names all begin with an 'I', so the mare will be christened Igezo, 'the charmer.' "

We celebrated with champagne, which we drank to the most unsuitable name the mean little filly could get, that of Igezo. The mare was kept at Captain Szücs' squadron. She was a strange animal, and her misdeeds were a constant subject for talk and laughter at the officers' club.

Captain Szücs liked Igezo in spite of her temperament, and, since he had no time himself, he had his sergeant ride and train her. She was a magnificent jumper, and won the jumping competition wherever she started, but she was a puller. She had a very strong herd-instinct, and gave a great deal of trouble when she had to leave the other horses. In the hunting field, she pulled outrageously and killed hounds. She did not kick them, but, with her ears pricked nicely forward, she leaped on them, hitting them with her front hoofs. They could not break her of it, so she was never hunted after the first few times. In the stable she bit at everyone. The rougher the grooms handled her, the meaner she got. Captain Szücs stopped the rough treatment and tried to use patience and kindness in handling her. He got excellent results, and even her stable manners improved. A few years after Igezo arrived, the Captain was transferred to another regiment, and another young officer, Lieutenant Daniel, took over the schooling of the mare. "I'll show her," he boasted, but the "showing" worked the other way around. Igezo soon got to the point where, if someone so much as lifted a stick in her presence, she immediately attacked the offending person. She ran out at the jumps when her new trainer tried to ride her; he finally put a gag-bit, or "corkscrew," in her mouth for one show. With her mouth bleeding, Igezo jumped into the spectators, making her way through their lines, biting and kicking with blood and saliva spraying out of her lacerated mouth. The mare got more vicious every day. In the stable they tied her front leg up so that they could clean her, and chained her head up high so she couldn't bite. Nevertheless she managed to leap forward, rear, and bash in the head of the brutal groom who tortured her. One night she tore her chain loose and kicked down the door of her stall.

We were dancing at the officers' club, when Lieutenant Daniel was interrupted by a breathless groom who told him that Igezo was free, and the sergeant major did not know what to do about it.

"The horse goes up and down the corridor between the stalls and attacks any one who comes in," the man told us. I suggested that he catch her with oats, but the groom only laughed bitterly. "That demon has been fooled and caught with oats so often, that, if anyone comes offering them to her, she won't trust him. There is no chance of her taking the oats, but she would probably take a bite out of the man's face instead."

"All right, I'll go and catch her!" the tipsy young officer's voice boastful but still a little doubtful.

The regimental commander's gay young wife, who sat next to me, was delighted at the prospect of an adventure. "Let's go see Daniel in the lion's den," she suggested.

We wanted nothing better, and we went, in spite of the commanding officer's protests. We must have made a strange procession as we picked up the long skirts of our evening gowns and walked to the stable. We stood upon the benches that the officers got for us from the tack rooms. In this way we could reach the high windows of the meticulously clean stables and enjoy the whole scene, as if we sat in a theatre. Inside the brightly lighted stable, Igezo, her head high, was pacing up and down the corridor between the sixty stalls. The horses turned occasionally to gaze at the nervous mare, then went back munching their hay peacefully. Soldiers guarded every door, two at each end and two in the middle of the stable that led to the tack and feed rooms. Near the doors the sergeant major was shaking an old oat bin, and the black smith, Palotas, was brandishing a red shiny apple and cursing at the horse in a most spicy and varied manner with sugared tones. The cursing was done to relieve Palotas of the anger caused by being called out of his comfortable bed at two o'clock in the morning. The sweet tone of voice was to fool Igezo into believing that, once she was in her stall, she would be showered with all the oats and carrots a horse could wish for. But Igezo had decided that this time she would not be fooled.

Then Lieutenant Daniel made his appearance, impressive and handsome in his dress uniform. He held a lump of sugar in the palm of his hand and spoke in a gentle, cultured voice that had charmed many a lovely woman, but Igezo, "the charmer," was not to be charmed. She lifted her head at the sight of her rider and charged at him in a clattering gallop along the brick passage between the stalls. Lieutenant Daniel made a hasty retreat, shutting the stable doors hurriedly behind him. But Igezo had miscalculated her distance, and we saw her crash against the closed doors.

Lieutenant Daniel must have thought that the horse would break through, for he lost his nerve and yelled, "Come on, help me! This creature is after me." We laughed until we nearly fell off our benches, then someone said that we should bet on who would catch the horse. Everyone contributed to the "pot," which was to be won by the captor of the "Lion." We decided to work in couples, but most of them could scarcely get through the door before Igezo charged. I had noticed that the mare seemed to dislike a uniformed figure more than a lady's, so I chose a young woman, who was a fine rider, to come with me. With thumping hearts, and no sugar, oats, or apples in our hands, we walked in as if Igezo was no concern of ours. The mare lifted her ugly head, and laid back her ears, but we moved on. We were nearly in the middle of the stable, when our courage gave out, and we stepped into one of the stalls. We sat down on the partition, that hung from the ceiling between each horse, and began to discuss our next move. We got into lion's den all right, but how could we tame her. I yelled at the soldiers, who stood in the middle doors, ready to help in case the mare charged, to get out and leave the stable clear of uniforms, which Igezo obviously hated.

They left after a second of hesitation, then Mara, my partner, said, "This is fine! What can we do now?"

"I don't know!" I answered, "Wait I suppose."

lgezo was standing in the far end of the stable, munching the straw bedding at the back of one of the stalls. I sat still wondering what steps to take, when suddenly Mara got up, her pale blue, star-studded evening dress streaming after her, and walked down the passage, with unhesitating steps, as if she were crossing a ballroom floor. lgezo was still pulling at the straw, when Mara reached down, took hold of the mare's halter and led her to a high partitioned box stall. She pushed the double bar in place and turned, as I hurried towards her.

"Now, let's hurry back to the casino," she said calmly.

At the door we were met by the laughing congratulating crowd. We went back to the club, and around five in the morning, while the gypsy band played the songs we had requested over and over, I turned to Mara.

"Why didn't you tell me what you were going to do?" I whispered. "You could have been badly hurt if the mare had recovered from her surprise."

"I didn't know what I would do myself!" she whispered back. "But when you said you didn't know what to do, Judith, I knew one thing, that I had to go to the lady's room. I had to get that horse back to its stall and get out of the stable, quick! So I did it! But, frankly, I was never so scared in my life!"

This episode strengthened me in my beliefs that sometimes the strangest events make heroes, and that Igezo, like most beings, whether horse or human, can be controlled by unwavering firmness. A few days later, at an officers' meeting, it was decided that Lieutenant Daniel, who had made a fool of himself before the soldiers, would be transferred to another regiment. The ladies were asked "not to use the regimental stables for their playground in the future." They also decided to have Igezo destroyed or sold. At Mara's and my suggestion the mare was auctioned off, and I bought Igezo for a ridiculously small sum.

Igezo was taken to my stables, and fortunately, my head groom, Ferenc Hornyak, loved her. He treated her gently, but she was a problem the first half year I had her. She bit most of the personnel, and even I was in the hospital because I didn't duck her flying hoofs soon enough. Finally she understood that she would not be mistreated, and from then on was my best, most reliable jumper. I always said that if I were ever in danger, I could trust my life to Igezo.

Igezo's performance, whether hacking or in the show ring, was of such an excellent quality, that I decided to breed her, in spite of her rather ugly conformation. I went to the squadron quarters to get her pedigree, but to my astonishment I was told that she had been sold to the army without one. This was a strange procedure for a stud farm that prided itself on the breeding of its horses. I wrote to Langos for the pedigree, and after a long delay, they sent it to me. Igezo's sire was Riado, a well known steeple-chaser and a fine thoroughbred stallion. The mare's dam was given as Vercse, but her sire and dam were not listed. I wrote and wrote again, asking for Vercse's pedigree. Finally my cousin answered me, stating that Vercse was some work horse on the farm. I thought it was strange that they had bred a "work horse" to such a fine stallion, but I gave up trying to get any information from Langos.

In the next few years Igezo gave me several very nice foals. They were lovely horses and showed no signs of having the "cold blood" of a work horse in them. I decided to go to Langos myself and find out something about the mysterious ancestry of Vercse. Without proof that the colts were purebred, I could not have them registered in the stud book at the Department of Agriculture. I went about it in a round about way, for my relations with the Langos family were strained anyway, because of the argument over Sarg's colts. I found out, during my visit, who Vercse's coachman was, and I went down to the stables to see him. I asked him about the mare and he answered my questions readily.

"Yes, yes, I drove Vercse," he said. "She was a good mare." "Where is she now?" I asked.

"Didn't the Countess know?" the old man said in surprise. "Vercse and her sister were hit and killed by a truck. Right after they were sent up to be driven as a parade team, it was."

"What?" I gasped. "Was Vercse Sarga's daughter?"

"Yes, Countess," the coachman answered. "Vercse had one foal before she died, a little bay filly that must have been the devil's horse. She bit and kicked like nothing I've ever seen-born mean, you'd say. The old count decided to sell her. He didn't even want anyone to know he'd bred such a bad-tempered horse. The Countess argued with him something terrible, the house servants said. She wanted to keep the filly for breeding. I don't know what happened to her though."

I stood frozen with shock, as I realized that, by some strange chance, I had bought Sarga's granddaughter. I had got back the clover breed I thought was lost forever.

Before lgezo was bred, I had won quite often with her, and, in 1936, won the tryouts for the Berlin Olympics against the official Hungarian military team. lgezo's sons became studs for the state remount depots. Her daughters were Itala, Italos, and lgezo II. All three are now in the United States with me.

In 1945 I was forced to flee from the Russians. The day we left, lgezo was taken desperately ill with colic. I could not stop my caravan of sixty-four horses and twenty-seven servants, for the Russians were only three and a half miles behind us. I couldn't bear seeing my mare suffer so. A veterinarian traveled with us, and, on the fifth day, I asked him to destroy her. He refused and told me that miracles could happen, that maybe she would pull through. But although for days she kept her place as the leader, bathed in the sweat of agony, she finally lay down and could not get up any more. And this just at the peak of excitement, with the Russians closing up faster and faster.

 It was at this moment that I heard my own voice with shocked distaste; a strange, high-pitched, hysterical voice that shouted at the veterinarian unit's commanding officer. He curtly told me to start and leave my dying horse in the village square.

"You go get on the road and leave me in peace!" I said. "I won't leave her! You go! You start! I will not desert Igezo, or my servants, or my horses."

I saw my faithful servants' worried faces around me in the flashing brilliance of the light from the bomb fires that were devastating a nearby town. Igezo's head was heavy in my lap, her ears hanging. Her breath was racking her body, then it got so quiet that I touched, fearfully, her cooling ears. The scared people of the village were watching the scene, their curiosity uppermost, even in this moment when they did not know when a group of Russians might appear. The Red army was advancing slowly across the country that the bomber planes had "softened," clearing out the straggling ends of the army that fled westwards.

My attention was distracted by a boy who tapped my shoulder, then plucked at my coat sleeve. He tried to say something, then Igezo raised her head in a last effort, gave a desperate help-seeking whinny; the call of a dying horse, that had wrung my heart so often ever since childhood. I knew what it meant, and it was almost with relief that I felt the mare's head get heavier and heavier in my lap. With a final trembling that shook her sweat-covered frame, Igezo stiffened and died. I turned toward the boy who stood at my shoulder.

"Ma'am! Countess!" the Austrian boy cried, "there is a trail still free and unknown, it winds up the 'Calvarien-Berg' and runs down the other side of the mountain. I will lead you there! Maybe you can pass the Tulln bridge to the northern side of the Danube! I think you can make it with horses!"

My coachman came running, "Countess, Countess, my wife is going to have her baby."

Hornyak, the head groom called to me. "Devole is down! She is foaling!"

Jani, the little son of the blacksmith ran up. "She has had it! She has had it!"

"Who?" I yelled at him, the funny side of the situation drowning the tragedy,

"Your Aunt Mari, or Devole ?"

"Devole. Mari is only lamenting", he answered disgustedly.

The veterinarian, his fat, short legged figure trembling with indignation came up to me.

"We are encircled, Countess, because of that horse. Seven-hundred horses and two-hundred eighty men, for whom I am responsible, will be prisoners of the Russians because of your horses. Several of my men have already been killed by a Russian patrol just outside of the village, and my two reconnoiters have not returned." A few bullets splattered on the wall of the church behind us.

"Down!" he called to the surrounding people. "We are already under infantry fire."

The bullets whizzed and ricocheted, but they did not seem dangerous somehow. The situation was so impossible, and the harm that I had done all these people, who stayed because of me, was overwhelming. I had a few young women in our convoy, and some white Russians who were anti-Communists, and therefore had joined the Germans. It was clear what the fate of them would be if they were caught by the Red Russians. Then as I realized it all with a shock, my wits returned, and I spoke to the boy who had offered to guide us.

"All right, go ahead! You are our guide. We will follow you!"

The coachman's wife, who had even forgotten to wail, was loaded into a carriage. A small group of soldiers protected our retreat against the cautiously advancing Russians in the narrow village streets. I don't think that it took us longer than ten minutes to disappear in the surrounding woods, and up the steep rocky trail.

We made it to the Tulln bridge, and the coachman's baby was born in the carriage, which the happy father upset in his excitement. We passed over the bridge, and it was blown up, just after we got out of the range of the explosion. We were in comparative safety on the north side of the Danube, when I saw the flames and the black billowing columns of smoke, that rose where the bridge had been. I said my thanks to St. Joseph, but I could not forget my old lgezo, who, by her unhappy death, delayed my convoy and prevented us from going ahead on our planned route-the road that would have taken us straight into the hands of the Russians.

Mokus

MOKUS was the daughter of Igezo II, a little chestnut mare out of old Igezo, was born on a dirty, Austrian farm. The farmer got 6,000 shillings a month to keep my dozen surviving horses in good condition for I had gone to the United States in the meantime to find a new home for my horses. The farmer rented the horses out, leaving the little one month old fillies without their mother's milk. He did not give them any food to make up for it, and they were near starvation. The little runts, driven by hunger, wandered about the farm trying to get a bite of the fine clover hay that the fat calves ate, or even an ear of corn from the pig pen. They were chased away with blows from every place they went, and I got frequent reports from the farmer. He said he did not know what to do, for the foals were terribly mean. He wanted me to send more money from "the blessed land of America," which in his mind was a country papered with dollar bills, that one just picked up to send to him. He really never expected me to return and only kept the foals living so that he could charge me for their feed.

I can imagine his astonishment when he received my wire, telling him to get the horses ready for transport to America. My man, who went for the horses, sent me a cable saying that they are not worth transporting and that the foals were hopeless. I cabled back telling him to ship them all no matter what condition they were in. The horses were sent and even survived a hurricane. They could not stand up during the storm, but fell and rolled between the box stalls, the partition of which broke under the weight of their heavy bodies. Even under these conditions they ate up everything, and thus survived.

The day of arrival came, and I went out on the pier to meet my horses. The S. S. American Importer glided in to dock, and it was not only my horses that I met, but also my past; even that came to join me in the new country.

I went up the ship and saw, in the comfortable box stalls, the tired, thin animals, that were once my lovely horses. I felt a funny choking feeling in my throat. But their eyes held the fire of an unbroken spirit, and I felt a little ashamed of myself at that moment.

After I patted their curious heads, I turned to the four little fillies peeking over the high partitions of the box stalls. I stretched my hand out to pet them and, as if on command, four pairs of ears were laid back. The only chestnut among the four greys leaped forward and snapped at me. As I laughed and jumped back, my eyes focused on her with complete astonishment. The little red filly had on the tip of her pink nose a sign; a sign that I had never seen before, but had heard of ever since I could remember. It was the Mark of Clover.

She was copper red, and she reminded me of my old home's red squirrel, so the name I gave her was "Mokus."

The horses were sent to Virginia, and today the four-year old Mokus is fat, and very sassy. She is small, with a large head and the build of her Mongolian ancestors. She has a remarkable jumping power for a horse of her size, and, though she is not mean, she is certainly deliberately mischievous. Mokus is too young to have accomplished any of the remarkable feats of her ancestors, but I have no doubt that she will someday, for she bears the Mark of Clover.

Epilogue

Dawn rises. I have finished the last episode during the night and concluded the chain of stories, that, over a thousand years, linked a line of brave animals-from the arid Asiatic steppes to the green pastures of Virginia.

I am tired and sleepy just the same as I was many years ago when rocked to sleep by the same stories' narratives. I want to remind you, dear Readers, that this is not a historical book: The names are distorted, the dates vague, and the locations anything, but precise. Yet, please, remember that these stories have been coloured by the imagination of several generations of minstrels, story tellers, old nurses, grooms, . . .

Now, my aim was to pass them on to you the way I heard them-the stories that would sink into oblivion, together with a certain type of life, of peoples and horses; a world to which we belonged; Old Hungary.

No doubt, people will call most of the events that connected the fate of the horses with my family's history a coincidence. They might be right. But as for myself, I can only feel gratitude toward the breed of Clover that stood me by.

I also want to ask you a favor, dear Reader: Do not lend this book to your friends; make them buy it. Because, as you may know, the breed of Clover eats oats-and how!

Sincerely

THE AUTHOR

Xenophon Press Library

30 Years with Master Nuno Oliveira, Henriquet 2011

A Journey Through the Horse's Body, Fritz 2012

A Rider's Survival from Tyranny, de Kunffy 2012

Another Horsemanship, Racinet 1994

Austrian Art of Riding, Poscharnigg 2015

Broken or Beautiful: The Struggle of Modern Dressage, Barbier/Conrod 2020

Classic Show Jumping: the de Nemethy Method, de Nemethy 2016

Classical Dressage with Anja Beran, Beran 2017

Divide and Conquer Book 1, Lemaire de Ruffieu 2016

Divide and Conquer Book 2, Lemaire de Ruffieu 2017

Dressage for the 21st Century, Belasik 2001

Dressage in the French Tradition, Diogo de Bragança 2011

Dressage Principles and Techniques: A Blueprint for the Serious Rider, Tavora 2018

Dressage Principles Illuminated, Expanded Edition, de Kunffy 2021

École de Cavalerie Part II, Robichon de la Guérinière 2015

Elements of Dressage, von Ziegner 2016

Equestrian Art: The Collected Later Works, Nuno Oliveira 2022

Equestrian Art: The Collected Early Writings (1951-1956), Nuno Oliveira 2022

Equine Osteopathy: What the Horses Have Told Me, Giniaux 2014

Equitation, Bussigny 2021

Federico Grisone's "The Rules of Riding," Grisone/Tobey 2022

Fragments from the Writings of Max Ritter von Weyrother, Fane 2017

François Baucher: The Man and His Method, Baucher/Nelson 2013

General Chamberlin: America's Equestrian Genius, Matha 2020

Great Horsewomen of the 19th Century in the Circus, Nelson 2015

Gymnastic Exercises for Horses Volume II, Eleanor Russell 2013

H. Dv. 12 German Cavalry Manual of Horsemanship, Reinhold 2014

Handbook of Jumping Essentials, Lemaire de Ruffieu 2015

Handbook of Riding Essentials, Lemaire de Ruffieu 2015

Healing Hands, Giniaux, DVM 1998

Horse Training: Outdoors and High School, Beudant 2014

I, Siglavy, Asay 2018

Horsemanship & Horsemastership Volume 1, US Cavalry 2021

Horsemanship Training Films 3 DVD set, US Cavalry 2021

Learning to Ride, Santini 2016

Legacy of Master Nuno Oliveira, Millham 2013
Lessons in Lightness: Expanded Edition, Mark Russell 2019
Mark of Clover, Kelly, 2022
Methodical Dressage of the Riding Horse, Faverot de Kerbrech 2010
Military Equitation or, A Method of Breaking Horses, and Teaching Soldiers to Ride, Pembroke, and *A Treatise on Military Equitation*, Tyndale 2018
My Horses Have Something to Say, de Wispelaere 2021
Principles of Dressage and Equitation, a.k.a. Breaking and Riding, Fillis 2017
Racinet Explains Baucher, Racinet 1997
Releasing the Jaw, Poll, and Neck DVD, Mark Russell 2021
Riding and Schooling Horses, Chamberlin 2020
Riding by Torchlight, Cord 2019
Riding in Rhyme, Davies 2021
Schooling Exercises In Hand, Hilberger 2009
Science and Art of Riding in Lightness, Stodulka 2015
Sketches of the Equestrian Art, Barbier/Sauvat 2022
The Art of Riding a Horse, D'Eisenberg 2015
The Art of Traditional Dressage, Volume 1 DVD, de Kunffy 2013
The Chamberlin Reader, Chamberlin/Matha, 2020
The de Nemethy Method: A training seminar, 8 DVD set, de Nemethy 2019
The Ethics and Passions of Dressage Expanded Edition, de Kunffy 2013
The Forward Impulse, Santini 2016
The Gymnasium of the Horse, Steinbrecht 2018
The Horses, a novel, Walker 2015
The Italian Tradition of Equestrian Art, Tomassini 2014
The Maneige Royal, de Pluvinel 2010, 2015
The New Method of Dressing Horses a.k.a. A General System of Horsemanship, Cavendish 2020
The Portuguese School of Equestrian Art, de Oliveira/da Costa 2012
The Quest for Lightness in Equitation and Equestrian Questions, Nelson/L'Hotte 2021
The Spanish Riding School & Piaffe and Passage, Decarpentry 2013
The Spanish Riding School: The Miracle of the White Horse DVD, US Lipizzan Association 2021
To Amaze the People with Pleasure and Delight, Walker 2015
Total Horsemanship, Racinet 1999
Training Hunters, Jumpers, and Hacks, Chamberlin 2019
Training Your Foal, Ettl 2011
Training with Master Nuno Oliveira, 2 DVD set, Eleanor Russell 2016
Truth in the Teaching of Master Nuno Oliveira, Eleanor Russell 2015
Wisdom of Master Nuno Oliveira, de Coux 2012